MARY CRAWFORD

Tempting Fate

HIDDEN BEAUTY BOOK 10

COPYRIGHT

Published on May 10, 2018, by Diversity Ink Press and Mary Crawford. Author may be reached at MaryCrawfordAuthor.com.

ISBN: 978-1-945637-59-9

Cover by Covers Unbound

HIDDEN BEAUTY SERIES

Until the Stars Fall from the Sky

So the Heart Can Dance

Joy and Tiers

Love Naturally

Love Seasoned

Love Claimed

If You Knew Me (and other silent musings)
(novella)

Jude's Song

The Price of Freedom (novella)

Paths Not Taken

Dreams Change (novella)

Heart Wish (100% charity release)

Tempting Fate

The Letter

The Power of Will

HIDDEN HEARTS SERIES

Identity of the Heart

Sheltered Hearts

Hearts of Jade

Port in the Storm (novella)

Love is More Than Skin Deep

Tough

Rectify

Pieces (a crossover novel)

Hearts Set Free

Freedom (a crossover novel)

The Long Road to Love (novella)

Love and Injustice (Protection Unit)

Out of Thin Air (Protection Unit)

Soul Scars (Protection Unit)

OTHER WORKS:

The Power of Dictation

Use Your Voice

An Everyday Guide to Scrivener 3 for Mac

Vision of the Heart

DEDICATION

To the tough kids who grow up to be fierce adults.

CHAPTER ONE

MINDY

I PUSH MY HEADPHONES tighter against my ears as I try to filter out the feedback assaulting my brain. Even as my fingers press against the cold plastic of my headphones, I know it won't do me any good. Still, I'm compelled to try. The noise isn't external. It's never been. I used to be able to sort out all the noise in my head, but lately I can't seem to. I don't know if it's the craziness of college life or simply because I'm away from home, but nothing in my life is making much sense.

I stare down at my chemistry notes. This should all be a simple review. I took this class during my sophomore year of high school. There is no new information here, so why does it all look like a foreign language? My carefully structured notes look like gibberish.

I lean back against my cushy down pillows and pull the quilt my Grandma, who I call Grummy, made me around my neck and angrily wipe tears from my eyes. This should not be so hard. After all, I'm Mindy Whitaker. I had my choice of full-ride scholarships to several Ivy League colleges. My dad started getting recruitment letters for me before I started high school based on my performance at a camp for gifted kids.

My parents have such high expectations for me I don't even know how to explain to them what a nightmare this is becoming. I take a deep breath and pull my computer off my nightstand and open it. My mom would kill me if I was anything less than honest. Still ... how do you even start that kind of email?

Before I can even finish booting up my computer, the door to my dorm room slams open. Melanie stumbles in and pushes her glasses up her nose as she takes in my appearance.

"Give me a break! What are you doing in your stupid Oscar the Grouch sweats? You promised me you would go to this party! It's at Kayden Colberg's house. Do you know what that means? His sister knows everybody at Gamma Iota Nu, this party could be my ticket in."

"Melanie, I have two exams on Monday. I can't afford to fail them."

"Aren't you a child prodigy or something? You won't fail your tests. You are just being a chicken because you don't want to be a grown-up. You should've stayed in high school."

"Mel, why do you want me there anyway? Like you said I'm only seventeen. Nobody will be impressed by me."

"Are you kidding me? All they'd have to do is turn on the radio. Those are your vocals backing up Aidan O'Brien. If people aren't fans of Aidan, they can check out your duet with Tasha Keeley."

"Uncle Aidan works with a bunch of session musicians, I'm not special. He's simply helping me earn money for college."

"Get real! You are personal friends with Tasha Keeley. I saw her the other day on your Skype call. She was asking for your advice on a song she was writing. That's more than a few background vocals."

"Okay, so I grew up around all those guys — but that doesn't explain why you need me at the party. I thought you got an invitation?"

"I did. Still ... I need to stand out."

"I'm not sure you want to get the kind of attention I would bring you. In case you haven't noticed, I'm kind of the essence of weird. If you want to fit in with everyone else, you probably don't want me. People tend to be creeped out by me."

Melanie looks at me with pleading eyes. "Please Mindy. I'm sure it's not that bad. You're used to talking to people — all sorts of people. You know me, when I'm around guys, I get all tongue-tied and say totally stupid stuff. Can you please just go be my wingman and make sure I don't make a fool out of myself? I've got a meeting with the women from Gamma Iota Nu next week. My grandma was a member of GIN and she'd be so proud if I got in."

I glance down at the notes I was trying to study. The rainbow of ink swims together. I let out a frustrated sigh. "Okay ... I guess I wasn't getting a bunch done anyway."

As I straighten my earrings in front of the bathroom mirror, Melanie comes up behind me with a sour look on her face as she scrutinizes my outfit. I'm wearing skinny jeans and a dark pink T-shirt which says, "Sarcasm — it's just one of my many talents" with a retro jean jacket.

She rolls her eyes. "Couldn't you sex it up a little? You're going to a frat party, not hanging out at an arcade in junior high." Melanie smirks and hiccups. She giggles. "Oops!" She sways on her high heels.

I raise an eyebrow. "Are you sure more alcohol is such a great idea?"

She lifts her water bottle up. "Nothing wrong with a little lubrication. You know how I hate to talk to people. This makes it easier."

I cringe. I have my own history with people who use substances to make life easier. It's ugly. But Melanie doesn't seem to be in a mood to hear my sad saga. "I suppose that might work — unless your brain becomes so pickled you can't put two words together."

Melanie sticks her bottom lip out. "I can't believe you're such a party pooper. Nobody would ever guess you're like a rock star."

I roll my shoulder. "Not really a rock star. I told you that."

Melanie giggles as if she's told the most hysterical joke on the planet.

"Just for tonight, please be. It wouldn't hurt if you told people you've got a recording contract or something."

"Why would I lie to these people?"

Melanie shrugs and then stumbles slightly. "Like they would care? Grow up! It's not like anybody's going to get hurt."

My stomach clenches as I follow Melanie up the porch stairs. I glance over at a couple having a hostile stare down. In rapid succession, random scenes play out in my mind, and suddenly the reason for tense expression on his face is clear. The guy looks like he's in shock. He's not saying anything. I totally get it. If the person I was dating just slapped me in the middle of a party in front of all my friends, I would be confused too. The thing is, this isn't the first time I've had a vision about this guy. I happen to know there is an amazing girl in our English class who has a gigantic crush on him. She's perfect for him. Sadly, I can't share what I know because it's not a matter of life and death. I quickly avert my gaze because it's rude to stare. Still, I feel awful because I can't do anything to make him feel better. As I pass him on the porch, I mumble, "Have faith in yourself, things will get better."

Melanie tugs on my hand. "Come on! What are you doing?"

"People watching."

"Knock it off. That's why people think you're creepy. Try to talk in normal sentences instead of like a weird fortune cookie, okay? Normal people talk about movies and music and how much their classes suck. Try not to embarrass me, please."

I laugh lightly as I attempt to cover how much her dig hurts. I don't know why this is so hard lately. When I was a kid, people couldn't shut me up. I'd talk to anybody, anytime, anywhere. I'm not sure what happened, but it just seems harder now. I don't seem to fit in anywhere. "I'll be on my best behavior, I promise."

A tall willowy brunette who lives three doors down from us in the dorms shoves a beer in each of our hands as she raises a skeptical eyebrow in Melanie's direction. "Mel, what were you thinking? Bringing the poster child for jail bait to the party of the year probably wasn't your smartest idea."

"Figured she could get us all tickets to see Tasha Keeley or Aidan O'Brien or something. She's with the band."

Jodi chugs her beer and covers her cough with a laugh. "Dude! This is California. Everybody says they're 'with the band'." Jodi looks over at me and snickers. A tall guy with long hair and a tattoo on his forearm comes over and places his arm around Jodi's waist. She glances up at him and asks, "Isn't that right, Kayden? Most of your friends are in some sort of band or another, right?"

He nods. "Yeah, but not everybody has the good fortune to be in Kayden's Cadence."

Despite the oddly tense situation, I smile at the wordplay. Jodi catches my change in expression. "Are you flirting with my boyfriend?" she demands.

I point to my T-shirt. "Nope, merely appreciating a good play on words. What kind of music do you cover?" I ask, addressing Kayden.

"I guess you could call it country/rap fusion," he answers with a shrug.

I grin even wider. "That makes your band name even more evocative. Congratulations."

Jodi narrows her eyes at me as she turns to Melanie. "I think you should send your little friend home. She doesn't seem to understand how to play at the big kids table."

Kayden looks as befuddled as I feel. "What are you talking about? We were just talking about the band." He turns back toward me. "Do you play for one of the local bands?"

I bite my lip as I try to decide what to disclose. "Not exactly. I play in a band with a few family friends up in Oregon."

Melanie takes a big, long sip of her beer without even pausing for a breath.

"Mel, you may want to take it easy. It's going to be a long night," I caution. "Maybe you should grab a bite to eat or something."

She scowls at me as she messes with her phone. "Shut up! You're not my mom. That's why I went away to college. If you don't want to see grown-up behavior, maybe you should just go home."

She pulls up the song Jude and I wrote — and then rewrote — after Logan and Katie were almost killed. Tasha and I ended up doing it as a duet. *Closer Than a Whisper* has become an anthem about love and acceptance. That's fine by me. It wasn't the original intent of the song, but if it's how people read the celebration of Katie's victory over her stalkers and her love story with Logan, more power to them. After Melanie struggles with her phone, she hits play. She snorts. "Does this seem like a small family band to you?"

As soon as the introduction plays and Tasha sings the familiar first few notes, Kayden eyes widen. "That's Tasha Keeley. I saw her on VH1."

A few moments later, Jodi Humphreys looks at me with her jaw slack with shock. "Oh my gosh! You're singing with her! Wasn't this song in the top fifty a few weeks ago?"

I shrug. "I don't know. Maybe. I don't keep track of all that stuff."

Melanie narrows her gaze at me skeptically. "Why the heck not? Don't you want to be popular?"

"It seems what I have to say is probably more important than how popular I am," I answer quietly.

Melanie turns toward Kayden. "Don't mind Mindy, some of us understand it's actually smart to make friends."

Jodi looks over her shoulder at me and instructs, "Obviously you're a noob at this party thing. What happens here stays here. Got it? Do you think you're capable of keeping a secret?"

It's all I can do not to roll my eyes. "More than you can possibly imagine."

Melanie sighs dramatically. "Whatevs. Jodi and I are gonna go talk about sorority stuff. Since you're not interested, just go hang out — or whatever." She takes off upstairs and pauses on the landing before she yells down the stairs, "Try not to look stupid m'kay?"

Why did I ever think college would be fun?

I promised myself I wouldn't be one of those pathetic homesick college students. Yet, here I am wishing I hadn't pushed so hard to graduate from high school early and get on with my life. I even miss my pesky little siblings. I wish Becca was here clamoring to try my makeup and Charlie was teasing me for wearing it. Fat lot of good it did for me to move on to college. Nobody cares if I'm smart or gifted here either. I'm just as much of an outcast here as I was at home — if not more so. At least at home, people accepted my differences. Here, people avoid me altogether.

Under the best of circumstances, large groups have always been a challenge for me. But, this party is far from ideal. My so-called gift has been malfunctioning more often than my Volkswagen bug. So, the visions I have been getting are scrambled and nonsensical at best. When you combine that with the added social stressors of the party and the various states of inebriation, my brain feels like it's going to explode from the pressure. I knew better than to come tonight. I don't know what I was thinking. I wish I could turn it all off. Unfortunately, my gift of precognition means I don't get to completely ignore everyone. I still get feedback from people whether I want to or not. It just happens.

Since my Aunt Tara — she's not really my aunt, but I've called her that ever since I was adopted — lost her baby and I couldn't stop it from happening, it's almost as if my special gift, as Tara calls it, is on the fritz. I mean, I still get visions but I can't make sense of anything anymore. I feel incredibly helpless. I have all this horrific information floating around in my brain and no way to funnel it to help other people.

All the psychic discord paired with the actual noise from the people at the party starts to become overwhelming, so I move from room to room seeking a quiet place. Remarkably, down in the basement there's a large television with a big blue screen and a pool table with a couple of large leather recliners. There's a guy leaning up against the wall texting on his phone and another sprawled out on a plaid couch doing something on his iPad. Aside from those two, there's no one else in the whole room. Gratefully, I sink down into one of the recliner chairs and pull my phone out of my purse and start to read a book.

I've been valiantly trying to push back all the discordant visions in my head to focus on my book to give my exhausted brain a break. Suddenly, the oddest thing breaks my concentration. I smell the guy before I actually look up and see him. It's not a bad thing. Unlike almost everything else in this house, he smells good. He looks good too — you know, kinda like the guys you see on the college brochures. In fact I'm not sure I didn't see him in the promotional video when I was choosing schools. As I look up and try to collect my thoughts, he extends his hand out. "Hi. I'm Joel. Joel Thackett. At the moment my major is biochemistry. Tomorrow it might be political science because I can't make up my mind. I'm a junior. So … I probably should figure it out."

I briefly shake his hand. "Hi, it's nice to meet you. I'm Mindy Whitaker. I'm only a freshman. I have a little time to figure out my major, but I'm confused too. I'm trying to decide between premed and prelaw. I'm interested in both. I have been since I was seven."

Joel scrutinizes me for a couple moments. "I'm sorry, you don't even look old enough to be a freshman. Besides, most of the freshmen around here would be up tapping in the kegs out on the patio."

I grimace. "Somebody already gave me a beer. You probably don't want to know what I did with it."

"Why? Did you throw it on one of the frat guys? If you did, did you at least catch it on video? That would be epic for my YouTube channel."

I chuckle as I slip my book back into my purse and scoot toward the edge of the seat.

"Sorry to disappoint you. It's nothing quite so dramatic. I know women who've had terrible things happen to them in places they thought they'd be safe, so I'm a little paranoid. I dumped it down the kitchen sink on my way through."

I hold my breath as I wait for his response. He might even live here for all I know. Slowly he smiles. "I wish I could get you to talk to my little sister. I've been trying to tell her she needs to do something like that when she goes to parties. Good for you. Not that I don't trust my friends — but I *don't* trust my friends."

He walks over to a small refrigerator tucked at the end of the couch and grabs me a can of Coke. "Will this work?"

I grin. "That's perfect!"

He tosses it at me and points to the pool table.

"You play?"

I freeze in place for a second. After a couple moments of indecision, I decide to be honest. "You probably don't want to play against me."

"Umm … why … are you afraid to lose?" He smirks.

"No. In my experience, guys don't like to lose. Since we just met, I'd rather not tick you off."

"I know you're new. You probably don't know this — but people don't usually win against me."

"Uh-huh … I should probably warn you I've been playing since I was seven. My dad has a table and so does my uncle."

"Sounds like a challenge to me. Mindy Whitaker, step

up and put your money where your mouth is."

I groan. "I don't actually have any money. You should see how much my textbooks were this term. If you're willing to play for bragging rights, you're on."

Joel shrugs. "Works for me. You wanna break?"

I raise an eyebrow. "Did you not hear me? Seriously … You don't want to give me that kind of advantage."

Joel just laughs. "What can I say? I'm a gentleman. My mamma raised me right. Ladies first. Besides, how much damage can you actually do?"

"Famous last words." I look down at the guy who was laying on the couch playing games on his iPad. He's now sitting up and watching our conversation like it's a tennis game. "Hey, what's your name?"

"Uh … I'm Brent Rigby."

"Okay Brent. Nice to meet you. So, you heard Joel say he's okay with me going first regardless of what the outcome is, right?"

"Yeah, I guess."

"I just want to make sure everybody understands. I don't want there to be any misunderstandings later."

"I don't know, I thought it was pretty clear I thought you said you didn't drink any beer," Joel jokes.

"I drank nothing. After the party is over, I have to go back and study. I've got tests on Monday."

Joel grins at me as he hands me a pool cue. "Then by all means let the party begin."

When my dad, Jeff, first taught me how to play pool, I was incredibly frustrated because he made me learn the mathematics of angles at the same time. It was slow and tedious for a kid. As a result, I see the game entirely different from anyone else I've ever played against. Consequently, the only person who can match me play for play is my dad.

I methodically clear the first five balls off the table, but I need the bridge for the sixth ball. When I walk over to the rack to get it Joel asks me, "How long did you say you've been playing again?"

"Ten years," I answer as I chalk up my cue again.

Joel's eyes widen. "You're only seventeen? Why are you in college?"

"I graduated early. I could've come to college even earlier, but I took a year off to travel with the band."

"The band?"

I sink the six, seven and eight balls before I answer. "I play acoustic guitar and provide backup singing for Aidan O'Brien and Tasha Keeley."

"No joke?"

"No joke. Do you have a particular pocket where you'd like me to sink the nine ball?" I glance up at him.

He shakes his head in dismay. "Obviously, I should've listened to you. I suppose I could make it tough and tell you to bank it and sink the nine ball cross side pocket. Something tells me you'd find that shot as easy as everything else you've sunk."

I wink at him as I do exactly as he asked. Much to my surprise, a bunch of people clap and cheer when the ball drops.

Everyone except for one voice which hisses at me, "I told you not to cause trouble and embarrass me."

I look around at the crowd in surprise until I spot

Melanie being supported by Jodi.

"I'm only playing a game of pool."

"I told you I was trying to impress Kayden's sister Kammie — you know the head of Gamma Iota Nu, the sorority I want to pledge to? The guy you're hanging all over is her boyfriend. Smooth move Mindy," she mocks, slurring her words in one long burst. "*Go home.* I don't want you as wing man. Heck, I don't even want you as my roommate. There's a reason no one likes you."

With as much dignity as I can muster, I walk over to the recliner chair and pick up my purse. From behind me, I hear someone whisper, "Wow, harsh."

Joel steps in front of me. "I can walk you back to your dorm."

I pull a card out of my purse. "It's okay I've caused enough drama. I'll just call the shuttle."

"For the record, it was fun to play against someone as talented as you. Maybe next time I'll be able to move a few balls around the table."

I look around at the faces of the people who are looking at me with a mixture of contempt and pity. "Something tells me I'm not likely to be invited back, but thanks for the offer."

CHAPTER TWO

ELIJAH

CANDICE FITZGERALD'S VOICE BUZZES in my ear like a bothersome fly at a Fourth of July picnic.

I'm pacing back and forth in front of the loading dock on the side of the public library. I'm here trying to write because the power is not functioning properly at my house. I was on a pretty good roll until my agent called to vent her frustrations over my career. "Douglas Hauser called me. He says your latest work doesn't have the same magic of *Behind Glass Bars*. I glanced at a few pages. I have to agree with him. What's going on with you?"

I run my fingers through my hair. "Jigger, jig, jig, first of all, jigger, jig, jig, what you viewed is just a draft. It's not even the final copy. Jigger, jig, jig, my work with Douglas is supposed to be confidential. It wasn't ready for public consumption, jigger, jig, jig."

"Didn't I send you to training to help you speak more effectively in public?" Candace asks me, without even trying to disguise her annoyance.

"You did, jigger, jig, jig. My stage fright is much

better. Thank you. Jigger, jig, jig."

"If it was so helpful, why are you still talking so strange?"

"Jigger, jig, jig, I've explained this to you before. It doesn't matter how many self-confidence classes you sign me up for or what kind of diction or speech therapy sessions I attend, jigger, jig, jig. I'll always have verbal tics because I have Tourette's syndrome."

"Can't you take medicine for it or something?" I can almost see her recoil through the phone.

Even though she can't see me, I still flinch. "Trust me, I take medication every day. If I didn't, the effects would be much worse."

Through the phone I can hear Candace click her tongue. "It's such a pity. You were such a talented writer too."

I let out an exasperated breath. "Don't you mean I *am* a talented writer? You guys didn't seem to have a problem with me when I was working on the screenplay for *Behind Glass Bars*, or when I released *Reflections*."

"Even you have to admit *Reflections* under-performed."

"Jigger, jig, jig maybe it under-performed by the publishers definition, but it was bigger than I ever dreamed."

"It's too bad you and your girlfriend broke up because I think part of the magic of *Behind Glass Bars* was her illustrations."

When this whole writing thing with Sadie took off, our parents got together with Mrs. Gable, our English teacher, and met with some publishing contacts she had from her former job. Eventually, we got a publishing contract and Candace Fitzgerald became our agent. Sadie and I have always written together under the pen name Anderson Fischer. Until now, I thought Candice understood my situation and was looking out for me. Now, I'm not so sure.

I climb up on a cement barrier and sit down. I shrug off my backpack and lean against it. "Sadie is not my girlfriend. She's just my friend and my writing partner. She's moved on to other stuff in her life now. Jigger, jig, jig, she told you that last year. I believe your words to her were something along the lines of 'Pictures aren't all that important. It's the words that matter.' Can't say I blame Sadie for being a tad offended. Jigger, jig, jig."

"Admittedly, I may have underestimated the value of her artwork to your project. Can't you simply call her up and make her come back?"

"You obviously haven't worked with Sadie much. Very few people *make* Sadie do anything. She'd probably help me if I asked her to. But I won't. Sadie has worked extremely hard to get where she is right now and I won't ruin that for her. Besides, I want to take my writing in a new direction which has nothing to do with Sadie."

Candace clears her throat. "Elijah, you are a talented young man. If you weren't, you wouldn't have received such a generous contract from us. We are happy to have you under our imprint. However, the demand for our brand is quite high. There are others like yourself coming up behind you and if you can't perform up to our expectations, we have to make room for new, fresh talent. Your fans want a certain product from you. Clearly you don't want to disappoint them. I suggest you read the terms of your contract before you make any big career moves. Not very many authors get the kind of chance you were given. You might want to think about that before you throw it all away."

My phone beeps in my hand. I pull it away from my ear and look at the screen.

"Candace, I'm about to lose you. My battery is dying and I don't have an extra charger with me. I'll call you tomorrow or the next day."

"Don't call me darling. You need to talk to Douglas and see if you can rescue the disaster of a manuscript you turned in. Last I checked, you're still on a deadline with us unless you decide to blow up your entire career."

With that stark pronouncement, my phone goes completely dead in my hand.

———•———

Thankfully, the porch light seems to be on when I finally get home after stopping by the local sandwich place to get a bite to eat. After the call from Candace, I don't feel much like writing anymore. I guess the utility company must be done working on the lines.

I clear off the spot on my grandfather's old roll top desk and plug my computer in as well as my cell phone. As I'm unwrapping my sandwich, a FaceTime call comes in from Sadie.

I accept the call as I throw on my gaming headset and slide into the executive leather chair I bought myself as a reward for finishing the screenplay version of *Behind Glass Bars*. "Jigger, jig, jig, how do you always do that?" I ask.

"Do what?" Sadie replies as she squints into the camera. She must be using her phone. "Did I call at a bad time?"

I shake my head. "No actually you called at a perfect time. Jigger, jig, jig, I just got off the phone with Candace. She thinks my new book sucks."

Sadie is silent for a moment.

"Sadie?" I prompt.

"I liked it," she answers with a shrug.

"But … you didn't love it, jigger, jig, jig?" I push.

Sadie shakes her head. "Sorry, I like other stuff you've written better. It's like you wrote it with your head and not your heart. I'm so sorry Elijah. I wanted to love it. I really did."

I slump back against my chair. I want to argue, scream and fight. I wish I could tell Sadie she's wrong. But, if I'm honest with myself, I know she's not.

"Sadie, I know it needs work. But I don't know how to fix it. The deadline is killing me. You know how I get. It's like I'm fixated on picking the perfect words and then I forget the emotion of the story."

"This story has tons of emotion too. You based it on Cody and Jasmine, didn't you?"

"I did. Jigger, jig, jig. Cody was always worried about being the villain in the story. I wanted to show him that he wasn't. He's been the person who made the biggest personal transformation throughout the whole process. I wanted to give him his own story so he could see how much progress he's made."

"I think you're almost there. You've got solid bones in your story. You need to give Cody a much stronger voice. Don't be afraid to show the readers what he went through instead of simply reciting facts. Cody gave you permission to write everything, didn't he? Even the part about the showdown with his dad?"

"Jigger, jig, jig, he did. I've been struggling with how much of his painful journey to share. Cody and I have become good friends. It feels like sharing all his personal stuff is a betrayal of our friendship. I know it's crazy. If you would've told me when we were still in high school Cody would be one of my closest friends I would've told you that you were certifiably insane. The guy bullied me almost every day from the time we were in the second grade. I guess it is possible for people to change."

"I haven't hung out with him much, but I think one of the reasons he gave you permission to tell his story is because he wants other young people to know they have the power to speak up against people like Scott. Even if they are not the ones who are being bullied. At the time you guys were going through this Cody didn't realize he was being bullied. He just thought Scott was picking on people like you. He didn't realize until he got out of the situation that he was a victim too. I think he wants you to be the voice he can't be."

I take a few bites of my sandwich as I consider her advice.

"You know, I never thought of it that way. I always figured he wanted me to tell his story as a sort of self-imposed punishment for what he did to us in high school. But I think you're right. I think he has a message he wants to share."

"So, you are one of the most powerful wordsmiths I know. Get busy and tell his story. You've known him longer than almost anyone around. You've seen the ugly side of him and how he's turned his life around with the help of Aidan. Go show the world how a bully can turn into a hero."

I groan. "I don't suppose you remember how much I hate editing and rewrites?"

Sadie chuckles. "I do. I also remember you telling me how it's easier to edit something previously written than to start with a blank page."

I grimaced. "I don't think you understand. Candace is talking about maybe taking my publishing contract away. I guess the publisher isn't happy with how well my books are selling —"

My cell phone rings, cutting short our conversation. I look down and see it's my sister Mariam.

I hold up my finger to my webcam as I say to Sadie, "Just a second, I have to take this. It's my sister and she *never* calls."

I hit the speaker button on my phone as my stomach sinks to my toes. "Jigger, jig, jig hello?"

"Elijah? This is Mariam. Get home as fast as you can. Some idiot tried to kill Dad. The doctors are saying he might not make it through surgery. I gotta go. They life-flighted him to OHSU. I'll call you when I know more."

Before I could say anything, the phone goes silent.

In an instant, my book deadline becomes my absolute last priority.

For a moment, I'm lost in time and space as memories of my dad flood my brain. Memories of Boy Scouts, soapbox derbies, arguing over sports scores, and repairing flat tires play randomly in my brain like a deranged game show.

"Elijah, do you want me to fly back to Oregon with you?" Sadie asks. "I'm sorry about your dad. Seth is such a nice guy."

"Don't you have a big art show this weekend?"

"I do. But if you need me, I'll work something out."

"That's totally cool of you, but I think I can handle flying by myself. Jigger, jig, jig, I'm not the same scared ninth grader you met all those years ago. Although, I'll admit the idea that my dad might not make it through the night scares the crap out of me, jigger, jig, jig."

"Okay, give me your driver's license number, your birthdate and your credit card number. I'll buy you the first ticket out while you go pack. You want window or aisle?"

"At this point, I don't care if I ride on the stupid wing, I need to get to Portland as fast as I can."

"I'll get you a ticket, a hotel room and a rental car. If you decide you don't need a hotel room, you can cancel it after you get there. I'll explain what's going on so they don't charge you a fee."

"Sadie Anderson, have I told you how grateful I am you're my best friend?" I ask as I pull my tennis shoes off and pull my cards out of my wallet and type the numbers in to Sadie. "Here are the numbers you need. Hopefully, you'll be able to find something this late which won't cost an arm and a leg."

Sadie gives me a reassuring smile. "Don't worry about it. I had a roommate once whose mom was a travel agent. She taught me all sorts of tricks. I've got you covered."

I scrub my hand down over my face. "You always do. Jigger, jig, jig I've been meaning to go home and visit. I never meant for it to be like this."

"Elijah, you can't beat yourself up over this. No one ever plans for these things to happen. We just have to hope and pray everything will be okay."

CHAPTER THREE

MINDY

I HOLD THE PHONE up to my ear while I use a makeup removal pad to take off the ravages of my mascara. "I just don't get it, Aunt Tara. I was only at the party because Melanie asked me to be there. I didn't want to go in the first place. How was I supposed to know who Joel was dating? I can't even keep the love lives of the girls who live on my floor straight. How am I supposed to know about everyone who lives on the entire campus?"

"I guess you can't — but I suppose you and I have a better shot at it than most," Tara quips.

"That's just the thing. I used to have a sense of those things, but I feel like I'm flying blind. I have an awful gut feeling I can't put into words. I was waiting for the shuttle to pick me up tonight and it's almost as if my feet didn't want to walk toward the bus. I knew Melanie and her friends didn't want me to be there — and trust me I didn't have any desire to be where I wasn't wanted — but it was almost as if there was something holding me there. I still don't know why I can't see anything. *Nothing.* It's so weird. It's never been this way for me."

Tara sighs. "I don't know what to tell you, Mindy Mouse. Maybe you're just trying too hard to force it. You know our gift doesn't work very well when we're too close to the situation. Perhaps all the turmoil of moving away to school and leaving your family has thrown a wrench into things?"

"I dunno. I wish whatever it is it would hurry up and resolve itself." I get up and strip off my jeans and change into some pajama pants. "I guess I never realized how much of a comfort my precognition skills were until they started to malfunction. They've always been such a natural part of me I never thought about what my life would be like if I didn't have them."

"It must seem odd. You spent so much time wishing for your gift to go away when you were younger, I bet you never expected to miss it. How is school going otherwise?"

"You *really* don't have time for me to tell you." I grimace. "By the time I finish telling you, Maddie would be old enough for college."

"That bad, huh? I had a rough start my first go around too. I ended up dropping out and starting over again later."

"I don't know what I want to do. It's nothing like I thought it would be. I figured being smart would be a huge advantage here. I'm not so sure it is."

I almost drop the phone when someone pounds on my door. "Melanie must be back. She must have lost her keys," I mumble into the phone as I get up to unlock my door.

When I swing open the dorm door, the campus safety officer shines his flashlight in my face and asks

"Mindy Jo Whitaker?" He is accompanied by a police officer.

"Aunt Tara? You might want to let my dad know I could use his help. Uncle Tyler might be handy too."

I hang up my phone and open the door wider to allow them into my room. "Yes, Officer, that's me. How can I help you?"

The officer consults his notes.

"Are you Melanie Lake's roommate?"

I point to Melanie's side of the room. "Yes. She lives here."

"When is the last time you saw Ms. Lake?"

"Earlier this evening," I hedge.

The police officer shifts uncomfortably. "Let's cut to the chase. We are aware you were at Kayden Colberg's party tonight. We would like you to come down to the police station and answer a few questions."

I look down at my PJs. "Do you mind if I get dressed first?"

The campus safety officer answers grimly, "That might be a good idea."

While the law enforcement officers go back out into the hallway, I throw on my jeans and a sweatshirt and put my long curly hair up into a scrunchie. I grab my cell phone and stuff it into my pocket.

As I open the door, I pull a piece of paper out of my notebook and look around for a pen.

"I guess I should leave Melanie a note so she doesn't worry about where I am."

The police officer clears his throat. "Unfortunately, I

don't think that's going to be a problem."

———— •♦• ————

I clutch my cell phone in my shaking hand as I ask Officer Monroe, "Do you mind if I call my Dad? I was on the phone with my family when you came into my dorm room. He's probably worried. I should let them know what's going on."

"Where does your dad live?" the campus officer inquires.

I blink back tears and swallow hard. "Oregon."

He turns to Officer Monroe and shrugs. "She's been cooperative, and it's going to be a long night. I don't see the harm."

Officer Monroe looks up in the rearview mirror and catches my eye. "Keep it short."

I nod and wipe away tears from the corners of my eyes as I dial my dad's number. As soon as we connect, my dad asks, "Are you okay, Princess Pumpkin?" Clearly Aunt Tara has queued them into the fact that something is going on if he's reverting to a childhood nickname for me he hasn't used in years.

"Yeah, I'm fine. I'm a little freaked out because I'm going to the police station to answer questions. I guess my roommate must be in some sort of trouble."

"Is everything okay? It's not like you not to know," he says, his voice full of concern.

"I don't know. Maybe I'm just adjusting to college, but everything is muddled right now."

"I'm sorry to hear that, Min. Did you have anything to do with your roommate's troubles?"

"No sir."

"Do you have information which might help them figure out how to help your friend?"

I shrug as more tears leak from the corners of my eyes. "I don't know. Maybe."

"Tell them what you know. You know the drill. Answer only the questions you are asked and try to keep the information limited to what the rest of us see, hear and feel. Just be as honest as you can be."

I lower my voice. "Okay, Daddy — I'll try. I miss you."

"Don't worry. Tyler and I are at the airport now. We're just waiting for a safety check on Aidan's plane. We'll be taking off shortly. Hang tight. You always have the right to ask for counsel, you know that."

"I know Dad. I didn't do anything wrong, I promise. I didn't let you down."

"I don't think you could, Mouse. You've survived tougher stuff. You'll do fine. I love you until."

"Me too, Dad. Bye."

The campus police officer looks back over his shoulder. "Feel better?"

I flash a wan smile. "A little, I suppose. My dad is awesome."

Officer Monroe shoots me a surprised look in the rear view mirror. "A lot of kids your age don't feel that way about their parents."

"Not everybody has a guy like Jeff Whitaker for a dad either."

Talking with my dad put me in a pretty good headspace. At least I'm no longer shaking. He is right. I've been through much tougher stuff. I rub my thumb over the scar tissue on my hand which never quite went away, despite many years of working with a plastic surgeon and hand therapist to overcome the horrific abuse I suffered as a child. My birth family cared more about drugs and alcohol than they did for me and my sister.

One day, my grandma was annoyed because I bothered her during her soap opera and she punished me by plunging my hand and arm into boiling water. For reasons I'll never understand, I was returned to my mother. Finally, I took matters into my own hands and ran away with Becca when she was only a few months old. After we were almost kidnapped during the escape, we landed in the hospital because we had been so neglected and malnourished.

In a roundabout way, that's how Jeff became my dad. He was dating Kiera back then. Becca and I were incredibly lucky. Kiera was the social worker who interviewed me after my Nana hurt me. I guess she could tell I didn't trust very many people so she gave me her private number and told me to call her if I ever needed her. When my Nana threatened to hurt Becca, I was planning to take the bus to the police station. I ended up calling Kiera after the bus driver wouldn't let us on the bus and I tried to hitchhike with a man and that didn't work out so well either. After all that drama, Jeff and Kiera worked tirelessly to adopt Becca and me.

At least I was fine until the officers escort me into a room with a one-way mirror. All the memories of one of the scariest days of my whole life crowd into my brain. Chills overtake my body and my teeth chatter.

I struggle to catch my breath as I reach over and grab a tissue from a nondescript tan box to blow my nose. It seems like I've been waiting here for a couple of hours. What I wouldn't give for my gift of precognition right now.

An older police officer enters the room with Officer Monroe. He reaches out to shake my hand. "Good evening, I'm Detective Jay Brannon." These days, I rarely think about my scars, but my trip down memory lane has made me more self-conscious than usual as I shake his hand.

Officer Monroe studies me for a moment before he interjects "Do you mind me asking — why the tears? You seem worse than you were during the ride in.

"You wouldn't understand. The last time I was in a room like this, it wasn't a good experience for me. It's a long story."

The detective crosses his arms in front of his chest as he says, "We've got nothing but time."

I shrug. "Okay, but don't say I didn't warn you. The last time I was this scared, I was trying to save my little sister from being burned. Ironically, I was trying to find a police station."

I grab a tissue and wipe my eyes, clear my throat and take a drink of water before I continue, "My Nana was convinced my sister was somehow evil so she was planning to mark her with her cigarette. I knew I had to do something. So when my grandma fell asleep, I grabbed Becca and all the money I had in my piggy bank and tried to catch a bus. I remember the bus driver laughing at me and a guy with scraggly blonde hair and cigarettes offering a ride in his car. I looked in the back of his car and he had a car seat, so I figured he had kids."

Officer Monroe flinches and takes a sip of his coffee.

"I didn't know what I was going to do. Becca was pretty heavy for me because I was only six. I couldn't walk all the way to the police station. I told the guy where I needed to go and he said he understood. So, I said I would go. I smiled at him and thanked him for being nice. He grabbed me and tried to kiss me. I was still holding onto Becca as tight as I could. I stomped on his foot and screamed. Then I ran. I went to the 7-11. I knew it was a store with lots of people because my biological mom used to buy beer there."

I pause to take a deep breath and collect myself.

"Kiera and Jeff came to rescue me. I remember sitting in the back of the store as I spoke to police officers and tried to tell my story while my sister screamed in the other part of the store."

"That must've been difficult for someone so young," Officer Monroe murmurs.

I nod. "Later, I had to come to a room eerily like this and try to identify the guy who tried to kiss me. I never did find him. Who knows how many other little girls or boys he tried to hurt? I'll never forget how scared I was of the big dark window. I was sure he could see right through it and know it was me looking at him. I remember being absolutely terrified. As scared as I was when I was six, I'm just about the same amount of freaked out right now."

"Try not to jump to any conclusions. We haven't even told you why you're here," Detective Brannon advises.

"That's part of the problem. You guys asked me to come here and I don't know exactly why — aside from the fact that Melanie hasn't come home from a party," I point out. "I think I have good reason to be scared."

Officer Monroe briefly leaves the room and comes back in with a cart. There is a breathalyzer test balanced precariously on the top. "I'm sorry this is so difficult for you. Usually when we see witnesses who are this emotional, there are illicit substances involved. Is that the case today?"

I shake my head. "No, sir."

Officer Monroe smiles at me. "You know, I've talked to a lot of college students during my career. You might be tempted to deny you've been drinking, but we're not here to bust you for alcohol use. We get that it's the thing to do. We need to know what we're dealing with. Do you mind if we get a baseline?"

"I'm not sure why the fact that my roommate didn't come home from a party gives you probable cause to test me — but since I've got nothing to hide. Go ahead."

Detective Brannon pulls out a legal pad and looks up at me. "When was the last time you consumed any alcohol, Ms. Whitaker?"

"I was six."

His eyebrows shoot up. "I beg your pardon?"

"My Nana was out of milk, so she poured some beer on my Rice Krispies. I didn't know any better so I tried to eat them. I threw up afterwards."

His mouth forms a grim line. "I see. Have you taken any other substances which might impair your function?"

"I had a headache on Wednesday. I took a couple of

Excedrin with caffeine."

Detective Brannon looks at me skeptically. "That's it? You were at one of the biggest parties on campus and you didn't drink?"

"No sir. I'd be happy to confirm it with a test."

Officer Monroe pulls out a form. "I need to see your ID so I can fill out these consent forms for the breathalyzer exam."

I try not to look nervous as I pull my ID out of my wallet. I grimace when I look at my driver's license picture. The officer studies it and looks up at me with a perplexed expression. "I've seen my fair share of fake IDs, but I've never seen someone admit to being only seventeen. What are you doing here and not back in high school getting ready for your homecoming dance or something?"

"If I was going to go to all the effort to fake an ID, don't you think I'd use a better photo? You'd have to look pretty hard to find a worse picture of me on the entire planet. To answer your other question — yes, I really am only seventeen. I'm here because I was one of those obnoxiously bright, precocious children who thought I should go conquer the world at an insanely young age. I am seriously second-guessing my choice these days."

While the officer is filling in the form, I blow my nose again and take a swig of water from the water bottle they provided. I glance over at Detective Brannon who is taking notes about I don't know what. "Will someone tell me why I'm here? What did Melanie do?"

Officer Monroe holds a plastic mouthpiece up. "Please blow into this for as long as you can. The machine will beep when you can stop."

I've seen this done on television, but I've never had to do it myself. It's harder than it looks — especially since I been crying. After what seems like forever, the machine finally beeps and I draw in a deep breath.

After a couple of seconds, the machine beeps again. Officer Monroe looks at Detective Brannon and shrugs. He pulls out a smaller handheld machine and holds it up to my mouth. "I hope you don't mind. This result is such an anomaly, we need to confirm." After I go through the whole routine again on the new gadget, Officer Munroe looks up at the detective in complete shock. "What do you know? She was telling the truth. Zero point zero." He turns back toward me. "We meant no offense Ms. Whitaker. College students almost reflexively lie about their drinking habits."

Something about their non-apology apology strikes me as amusing. I raise an eyebrow. "So far we've established I'm an atypical college student and I tell the truth. So, can we get on with why I'm here?"

"What can you tell me about what happened tonight?" Detective Brannon asks.

"As you can imagine, I'm finding it a little challenging to make friends here because I'm younger than everyone else and I'm pretty much the definition of lame. Melanie is my roommate, and she discovered I'm friends with Tasha Keeley. Apparently, for whatever reason that makes me valuable in her social circle. So, she thought I could help her impress some people from this sorority, Gamma Iota Nu. I guess she wants to rush them next week."

"Are you part of the sorority?"

"Are you kidding me? I don't understand people well enough to do the sorority thing. So, anyway ... Melanie tells me Kayden's sister, Kammie, is a power player in the sorority or something so Melanie wanted me to go to this party and be her wingman. It was pretty much the last place I wanted to be — but I also didn't want to tick Melanie off because roommate drama is no fun."

"Aside from Melanie Lake, did you know anybody at the party?" Detective Brannon asks.

"I didn't think I would know anyone, but Jodi was there. She lives three doors down from us on the same floor in the dorm. Her boyfriend is the Kayden Colberg dude who owns the house."

"Anyone else?"

"No. I mean, I saw people I go to class with, but I didn't know anyone else's name until I got there. I played pool with this guy named Joel and there was this other guy watching us play. I think his name was Brent or Brett."

Detective Brannon pauses and looks up from writing his notes. "Obviously, you weren't drinking, but what about the people you were with?"

I grimace. "This feels a bit like being a snitch in school. I try to stay out of other people's business."

"I understand. We're just trying to help Melanie here."

"It's funny you should say that. Melanie was the drunkest person I saw tonight. She started partying way before we actually went to the party. She said she needed to loosen up before she started talking to the guys. I don't know what she had in her Gatorade. Sometimes she drinks vodka and other times, she drinks Everclear."

"Do you know how she gets it? Isn't she a freshman like you?" Officer Monroe asks.

"As far as I know, the juniors and seniors buy it for her. I've never really asked her. She doesn't seem to have any trouble getting it."

"So, you thought she was impaired before she went to the party?"

"I'm not an expert or anything, but Melanie acted like my birth mom did when she was buzzed on alcohol. She thought everything was funny and her voice was kinda whiny."

"To your knowledge, did Melanie drink more while she was at the party?"

"Uh-huh. I tried to get her to slow down, but she was having too much fun."

"What happened next?" Officer Monroe asks.

"She told me that she and Jodi had to talk about sorority stuff. They told me to stay out of trouble and leave them alone."

Detective Brannon leans forward in his chair. "Did you see her again after that?"

I nod. "It wasn't pretty. The next time I saw her, Jodi and her friend were practically holding Melanie up. But that didn't stop her from being completely ticked off at me. Remember I told you about that guy, Joel Thackett? In addition to being a self-professed superb pool player, he happens to be Kammie Colberg's boyfriend."

Detective Brannon thumbs back through his notes. "Kammie Colberg?" He asks quizzically.

"Powerful sorority sister in Gamma Iota Nu," I explain. "Apparently, I committed some huge social sin by playing pool with her boyfriend, even though he's the one who invited me to play. Melanie was livid. She told me to go home. She said she didn't want to be my roommate anymore."

"Did you know this guy had a girlfriend?"

"No! How would I even know that? He just asked me to play pool."

"Where you guys actually playing pool or doing more?"

"We were playing pool. More precisely, I was clearing the table while Joel watched."

"Okay, point taken," Officer Monroe concedes with a fleeting smile.

"So, what happened after Melanie demanded that you leave," Detective Brannon asks. "Did Joel take you home?"

"He offered, but I didn't want to start another fight so I just called the campus shuttle."

"Do you remember if you took the red one or the yellow one?"

"It was definitely yellow. I remember thinking it looked like a big ole' obnoxious banana."

Officer Monroe looks at Detective Brannon. "I'll call Chet and ask him to upload the security footage from the bus."

"Why would you need it? What's going on here?"

Detective Brandon shifts his chair toward me so he is directly looking at me. "There is no easy way to tell you this. Something happened to Melanie Lake tonight. We are trying to determine whether she passed away from natural causes or whether her death was a homicide."

I feel like the detective just sucker punched me.

"Melanie is *dead*? I just saw her a couple of hours ago. Yeah, she was drunk — but she wasn't dead," I repeat out loud as I try to process the news.

"I hate to ask this. Did you go anywhere after the shuttle dropped you off at your dorm room?" Detective Brannon presses.

"No, I didn't! If you must know, I cried for a while because I was upset at myself for my epic lack of social skills. I called my Aunt Tara — we're not actually related but everyone in my family treats us as if we are. I told her all about my horribly awkward night at the party and I whined about how much I don't fit in at college. I changed into my jammies, then you guys showed up and I changed back into street clothes. That's how my horrible, no good, awful, can-I-please-wake-up-from-this-nightmare night has gone."

"I'm sorry for your loss." Detective Brannon hands me a tissue.

"As horrible as my night was, I'm alive. I can't imagine what Melanie went through."

Detective Brannon lays his hand on my shoulder. "Ms. Whitaker, you can't think that way. These things happen. You can't hold yourself responsible. Even if you would've known, you might not have been able to stop it. Sometimes, fate has a mind of its own."

I sigh. "I don't think you understand. There was a time in my life when it almost seemed as if I could tempt fate and give it a helping hand. Unfortunately, I think those days are behind me."

There is a knock on the door. Officer Monroe stands up to answer it. Another officer peeks his head in the door and says, "Ms. Whitaker's father is here and he would like to see his daughter."

Detective Brannon glowers at the younger officer. "Normally, I would tell him to wait, but we are finished here anyway."

"Understood, Sir."

As soon as I see my dad in the doorway, I run into his arms and give him a huge hug. "I'm sorry Dad. I should've followed my gut feeling and not gone to the party at all. I was just trying to be a good friend and fit in. I don't know what happened to Melanie. I still can't get over the feeling I somehow should've stopped it. I don't think college life is for me. Maybe I should come home."

My dad simply holds me tight for a few moments while he absorbs my fear. "Princess, I'm not sure you need to make those decisions at this very moment. Let's let Tyler talk to them about what the safest route is for you right now. Your roommate could just be staying with friends or something."

"No, Dad ... they know where she is. Melanie is dead."

"Oh ... in that case, taking a term or two off may not be such a bad idea."

My dad catches the eye of Detective Brannon over my head. "My daughter has had an exceptionally long night. Do you need anything else from her?"

Detective Brennan consults his paperwork. "Assuming the evidence backs up her statements, we shouldn't require anything further. I have her contact information if I need more." He turns to me. "Thank you so much for being so forthcoming. We will try our hardest to determine what happened to your friend, Ms.

Whitaker."

"That's all I can ask. Nobody deserves to die because they went to a party."

CHAPTER FOUR

ELIJAH

I ALMOST WALK RIGHT past the small secluded waiting room. It's been a while since I've seen my sister and I almost don't recognize her. She cut her hair since I last saw her. At the moment, she's hunched over her laptop computer with a grim expression on her face. I look around the small area, and I don't see my mother.

I walk over to Mariam and put my arm around her shoulder. She must be playing music through her earbuds because she jumps when she feels me touch her. "Where's Mom?"

Mariam sticks her hand around my waist and squeezes. "She's had enough waiting for now so she went to go get fresh coffee and take a little walk. The doctors say dad will be in surgery at least three more hours."

"Jigger, jig, jig, I thought you told me he had surgery yesterday?"

Mariam blanches. "He did. They had to remove his spleen and insert a tracheotomy tube. He had a fractured rib which tore up some blood vessels and caused internal bleeding. Today, they're trying to stabilize an injury to his T-1 vertebrae so he doesn't end up paralyzed. He has bleeding from a skull fracture. Apparently they're going to try to remove a blood clot too."

"Is he out of the woods, jigger, jig, jig, yet?" I shrug my backpack off and sit down in one of the nondescript chairs in the waiting room.

Mariam shakes her head. "No, this is only the beginning. They don't even know if the surgery will help. Apparently there are parts of his vertebrae which were nearly pulverized in the accident. They're trying to reconstruct it piece by piece."

"Jigger, jig, jig, what happened? Dad usually works a long way away from the flaggers. How was there a vehicle anywhere near where he was working?"

"I don't know. I was just looking at the pictures a few of his coworkers sent me of the accident scene. They're weird. I was talking to dad about this project the other day. They were about to wrap it up. Dad couldn't tell me much. He said something about it didn't sit right with him. Parts of it which should have taken a while to complete seem to be rushed and other parts which should have been routine seemed to take a long time. It struck him as strange. He was being extra meticulous about his inspection. It was starting to rub several contractors the wrong way. He said he was getting a great deal of heat from his supervisors to hurry up and finish approving the project."

I stare at my sister with my mouth wide open. "Mari, are you saying what I think you're saying, jigger, jig, jig?"

Tears spring to her eyes. "Don't pay any attention to me. I'm exhausted. I haven't slept in days. I probably don't know what I'm talking about. I just know Dad is super careful in his job and he doesn't say anything unless he's got a reason to believe something is amiss. Maybe he was trying to tell me something. You know what I mean?"

"Jigger, jig, jig, you're right. Dad is a very cautious man. Still … that's a big leap to make."

"I know. I know! I could just be going insane because I'm so tired. It may be nothing but delirious ramblings. I'm not sure about anything anymore. It seems strange there were so many people standing around watching all this happen and every single one of them has a different story to tell."

I fish the hotel key out of the pocket of my jeans. I walk over to where Mariam is sitting and place it on the table in front of her. "Go. Find Mom and get yourselves a decent meal and then take a nap. Jigger, jig, jig, if the doctors have something interesting to say, I'll text you. Otherwise get some rest. Like you said, it'll be hours before they have any news. You might as well get a little sleep. I'll take this shift, jigger, jig, jig."

My sister rubs her eyes with the heels of her hands. She stands up and stretches. "I should probably stay and present a united Fischer front and all that — but I'm so exhausted I'm not sure how much longer I can stay conscious. I'm almost positive Mom feels the same way. A nap and a hot shower would work wonders."

"Sounds good. Don't worry about the key. Jigger, jig, jig, I had the front desk make extras. Sadie got us in at the Marriott."

Mariam shakes her head and chuckles softly. "You guys don't even live in the same city and that woman still takes better care of you than any wife. Are you sure you don't want to marry Sadie?"

I roll my eyes. "Jigger, jig, jig, not you too! No one seems to understand Sadie has never been anything other than my best friend. I agree she is amazing, but we're merely friends. Besides, I think her boyfriend would probably object if I marry her."

"It's too bad, I think you probably let a great one get away," my sister comments as she packs up her computer and her oversized purse and slings it over her shoulder. "You know where I'll be. Call me if anything happens, promise?"

"I promise. Unless it's life or death, I can handle it."

"I know. You may be my little brother, but I still trust you."

<hr>

I stare at the document in front of me for what seems like forever before I close it down and open a blank file. Sadie is right. I missed the mark. I didn't miss it by mere inches, I missed it by miles. If I'm going to do Cody and Jasmine's story justice, I have to tell it with nothing but total honesty. To do that, I have to start over from scratch. I can't just edit what I already have. I have to dig deep and put Cody back in the story — this time front and center. I can't just hint at his presence, he has to be the star.

I pull up the playlist Cody sent me and put in my earbuds as I re-frame the story in my mind. Cody cares a lot about his younger siblings. What would he want them to know if he had only a limited amount of time left to share his knowledge? What if they didn't listen?

In no time at all I have a rough outline of my revised

story. I can already tell it has more life and movement than my completed manuscript. Just as I was about to settle into writing my first draft again, someone knocks on the doorframe to the small waiting room. It takes me a few moments to leave my world of fiction and become re-acclimated to the real world. I'm startled when I recognize a familiar face.

"I'm sorry to bother you. I don't know if you remember me, but I'm Tyler Colton. I'm looking for your sister."

"Jigger, jig, jig, of course I remember you. You were at our launch party for *Behind Glass Bars*. Your wife said you threatened to show up in your army fatigues. Jigger, jig, jig, I didn't realize Mariam knew you."

Tyler grins at me. "Like nearly everyone else, she doesn't really know me. She knows Heather. Heather provided a wedding cake for a wedding your sister was involved in."

I narrow my gaze at Tyler. "Jigger, jig, jig, so what do you want with Mariam?"

"Mariam is aware of my law enforcement connections and she wanted to know the name of my favorite accident reconstruction expert. We happened to be in Portland when I got her text, so I thought I'd stop by. How is your dad, by the way?"

"Umm … wow! Jigger, jig, jig, she's really serious about her concerns about Dad's accident. I'm not exactly sure how he is. He was already in surgery by the time I arrived from California. I sent Mariam and my mom back to my hotel for some much needed rest, jigger, jig, jig."

"From the sound of things, that was probably a good idea. I know when my men are hurt, the hardest part is the sitting around waiting for things to happen. The not knowing part is hard."

"Thank you. If you want to give me the name of your guy, I'll be sure to give it to my sister."

"Actually, the best guy I know in the business is a woman. Her name is Claudia Featherstone. If anyone can solve the puzzle of what happened to your dad, it's her. She used to work out of the city of Seattle, she's freelancing now. Here is her card."

"Jigger, jig, jig, thank you so much. I'm sure Mariam will appreciate this." I pull my wallet out of my back pocket and carefully file the card away.

I'm startled when I hear another person clear their throat. "I don't know if you need another referral, but I'm Jeff Whitaker. I've been a member of the Oregon bar for several years now. I don't do workers comp or personal injury law, but I have friends who do. If you'd like some recommendations, I'd be happy to get some."

"Jigger, jig, jig, Whitaker? Are you Gabriel's uncle and Mindy's dad, jigger, jig, jig?"

His eyes widen. "I am." He studies me for a moment. "Oh … wait. You went to the prom with Gabriel and Sadie a few years back, right? I remember taking pictures of you guys for my sister when I picked you up."

"Quite a few years ago now, jigger, jig, jig," I reply as I feel my face turn red.

"I used to stutter when I was younger, it can get awkward," Jeff comments. "Sometimes in a high-pressure case, I still do it in court."

"Some people don't understand, jigger, jig, jig," I concede.

Jeff turns around and checks the hallway behind him.

"It's too bad Mindy had to take a phone call, she'd be thrilled to see you. You are still one of her favorite authors. Your book had a profound impact on her life."

"Honestly, I'm not sure Sadie and I were quite prepared for all the changes our book would bring for everyone involved."

"It seems a lot of people thought *Behind Glass Bars* was pretty impressive — and not just my daughter, although she does have exquisite taste in books."

I hear a chuckle before a slightly husky, melodic voice I will never forget says, "Dad, way to work a complement for me and my favorite book into the same sentence. I don't mind, of course. But, it is a rather strange conversation to be having in the middle of the hospital."

Jeff steps out of the doorway so Mindy can see me sitting behind my computer.

"Oh. My. Gosh. This. Is. So. Not. Happening. To. Me." she hides her face in her hands for a moment and then puts them down at her side. She clenches and unclenches her fists in frustration. She walks up to Tyler and pokes him in the chest. "You could've warned me. But no! Instead you told me you were dropping off a business card for someone who had been a bridesmaid in a wedding Aunt Heather catered. I am a complete mess. My sweats were a gag gift from Aunt Donda. They have Oscar the Grouch all over them. Just for the record, Elijah doesn't look like he's been a bridesmaid in any weddings recently."

"I'm sorry, Mouse. I forgot you knew Elijah. I wasn't expecting him to be here. I actually thought I was meeting his sister Mariam."

I feel compelled to intercede. "It's not Tyler's fault. I sent Mariam home because she and my mom are exhausted. I just got here and I'm too keyed up to rest. So I thought I would take a shift while we wait for my dad to get out of surgery. Don't worry about impressing me. Have you taken a good look at me? It's been a couple days since I've shaved and I'm not even sure I know where my contact lenses are."

"What happened to your dad?" Mindy asks.

I run my hand through my disheveled hair. "My dad was inspecting some construction on a bridge and someone ran over him. That's all I know. He's fighting for his life and no one knows why. I wish I knew. At this point I have more questions than answers."

Mindy swallows hard and wipes away tears with the back of her hand. "I'm sorry. Normally, I would be able help you find answers. But for some reason I can't — in your life or in mine."

Something about the sadness in her eyes is unsettling. I reach out and brush the hair out of her face.

"Mindy, it's not your job to solve the problems in my life. But, thanks for offering."

"Still, I wish I could —"

"I know you're probably busy with school, but I'm working on a special project and I could use a little constructive input. Would you be interested in helping?" I offer before I have a chance to formulate my thoughts completely.

I walk over to the table where I was taking notes in my journal and I tear off a piece of paper. Taking the pen I keep tucked behind my ear, I jot down my cell phone number. "Send me a text so I have your number. I'll be in touch."

If Mindy's smile as she leaves the waiting room is anything to go by, my impromptu offer brightened her day as much as it did mine.

———————◆●————————

I don't think I've ever seen anyone hooked up to so many machines in my life. I guess I've seen things like this on television — but they don't prepare you for all the noise and the blinking lights. Even though my dad is laying perfectly still, pain radiates off of him as if it's a physical being lurking above his body.

Even though my mother works in the healthcare industry as a nursing home inspector, she is completely distraught. I can tell she wants to touch my dad, but she is afraid of causing more pain. She has found one small area on the back of his hand not covered with adhesive tape, IVs or monitors. She is stroking his hand and softly speaking to him in a mixture of English and Yiddish. I'm not sure if she's talking to my father, yelling at God, or both.

Mariam is hunched in the recliner chair in the corner of the room with her knees drawn up to her chest. She is running her finger over the raised print on Claudia Featherstone's business card. "Mr. Colton didn't tell you anything else about her?" she presses as she looks up at me with red-rimmed eyes.

"Only that she freelances now, jigger, jig, jig, and that she is one of the best he's ever worked with."

"Do you think it would be okay if I called her?" She bites her lip and studies the card.

"Jigger, jig, jig, I don't think he would have given me

the card if he didn't want you to call. After all, he went to all the effort of dropping it off in person."

My mother turns to Mariam and chides sharply, "Don't you go messing around where you shouldn't be. We can't afford to lose your dad's health insurance right now."

"Mom, I'm not planning to sue anyone tomorrow or anything. I just want to know what happened. Not everyone who saw the accident seems to be telling the same story. I want an expert to talk to them before they all get their stories straight."

"Well, don't you go and make yourself a troublemaker. Your father has enough to worry about without having to find a new job. We don't even know if he'll end up in a wheelchair for the rest of his life — if he makes it through all of this. Do you understand?"

My sister looks crushed.

"Jigger, jig, jig, Mom, Mariam isn't trying to cause any trouble. She's simply trying to find answers in case we need them later. I don't think Mr. Colton would recommend someone who would make things harder for us. He's totally come through for me in the past. His friend, Mr. Whitaker, even offered to refer us to an attorney if we need one."

My mom looks over at my dad as a fresh alarm starts to go off and a nurse rushes into the room to adjust the sensor and turn it off. She slumps back into the chair. "I suppose you two are right. It's probably not too early to think about these things."

My mom gingerly grabs my dad's hand again. "I wish I could go back to the way things were a couple days ago when I was kissing your dad goodbye before he went to work. He asked me if I wanted to go out for dinner. I told him not to bother because I needed to have my hair done and I wasn't fit to go out in public. Seth wanted to stop and cuddle for a moment. I told him he was being silly and he needed to go to work. I wish I would've stopped and hugged him and told him I loved him — but I didn't. I treated his love like it was a big joke. I'm so angry at myself. What if he was thinking about the conversation and not paying attention to his job? What if I would've stopped and given Seth a hug and kiss and reminded him how much I loved him?"

Mariam gasps. "Mom, you can't do that to yourself. You had no way of knowing what would happen. None of us did."

My mom vehemently shakes her head. "That's not true. I knew your father's job had risks. I should've been living and loving him like every day mattered."

Her words echo all the way down to my soul.

CHAPTER FIVE

MINDY

MY SIX-YEAR-OLD brother, Charlie is staring at me as if he's never seen me before. I throw the grated cheese into the scrambled eggs and stir them before I scrape them out on the platter and carry it over to the dining table. After I finish setting the table and putting serving spoons on the table, I call Becca to breakfast. I pull a chair out for Charlie and wait for him to sit down before I sit in the chair next to him. "Did you have a question?" I ask, as he continues to stare.

"Did you kill somebody?" My little brother narrows his eyes at me in a move so similar to my dad's, it's spooky. I feel like I'm being cross-examined.

"No! Whatever gave you that idea?"

"I heard Dad talking on the phone to Aunt Tara. He told her he had to fly on an airplane to go help you because somebody died. People die all the time and you don't need the help of a lawyer man like Daddy. I figured you must have killed her."

"You misunderstood, Charlie. I didn't kill her. As far

as I know, nobody knows exactly why Melanie died. I wasn't even around when she passed away. I was back in my dorm room talking to Aunt Tara."

"So why did Daddy take Uncle Tyler with him?"

"I think Dad was afraid I would feel scared and alone and he wanted to make sure I had as much help around me as I could in case I needed it."

"So how come you're not still in school? Did they cancel school?"

I shake my head. "No, I don't think they canceled school. But, Melanie was my friend and my roommate. Since no one knows why she died, it makes Uncle Tyler and Dad feel more comfortable when they can keep an eye on me."

Charlie puffs out his chest. "I can help watch out for you too. Grandpa says I'm becoming a strong young man."

I reach out and ruffle his hair. "I'm sure you are Charlie. I can already tell you've grown in the few months I've been gone."

"Are you going to quit college?" Charlie asks with an anxious expression. "If you do, I bet Mom will be super ticked off. Every time I get a bad grade, Mom always tells me I need to do better because college is super-duper important."

Becca comes in from the kitchen carrying a plate of toast and a carton of orange juice. "Come on, Charlie. Let's leave Mindy alone. She just barely got here. It's too early in the morning to make any decisions. Let's eat breakfast in peace, okay?"

"Okay! But I'm not wrong. Mom and Dad wouldn't let me drop out of school! They wouldn't even let me miss a day when Lucky died."

"Charlie!" Becca scolds. "We weren't going to tell her until Christmas break, remember?" Becca looks at me and explains, "We didn't want to upset you during your first week of school."

"I appreciate it. But Uncle Tyler told me ages ago. He thought Dad might need some extra hugs — even if I had to give them over Skype."

I eat a few bites of my eggs before I turn to Charlie. "I honestly don't know what I'm going to do about school. I don't think I'll stop college forever. I might take a break for a while and travel with Uncle Aidan and the band while I figure out what I want to do. I haven't decided whether I want to go into the medical field or whether I want to be a lawyer like Dad. I should probably figure that out before I decide where I want to go to school. I figured going away for college would be like the coolest thing ever. I guess I was wrong. Bullying is as big a problem as it ever was in high school. I guess I thought I would find my own tribe of super cool, smart kids like me. But that's not the way it worked out."

"Have you met everyone in your whole school?" My little sister rolls her eyes. "There are a lot more people at your college than back in high school. Maybe you just haven't found people you click with yet. You've only been there a few weeks. You were probably hanging out in your room as usual. Have you even taken your nose out of your precious books?"

I avert my gaze as I shrug. My little sister doesn't even need to live in the same state as me to know exactly how I spend my time. Suddenly, she seems way older than twelve and a half.

"Have you played your guitar for them?" Charlie asks. "You always make lots of friends when you sing and play your guitar. Do they know you have a song on the radio?"

I grimace. "Yeah, a few people know."

My sister laughs out loud. "What gives? You say it like it's a bad thing. Uncle Aidan pays you for singing. Did you forget? The better the single does, the more you get paid, remember? Besides, it was totally cool when my friends and I were at the mall shopping for school clothes and the song came on and I was able to tell them it was you."

"That's just it. I wish I could play. I miss music a lot. I haven't played much around campus because I don't know if people want to hang out with me because they think I know famous people like Uncle Aidan or Tasha and Jude — or if they really like me."

Becky shrugs. "Seems simple enough to me. If they only hit you up for concert tickets, they probably are fame seekers. If they hang out with you when you have the flu or if they help you study for a big test, they're probably your friends. It doesn't take a rocket scientist to figure it out. I think you can totally handle it."

I grin as I put jam on my toast and take a bite. "Who knew it could be so simple? If only all my problems could be solved so easily."

"Speaking of problems, can you help me figure out what to wear to Addison's slumber party? She's having a Star Wars movie marathon. She's inviting a bunch of boys from our class."

"There'll be boys at this slumber party?" I ask as my eyebrows climb in surprise.

"No! They have to go home at midnight. But, they'll still be there."

I wink at her. "Gotcha. So, in other words, you want to look spectacular, but you don't want to look like you're trying too hard."

"Oh my gosh! You totally get it. How do I dress up without looking like I'm dressing up?"

"It's a battle I fight every single day when I get dressed in college."

"I thought everybody wore pajamas to class in college?" my sister replies.

"It's a delicate balance. The idea is to look as casual as you can while having your makeup and hair look as flawless as possible. It drives me insane. Nobody looks that good rolling right out of bed."

Charlie grabs a piece of sausage off of the platter as he comments, "Geez, no wonder college is so stressful. Girls are strange."

Becca and I look at each other and burst out laughing as I say, "You have absolutely no idea."

———◆———

My dad slides a mug of steaming hot milk in front of me, and breaks my concentration. I smile when I smell vanilla. I can't believe he remembers my favorite bedtime snack. When I was a kid and had a hard time sleeping, he used to fix it for me and hold me in his lap as he reviewed case law for his trials the next day.

When he sees the two newspaper articles I have up on my computer screen, he frowns. "Princess, you cannot do this to yourself."

When I lift my heavy hair off my neck and twist it into a knot, he pushes my hands aside. He grabs a wide-tooth comb off of my desk and divides up my hair. He methodically French braids it as he's done since the first day we met.

I exhale and fight back tears as I fervently wish I was a child playing with Barbies. I remember my dad indulgently playing the role of Prince Charming coming to save the day. These days, I'm not so sure any guy would have the superpowers necessary to save me. Heck, these days even I've lost my superpower.

When he finishes braiding my hair, he taps me on my shoulder and I hold up my wrist so he can remove the scrunchie I habitually wear there. After he twists it around the end of my braid several times, he spins my little office chair around so I'm facing him.

"You want to tell me why you're torturing yourself like this?" He gestures toward the computer screens.

"Dad, it says here they're looking at several persons of interest who were around Melanie right before she died. They could mean me, right?" My voice breaks as my fear leaks through.

"Mouse, unless there's something you haven't told me about the situation, you don't have anything to worry about. You were a couple of miles from where Melanie died."

I lean back in the little roll around chair and flick tears from my eyes with my fingertips. "That's true. But Melanie was pissed with me when I left. People will remember the drama. She was screaming about how much she hated me and never wanted to see me again."

"People say a lot of awful things when they're drunk.

I'm sure the people at the party knew Melanie was wasted."

"What if everyone thinks I was ticked off at her for what she said and wanted to get even?"

My dad leans over and kisses me on the forehead. "If they could even think that about you, they don't know you very well."

"That's what I'm afraid of Daddy. Hardly anyone knows me there and the people who do know me think I'm creepy. The rumor mill was terrible before this happened, I can imagine what people are saying about me now."

"I'm sorry Mindy, but, sitting here stewing about it won't help you. I think you should go out on this leg of the tour with Aidan. He was telling me he really needs you. This isn't simply a bogus pity offer. Stella has to go in and have surgery for vocal polyps. He needs you to sing backup."

"What if they need me for this case?" I ask as I look back toward my desk.

"Well, that's the nice thing about modern technology. Aidan can stick you on a plane if he needs to. Otherwise, everything else can be done over the Internet."

"Are you sure?" I ask skeptically.

"Yes. I've even been known to conduct depositions via videoconferencing." my dad answers with a chuckle. "You'd be amazed how much the Internet has changed the justice system."

I lean forward and hug my dad. "Thank you, Daddy. I can't sit around and wait another day. This is driving me absolutely crazy."

"Believe it or not, your Uncle Aidan will be even more excited about the news than you are. I think he's been holding his breath waiting for you to decide."

"I always lose myself in my music, but this time I hope I find myself too. I'm tired of feeling lost."

"I hope you find what you're looking for too. But remember, sometimes answers come when you stop looking for them."

———◆●———

"How does it feel to be back on stage?" Katie asks me as we take a break during a sound check.

I take a bite of my granola bar while I ponder how candid to be. "Honestly? Weird. I thought I closed this chapter in my life. Music has always been a creative outlet for me to burn excess energy. It's like my brain is busier than everyone else's. I have to keep it occupied with something. After Jeff and Kiera adopted me, Uncle Aidan taught me to play the piano on a whim. He didn't realize I would pick it up quite so fast. After I got bored with piano lessons, he taught me how to play the guitar. I suppose it's my favorite."

"How did you get started singing?" Katie asks.

"My grandma from my dad's side of the family got lung cancer and my grandpa from my mom's side of the family fell in love with her. So, I wanted to sing a song which said all the things Grandpa Denny couldn't say out loud. Uncle Aidan helped me sing it at their engagement party."

"What a sweet story," Katie says with a sigh.

I shrug. "Yeah, everybody seemed to like it so that's how I started singing with Uncle Aidan and Tasha."

Katie studies me carefully. "You're an exceptionally talented singer with tons of fans. Why do I get the feeling you're not overly excited about that?"

I take a gulp of my water before I lay it all out.

"I don't know what I'm supposed to be doing with my life," I confess.

Katie raises an eyebrow. "Welcome to the club. I don't think any of us do."

"No, I don't think you understand. From the moment Kiera wheeled into the little conference room when I was a kid, I knew she would save my life. I also knew I would do everything in my power to repay her and Jeff for the kindness they showed Becca and me. I knew my life would go in one of two directions. I figured I would be a lawyer like Jeff or a doctor like Uncle Jaxson. Although I've always known I probably couldn't fix my mom, I could work on finding a cure for autonomic dysreflexia so my parents wouldn't have to live in fear of a random injury putting my mom's life in danger."

Katie pulls the neckline of her shirt to the side and shows me the scar from where she was shot. "Mindy, if anybody knows about plans being derailed and changed, it's me. Who knows? This might simply be a small bump in the road or it might be a new path for you. A new path doesn't necessarily mean an inferior one. Just because things aren't turning out the way you planned doesn't mean they won't turn out the way they should."

"It would be nice if life was as simple as a motivational poster."

Katie grins at me. "Look at me. I left what should have been a picture-perfect wedding because I found out my fiancé was a narcissistic jerk. While I was trying to drown my troubles in Jack Daniels, I found the love of my life. There was nothing predictable or even motivational about that. I guess it was simply meant to be."

"I'm not sure I know how to believe in meant-to -be anymore. If things were 'meant-to-be' why would I know something was wrong with Aunt Tara's pregnancy with Adriana, but not be able to stop it from happening? Why couldn't I convince Melanie not to go to the stupid party? What good does it do me to see the future if I can't change it? I am a failure at everything."

"I don't know the answer, Mindy. All I can tell you is I am grateful for what you can see because you saved the life of the man I love. You can't say you never change the future."

I lean my elbows on the table and bury my head in my hands. "I can't even do that anymore. I've lost part of who I am. I can't see the future and I can't fix the past. My Nana was right. I'm worthless. I don't deserve to be loved."

Katie stands up and walks around the table. She puts her arm around my shoulder. "Mindy, you just have a good old-fashioned case of survivor's guilt. I know, it's hard. I've been in your shoes. None of this is your fault. There are hundreds of people in your life who love you simply because you are you. Never forget that."

Before I can fully absorb the impact of Katie's words, Maddie, Uncle Aidan and Aunt Tara's daughter comes screaming around the corner in her bright purple wheelchair so quickly I'm afraid she might tip it over. I can't help but smile at the eager expression on her face. She reminds me so much of myself — from her wild hair to her sometimes watchful expression.

"Careful, Madison, you'll leave skid marks on the floor if you don't slow down," teases Katie.

Maddie looks down at the floor with a puzzled expression. "I am?"

"I'm teasing, you little speed demon. Did you need something?" Katie answered with a grin.

"Oh … yeah. My dad said to tell Mindy they're ready for her on the stage."

"Thank you Maddie, I'll be there in a second."

"Daddy says if I keep practicing I'll be as good as you," Maddie says as she starts to wheel away. "I can't wait."

Katie winks at me. "See? What did I tell you? People love you. You have fans everywhere you look."

CHAPTER SIX

ELIJAH

MARIAM HANGS A NECKLACE made from a glow stick around my neck and hands me an artificial candle. "Smile! This is supposed to be a celebration."

"Jigger, jig, jig, are you sure this is the best time to do this? Dad is due home from the rehab center on Thursday."

"That's why this is the perfect time. Mom is out playing bingo with Aunt Lila. She told us to go out and have a little fun. The people remodeling our bathroom won't be here until Monday. The neighbor guy who's helping with the ramp can't come until Sunday. You have no legitimate excuse not to celebrate tonight."

"Still, Dad might want a few visitors at the rehab center," I argue.

Mariam snickers. "Actually, he doesn't. He made a friend during physical therapy. They went in together and bought a pay-per-view fight. They're planning to watch it tonight and play cards. He told me they don't want any young'uns around because they don't want to censor their language for sensitive ears."

I snort with disbelief. "The accident must have affected Dad's memory. He obviously has forgotten who his children are. We've both been known to cuss like sailors, jigger, jig, jig."

"Oh, I think he knows. I think he was just looking for an excuse to give Mom a break from her twenty-four-hour/seven-day-a-week vigil. She told him Aunt Lila would be in town. He knows they like to go to the senior center to play bingo. He merely told them the story as a fantastic excuse to encourage them to go play. Whether or not he really has a pay-per-view boxing match to watch is anybody's guess."

I shrug. "Jigger, jig, jig knowing Dad, they probably did buy a fight because Dad totally gets into that kind of thing."

"Speaking of stories — congratulations on completing your new manuscript. What does your editor think of it?"

"Douglas seems to like this one much better. Jigger, jig, jig, although Candace is blowing a gasket because I moved back to Oregon. She thinks the public perceives me as a much edgier writer when I live in California. Jigger, jig, jig, I don't see how it makes any difference. I can create my books anywhere I have a computer."

"I'm sorry, but this woman sounds like she misplaced her heart somewhere. It's not like you just got a hair up your butt and decided you didn't like the view from your front-room window. You moved because your father was in a life-threatening accident. She needs to get a clue."

"This isn't the first time I've had that thought. Jigger, jig, jig, trust me."

"Maybe you need to stop thinking about it and do something about it."

"Do what?" I ask.

"I don't know. There must be something you can do. You shouldn't have to put up with someone like her," Mariam replies. "What does Sadie think?"

"Well, Sadie has never been one of her biggest fans. She thinks I can do better. I'm not sure. Jigger, jig, jig, maybe Candace is right. Perhaps without her I would have never gotten a contract at all and I should simply be grateful."

"Or maybe, you could be doing a hundred times better if you had an agent who understood where you are coming from and where you want to go," Mariam counters.

Mariam sucks in a deep breath as the house lights go down and four figures show up on stage. "Here we go. This is so cool!"

———————•●————————

Cool indeed. Sometimes my sister has a gift for dramatically understating things. This is one of those times.

The spotlight is intended to draw attention to Tasha and Aidan who are standing center stage singing a duet. Jude and Mindy are in the shadows accompanying them with their guitars. As awesome as they all sound, the rest of them might as well not be on stage. Mindy draws all of my attention.

There aren't any Oscar the Grouch sweatpants to be found today. It's hard to believe the sophisticated sexy woman in front of me is the same woman I saw the other day. Her wild curly hair is falling in soft curls around her shoulders as she sways with the music. I don't know if I've ever seen her wearing makeup, but she looks amazing. The spotlight highlights her pale skin and makes her smokey eye makeup and her deep rose colored lips stand out even more. She opens her eyes and looks out into the audience — seemingly at me — as she sings vocals with Jude. My heart seems to skip a beat.

When the song ends Aidan motions Mindy over toward the center of the stage. She looks puzzled as she joins him. Obviously, they haven't rehearsed this because Tasha and Jude look confused as well. Aidan slips his arm around Mindy's shoulders as he whispers, "Relax. This is nothing bad, I promise." Of course his microphone picks up everything, and the audience laughs as Mindy slumps with relief.

Aidan turns to the audience and announces, "You all know Mindy is a phenomenal singer. You'll get a chance to hear her and Tasha sing their latest single in a moment. But, if you think it's great when you hear it on the radio, you are in for a treat because it's magnificent live."

"Okay … but it won't be unless you let Tasha and me reset for the song," Mindy mumbles as she blushes.

"I will. But I have a little something I need to do first. You all might not know this, but Mindy is more than just a singer here at Silent Beats. I have known her since she was six years old. She is more like my niece. In fact, if she's not paying attention, she is likely to call me Uncle Aidan and I'm just as likely to call her by her childhood nickname, Mindy Mouse. But, I guess I probably shouldn't do that anymore because after today, Mindy officially isn't a kid. Happy eighteenth birthday, kiddo!" Aidan announces as he pulls out a funny little cardboard crown and sticks it on her head.

Jerome, the bass player wheels out a beautiful cake. Mindy reaches up and hugs Aidan. "It's not very nice of you to make me cry before I have to sing. But thank you so much for the birthday surprise."

Tasha walks over and gives Mindy a high five. "Blow out your candles, Birthday Girl!"

Mindy gives her a somber look. "I will. I have to decide what to wish for first."

"That's just a silly superstition. More than anyone else I know, you are in charge of your own destiny. If I were you, I wouldn't worry about tempting fate."

Mindy shrugs. "I suppose you're right. Besides," she says as she points to us, "these guys came for a show, so I guess we better give them one." She leans forward, holds her hair back and blows out the candles. When there's a stubborn one which won't extinguish, she blows on it several more times before it goes out. Mindy laughs out loud and then walks over to the mic near center stage. Jude grins at her before he walks over to her stool, grabs her guitar and hands it to her. She blushes and puts it over her head and then steps back up to the mic. She seems to take a moment to center herself before she starts to play the haunting melody.

Once again, I am adrift in the music as Mindy begins to sing about love almost lost.

———————◆●◆———————

Grinning from ear-to-ear, Mariam is practically jumping up and down when the house lights finally come up. "This is the best concert I've ever been to. All I can say is someday I want a guy to look at me the way Jude looks at Tasha. It's like he forgot the audience was out here."

"Jigger, jig, jig, I agree. There's some serious chemistry between them. Although, if Tasha Keeley was my girlfriend, I'd probably feel the same way. She's quite easy on the eyes."

"Oh really? I could've sworn the only person you noticed on the stage was Mindy Whitaker. You seemed extraordinarily taken with her," my sister teases.

Mariam always knows how to get under my skin. I feel my face heat as I blush. "Jigger, jig, jig I think she's interesting. I met her a few years ago, she's changed a lot."

"In other words, you like her," Mariam presses.

"What would be the point, jigger, jig, jig? She'd never be interested in me."

Mariam cuffs me on the shoulder. "Why wouldn't she be? You're smart, funny, and an above average writer. My friends swear up and down you're cute. Why do you think she wouldn't like you?"

"You're my sister — jigger, jig, jig, you have to say that. Well not the cute part — jigger, jig, jig, that's a little weird. Seriously, have you heard me talk? I still randomly hit myself in the face. Sadie knows Mindy pretty well. She says Mindy is scary smart and can be anything she wants to be. Sadie says she wouldn't be surprised if Mindy is the President of the United States one day."

"And what would Sadie say if you told her you had a thing for Mindy?"

I stare down at the ground and roll my shoulder before I admit, "Sadie would tell me to go for it."

"So, what's the problem?"

I groan. "I don't know. It's just easier to talk about

this stuff than to actually do it."

Mariam gathers up her cell phone and her purse. She starts filming me with her phone as she backs up the aisle. "I don't know. I think you're too scared to try. I think we should set up a wager. What do you think the stakes should be —" she teases before she backs into someone.

"Sorry," Mariam murmurs.

When the guy turns around, his expression changes from annoyance to recognition. "Fischer! How are you? Last time I saw you, we were wearing ugly suits and our shoes were too tight."

I grin. "Jigger, jig, jig, good to see you, Gabriel. Sadie would be so jealous. She still refers to you as 'the one who got away'."

Gabriel's eyebrows climb. "Seriously? I always figured there was a little something-something between you and Sadie."

Mariam stifles a giggle beside me. "See? I'm not the only one who doesn't understand what's going on between you and your 'best friend'."

Gabriel does a quick assessment of my sister and turns to me. "Who is this vision of loveliness?"

"This pesky thing is my older sister, Mariam. Jigger, jig, jig, she was away at college when we met." I turn to my sister and add, "Mariam, this is Gabriel, Mindy's cousin."

I'm not sure what Gabriel read in my sister's expression, but his face grows tight. "My grandpa was black," he explains in a low growl.

Mariam looks mortified as she covers her mouth with her hand. "Oh, I'm so sorry. I didn't mean to be rude. I've been researching genetics and you and Mindy look so different. It took me by surprise."

Gabriel relaxes. "Mindy and Becca are adopted. Charlie looks more like Uncle Jeff. Although, in an odd coincidence, he has an awful lot in common with Becca and Mindy. In many ways, it's hard to tell they're not related by blood."

Gabriel's phone beeps. After he looks down at it, he makes an abrupt offer. "Hey, we're having a little party for Mindy's birthday backstage. You guys want to come?"

"Jigger, jig, jig, are you sure she wants us there?" My hand flies up and hits the side of my face. I hate it when this happens. I've gotten a little better at controlling my physical tics, but when I'm nervous, all bets are off.

I have to give Gabriel credit. He doesn't say anything about my odd behavior. His only reaction is a slight widening of his eyes as he watches me trying to regain control of my body. After a few moments, he grins. "Are you kidding? You are like one of her favorite authors. She reads every book you've ever written. She cyber stalks you if you appear on a blog or a local TV show. It would totally make her day."

Tempted by the offer, but torn by my sense of responsibility, I glance over at Mariam. "What do you think? Should we go home and check on Mom?"

Mariam adamantly shakes her head. "You heard Mom's instructions. She'll be out with Aunt Lila. She told us to have as much fun as we wanted. Life will close in on us fast enough once Dad is home. I say let's party while we can."

"Jigger, jig, jig, my sister has spoken. I guess you can consider us official party crashers."

Gabriel grins widely. "I can't thank you enough. You are going to turn me from a zero to a hero. It's been a long time since I have been able to surprise my cousin with anything. This will totally freak her out."

My sister is practically bouncing with joy as she walks next to Gabriel, navigating the labyrinth of hallways backstage. All I can think of is whether Mindy's freak out bodes well for me or not.

CHAPTER SEVEN

MINDY

I FORGOT HOW MUCH effort it takes to be on stage. Usually, I draw a ton of energy from the crowd. Today, it didn't seem to work out that way. Today felt much more like the survival of the fittest. I barely made it through. Maybe it was because Uncle Aidan threw me off my rhythm with his strange birthday announcement, or maybe it's simply because I'm rusty and haven't played my instruments in a while. Perhaps it's because I haven't sung since I can't remember when. Either way, I've felt a couple beats behind all night.

I know Uncle Aidan meant for the birthday announcement to be a big happy surprise. It probably should have been, but it made me feel naked and exposed. I'm far different from the girl I once was long ago when Uncle Aidan and Aunt Tara first met me. Back then, I could see so clearly what my life was meant to be. I knew what gifts I brought into the world and how to give back to make everything balance. These days, I don't know anything. Everything is a tangled mess and I don't know how to untangle it. I don't know how to function anymore.

Fortunately for me, Jerome is in the middle of teaching my little brother how to play a couple of spoons on his knees. What my brother lacks in musical ability and timing, he makes up for in joy and enthusiasm. The partygoers are enjoying the impromptu show and Charlie is happy being the center of attention.

I curl up in the corner of an old beat up leather couch and sip on some hot tea as I observe the chaotic scene in front of me. It's weird to feel like an outsider at my own birthday party, yet somehow I do.

I'm startled out of my thoughts when someone comes up beside me and sits down. "Jigger, jig, jig, I thought you might want a little cake," Elijah offers as he extends a piece of cake and napkins toward me.

I take a moment to study him. I thought he was cute when I met him several years ago, but he's an interesting mix of cute and hot these days. Like me, Elijah must have contact lenses now. He has just a hint of facial hair and very sexy piercings. Even though he looks much more sophisticated, he still has that adorable crooked smile as he offers me cake.

I wave it off as I hold my hand over my stomach. "Oh no thank you. As much as I love Aunt Heather's cakes, I've had way too much. I really need to eat real food. I've got the jitters from too much sugar."

Elijah looks around the room. "I can get you some if you point me in the right direction, jigger, jig, jig."

I shrug. "I looked for some earlier and came up empty. Apparently, the event staff was a little too helpful and removed everything."

"How attached are you to your party?"

I smirk. I gesture at the distance between the couch and the rest of the people at the party. "Obviously, not much — they don't even seem to miss me. Why?"

Elijah pulls his cell phone out of his pocket and checks the time. He grimaces. "It won't be glamorous, but I could take you somewhere to grab a bite to eat. It might be a truck stop or a fast food place at this time of night."

I grin. "Are you kidding me? My grandpa was a truck driver. I have an unabashed love of truck stops. I would love to go grab a bite to eat."

Elijah looks around the room again. "Let me tell my sister what we're doing."

I point over to my right. "Does your sister have dark hair and cute dimples like you?"

Elijah blushes before he answers. "Yeah, I suppose. Why?"

"She's over there … under the spell of my cousin Gabriel. It looks like he's drawing her portrait. Let's go talk to them."

Elijah seems a little surprised when I grab his hand and walk across the room toward Gabriel.

"Hey it's great to see you haven't lost your touch," I commented as I look over his shoulder. I look over at Elijah's sister. "It's Mariam, right? I wish I was brave enough to cut my hair like yours. It's such a cute style. Would it be all right if Katie, my security guard, gave you a ride home?"

Not surprisingly, Mariam looks confused by my weird request. "Why?"

Elijah steps forward and explains, "Mindy is a little hungry after her performance, so I offered to take her out to eat."

Mariam's eyes go wide as she studies her brother. "Oh … cool! Um … you don't need to bother your security staff. I wouldn't mind if Gabriel took me home," she stammers. She looks at Gabriel and adds hastily, "I mean … if you don't mind."

Gabriel appears a little surprised but quickly recovers. "Have you moved since Elijah went to the prom?"

Elijah and Mariam shake their heads no.

"Okay, we should be good then. I still have Elijah's information in my contact list."

Gabriel winks at me. "Have a great time celebrating your birthday. Make it memorable, but not too memorable."

Elijah's eyes widen as he watches the waitress bring me my food. I can't help myself as I laugh out loud at his reaction. "What's wrong? Haven't you ever seen a girl eat before?"

"Jigger, jig, jig, not recently. I live in California, remember? My agent and I went out a while back and I swear her whole meal was a cucumber with some weird smears of organic vegetable purée with a glob of frothy whipped stuff on the top. Whatever it was, it was supposed to be exotic and cleansing. The only thing exotic about it was the price. It was forty-five dollars, jigger, jig, jig."

I pour steak sauce on the edge of my plate and ketchup over my cheese fries as I shake my head. "I'd be ticked off. I like food too much to be part of those trendy diets. There were a few girls in my dorm who were part of a vegan club and they wanted me to join, but it wasn't my thing."

Elijah looks down at his pancakes and scrambled eggs. "Jigger, jig, jig, I think I ordered the wrong meal. Whenever I think of truck stop diners, I think breakfast."

I smile at Elijah. "Don't worry, you can't go wrong here. Any meal is great. The hash browns are amazing. It's funny, when I think of this place, I think of stories. Warm, happy stories. You haven't met my grandpa, Denny, yet, but he tells the best stories ever. You should get him to write a book. He was a truck driver for decades. He's traveled all across the United States in good times and bad. After his first wife died, he had to take my mom on the road. He was a single dad before being a single dad was cool. He sometimes took my mom with him on the road, so he has a million and one stories about her. I love listening to him."

"Jigger, jig, jig, you should really write those stories down while you can. I'm afraid to think of all we may have lost with my dad."

"I'm so sorry. How is your dad doing?"

"It's hard to tell. He's still at the rehab center, but he'll be home soon."

"I'm sure that'll be easier on your mom."

"In some ways, I suppose. But I think she's worried about being able to take care of him, jigger, jig, jig. She'll have nurses and care providers for a bit while he is still in a cast. I moved back to Oregon to help, jigger, jig, jig. I got a townhouse not far from where I grew up. Mariam is around too. She graduated from college, but she hasn't found a job yet. Jigger, jig, jig, she thought she had a research position, but the grant they were counting on fell through. So, she's still looking for work."

"It must be really frustrating for her."

"It was, jigger, jig, jig. Maybe it will work out in the long run because she'll be able to help Mom too. Mariam is staying in the extra room in my townhouse. It's totally strange to be roommates again. It feels a bit like we're reliving our junior high school days."

I groan. "I can totally relate. I've unexpectedly returned to the nest too. As much as I love my little sister and brother, I miss my privacy."

"Jigger, jig, jig, why are you home? I thought you were studying medicine or law or something in California."

The corner of my mouth hitches up. "Or something — seriously, for a really bright person, I was having a terrible time figuring out what my major was."

"You dropped out of school because you couldn't pick a major, jigger, jig, jig?" Elijah's brows furrow with confusion. His hand comes up and hits the side of his face.

Without meaning to, I reach out in an attempt to rub away the pain in his jaw. I wince. "Doesn't it hurt when you do that?"

Elijah draws in a sharp breath and lets it go. "I've been like this for as long as I can remember. I hardly notice it anymore."

I watch Elijah fight the involuntary movements in his hands and watch a muscle twitch underneath his eye. "You have no way of controlling it or predicting when it will happen?" I confirm.

Elijah shakes his head and a sad expression crosses

his face. "I wish. Have you ever been in church or someplace quiet and needed to sneeze? The harder you try not to sneeze, the more you need to, right? That's how it is with my tics. If I try to control them or suppress them, it becomes painful and they get even worse. I hate them. I wish they would simply go away." His hand swings up and hits him square on the nose. He sighs wearily. "I'm tired of being weird."

I nod. "I understand."

"How could you possibly understand hating a part of yourself so much you wish it away every single day of your entire life?"

I carefully pick through my cheese fries and take a few bites. "I know more about that than you might think."

"Jigger, jig, jig, I don't think that's possible."

I sigh. "It's not only possible, it's the story of my life." I wipe my hands on a napkin and lean back against the vinyl booth as I try to explain my very strange existence. "Imagine everyone you meet has a television above their head with a different program playing. Sometimes, all of it is in English. Sometimes it's not. Sometimes you can tell what the actors are doing and sometimes you have no clue. Sometimes the station is coming clearly, but other times it's fuzzy and muddled."

Elijah's eyes widen. "Seriously? Does the other person know you see this weird television above their head? Does it get confusing to pay attention to the actual conversation and still see things no one else can see?"

"Oh, absolutely! That's why most of the time people think I'm slightly out of it," I answer with a grin. "Most of my friends and family know by now. Everyone is mostly used to it. But when I was a little kid, nobody knew. Well, I guess my birth family knew because they thought I was possessed by the devil. That's why my parents and my grandma beat me so bad. My grandma always said she was trying to beat the evil out of me."

"How long has this been happening to you?"

"Honestly, I don't remember a time when it didn't. That's what makes it so weird now. It's like all those wishes I made as a kid to wish my abilities away have come true. You have no idea how many times I wished I could just turn those invisible TVs off. Now that my ability is gone, I miss it. I never in a million years thought I would ever say that."

"So, let me get this straight — jigger, jig, jig, all those years ago, you knew *Behind Glass Bars* would be a huge hit? Why didn't you tell us? It would have saved us a bunch of sleepless nights and helped us get through some tough times when we were trying to get it ready to be published."

I lean forward and catch his gaze intently. "You have no idea how often I want to reassure people and share all the great news I see. Unfortunately, I can't. It's against the rules. If I interfere, it might change the path of the future. If I had told you what a groundbreaking novel it would be, you might not have pushed the boundaries quite so far. You might've been tempted to take the easy road if you guys had known success was already guaranteed."

Elijah is quiet for a few moments. "So, you see this stuff about everyone — whether you want to or not? Jigger, jig, jig, even if you don't know them — like the guy who pumps your gas or the person who is simply standing in front of you in line at the grocery store?"

"I used to," I answer as I take a sip of my drink and fight back tears.

"Jigger, jig, jig, you see random stuff about their lives like if they're about to have a baby or if they'll get a promotion at work or a good grade?" Elijah frowns and swallows hard. "Jigger, jig, jig but, that's not all you see, is it?"

Involuntarily, my eye twitches as I shake my head.

"It must be awful to know when someone's father is going to die or jigger, jig, jig, if they're going to be evicted from their house or if a family is going to get killed in a car crash —" Elijah rambles as if thoughts are tumbling around in his brain. He pauses and studies me carefully for what seems like an eternity. "Jigger, jig, jig, or if you know someone is about to get shot. Suddenly the story I heard about Logan and Katie makes a lot more sense now," he adds with a sense of wonderment. "Wow! That must be a trippy burden."

"It can be. Fortunately, I can make an exception to my 'no interference' rule for matters of life and death."

"What's that best thing you've ever been able to tell someone, jigger, jig, jig?"

"I got to tell my mom that my little brother would be fine despite the fact that her pregnancy was considered high risk."

"Jigger, jig, jig, how fun. Was she surprised?"

"I don't know if she was surprised so much as profoundly relieved. My dad is a huge worrywart so for once my precognitive abilities made things so much easier."

We eat in silence for a few more moments before Elijah gazes up at me with a serious expression, "What's the worst news you've ever had to share, jigger, jig, jig?"

"The worst thing I ever had to do was tell my Uncle Aidan that my Aunt Tara had miscarried their daughter and no matter how quickly they got to the hospital, nothing could be done because she was already gone."

Elijah looks stricken. "Jigger, jig, jig jigger, jig, jig, I'm sorry." His right hand comes up and strikes his face with an astounding amount of force. He shoves it back down to his side and sits on his hand. "I was wrong jigger, jig, jig. You do understand what it's like to wish you were normal. A few random words and physical tics are nothing compared to what you go through," he insists.

"Life doesn't work that way. We all deal with stuff. I don't think ranking the stuff we deal with helps anybody. Actually, I don't think there's really a way to do that. I used to think my so-called gift was a huge burden and that it was probably the reason I have a hard time making friends. Yet now it would be a stretch to say I have any pre-cognitive abilities at all these days and I'm still having a tough time."

"You might be right, jigger, jig, jig." Elijah shoots me a ghost of a smile. "Jigger, jig, jig, isn't that weird? You know, the whole time I was growing up, I thought everything would be different if I was popular and people knew who I was. Well, my friendship with Sadie and the whole social experiment which led to *Behind Glass Bars* made me more well-known and popular than I ever could have imagined, but I'm still lonely and I still feel as awkward and shy as I ever did. Everything I thought would happen if only I was popular ... never really did."

"As a kid, I just wanted to be normal so my family would accept me and stop thinking I was evil."

Elijah looks furious. "No one should jigger, jig, jig have ever thought that about you. Kids can't be evil. Jigger, jig, jig, that's just wrong."

I flash him a teary smile. "You would get along famously with my dad. That was one of the first things Jeff tried to teach me from the first moment we met, even before he and Kiera adopted me. He tried to drum two things into my head: First, kids can't be evil. Second, it wasn't my job to worry about the world. It was only my job to try my best at school and to have fun."

Elijah nods. "Sounds like something my dad would say. Pretty solid advice, jigger, jig, jig."

"It was great advice. I did a pretty good job of absorbing his advice about kids not being evil. I'm still not so great about not worrying about the whole world. Right now, I would give anything to get my gift back. There are so many people who need answers. These people have serious problems and they need my help. For the first time in my life, I'm helpless. I have no answers for anyone. I have never felt more worthless in my whole life."

Elijah makes a series of odd facial grimaces. This seems to go on for a couple minutes. He appears frustrated with himself. Finally, he takes a deep breath and lets it out. "Jigger, jig, jig, jigger, jig, jig you're not worthless to me. Mindy, regardless of whether you can see the future, you mean a lot to me." He looks down at his cell phone and he raises an eyebrow. "We've been talking for more than an hour and a half, jigger, jig, jig. I can't remember the last time someone besides my family had the patience to listen to me talk so long. Most people give up or they get freaked out if I make faces or hit myself."

I flinch at his disclosure. "I hope you don't think I'm that kind of person. I wouldn't treat you like that." I take a long drink of my soda to avoid saying more. People like that make me so angry.

"Jigger, jig, jig, I know. I wasn't trying to suggest you were. I don't think most people mean to be. They're just uncomfortable with what they don't understand."

"I understand more than I'd like to," I confess as I wipe tears away.

Elijah's expression gentles. "I'm sorry you're in a position where you have to understand, but it's kinda nice not to have to pretend I've got everything under control when I totally don't. Jigger, jig, jig, I like just being me."

For the first time in several weeks I feel like I can take a deep breath and let it go as I wipe away tears. "You took the words right out of my mouth. Can we do this again … soon?"

"Anytime you want," Elijah offers with a smile.

"You might be sorry you said that," I admit. "I seem to have a lot more free time than I used to."

"I'm a wildly creative person, I'll probably find ways to occupy your time," Elijah responds with a gleam in his eye.

Something in his tone makes me sit up and take notice. It seems a lot more than Elijah's appearance has changed over the last few years. My stomach tightens and flutters a little with anticipation. Maybe coming home wasn't such a bad idea after all.

Chapter Eight

Elijah

As I loosen the tie-down around my dad's wheelchair, I thank God for that awkward day which brought Sadie into my life. Without her, I would've never been brave enough to become an author. If I had never started down this path, I could never have helped my parents out with the added expenses my dad's accident has brought on. Maybe they'll be resolved and covered by workers' compensation or by his firm, but right now all that's up in the air. My dad's recovery can't wait around for them to decide who's to blame. Quite frankly, I'm not sure anyone will ever step up to the plate and do the responsible thing.

Today hasn't been too bad. Speech therapy tires my dad out, but not nearly as much as physical therapy. Dad seems strong enough to participate in what is quickly becoming our post-therapy ritual. I open the door to the little mom-and-pop diner and prop it with my hip as I help my dad steer his wheelchair through the narrow opening.

As Kerri Witherspoon, our favorite waitress, sees us

she exclaims, "Seth Fischer, I swear you get more handsome every time I see you!"

It takes my dad a few moments to write, "BS, but thank you."

"I kept a piece of chocolate silk pie back for you, or Arnie may have custard with real vanilla beans. Which would you like?" Kerri asks him as she escorts us to our usual table.

After a few moments, my dad writes, "Both. Will you marry my son? He needs a wife."

The waitress and I read the white board at about the same time and both of us turn about the same shade of red. "Jigger, jig, jig, Dad! I don't need your help. I'm sure Kerri is a really nice person, but she doesn't know anything about me jigger, jig, jig."

Kerri sighs happily as she moves the menus she's holding to the side to give my father a clear view of a sparkling ring on her finger. "Sorry to disappoint you Mr. Fischer — but my Xander surprised me with a proposal for my birthday." She moves her hand closer to my dad so he can see. "Isn't it beautiful? I had no idea Xander could be so romantic. We've been dating since I was a seventh grader. I figured he'd wait until we were finished with college, but he didn't. You could have knocked me over with a feather."

My dad smiles as he writes, "Congratulations." Looking at me he writes, "Another one gone."

Before I can answer him, my phone beeps. As I take it out of my jacket pocket to check it, Dad mouths, "Sadie?"

I shake my head and answer, "Jigger, jig, jig, Mindy."

I wasn't aware that my dad even knows who Mindy

is — but whatever. The mere mention of her name throws my dad into a flurry of writing. He doesn't even look up when Kerri delivers a piece of apple pie for me and two desserts for him. He just keeps writing on the whiteboard.

When he finishes, he pushes it over to me with a flourish.

"Mindy? Is that the musician gal your sister can't shut up about? I heard you went on a date and it lasted a long time. This must be something big. First girl since Sadie. Your sister said she's young. True? She's barely legal?! You're 22. Be careful!"

"Dad…" I respond with a sigh. "I'm aware of how old I am. I also know how old Mindy is. Yes, Mindy is a musician, but that's not all she is. It's really complicated. I've known Mindy for years. She helped me with *Behind Glass Bars* several years ago. Sadie knows her too. Sadie thinks Mindy is one of the coolest people she's ever met."

My dad looks at me and motions for me to return the whiteboard to him as he struggles to use a napkin to erase it so he can write more.

My dad's handwriting looks almost angry as he pushes the board back to me.. "If this Mindy gal is so much like Sadie, why don't you date Sadie?"

I try very hard to be patient with my family about the whole Sadie issue, especially after my dad's head injury, but I don't know how many ways I can explain this. I take a deep breath and try again. "Jigger, jig, jig, would you want me to date Mariam?"

My dad scowls at me. He shakes his head vehemently.

"Then don't ask me jigger, jig, jig to date Sadie. Jigger, jig, jig, it would be the same. She's my best friend and like a big sister to me."

A single sarcastic sentence scribbled on the whiteboard is his answer. "Sadie is younger than you."

I shrug. "It's never seemed that way. Sadie is so much better at keeping her life together — I always seem like the little brother tagging along trying to keep up."

My dad shakes his head in dismay. He erases the board and writes one last instruction. "If you like this Mindy gal, don't screw it up."

<hr>

"Jigger, jig, jig, I've really screwed up this time," I lament before I even have a chance to completely put my headphones on and look up at my webcam.

"What do you mean? I'm sure it's not that bad. You always do this to yourself."

"Jigger, jig, jig, don't take this the wrong way, but you like me, right?"

"Duh!" Sadie says with a laugh. "Are you feeling all right? Geez, Elijah! We've only been best friends for almost a whole decade. Of course I like you."

"Okay, it's not such a stupid question, jigger, jig, jig. I took my dad out for a treat today and the waitress was telling him about her love story, jigger, jig, jig. They've been together since the seventh grade and they recently got engaged. Jigger, jig, jig, so why isn't that our story? Mariam was teasing me the other day. She said you treat me better than a wife — she's not wrong. I know you love me. So, why aren't we *in love*? Jigger, jig, jig, did we screw up somewhere? Did we miss our chance?"

Sadie is silent for a long time. Only then do I take a

close look at the screen and notice that she's wiping off some weird green glop from her face. "Jigger, jig, jig, what's that?"

"You just now noticed I look like some weird deranged version of the Incredible Hulk? Way to be observant. I have been going around to galleries in the city trying to get my work featured. I wore makeup, and it makes me break out. So, I'm trying to fight back before it gets horrendously bad. This stuff is supposed to clean my pores."

"Sorry, I wasn't paying attention, jigger, jig, jig."

"It's all right. I've been your friend for a long time, I'm used to it. Every time I have a painful breakup, I ask myself those same kind of questions. Why aren't we more than just best friends? I don't have a great answer. You understand me better than any other human being on the planet — including my parents. You probably know me better than I know myself. I trust you to love the sides of me which aren't so perfect or pretty."

"We are astonishingly real with each other. You know all of my flaws."

"There were times when we were growing up, I wondered if it be easier to date you than to put myself out there and pursue other relationships. But I didn't want to ruin our friendship. As much as I love and cherish you, I'm not willing to risk our relationship just to call you my boyfriend. Does that make any sense?"

"Jigger, jig, jig, yeah, it makes total sense. A bunch of guys I knew in high school went through girlfriends faster than they could change socks. I didn't want to be that guy with you."

"So, why are you asking me about it now?" Sadie

asks.

I shrug. "It's weird being back home with my family. It's like nothing has changed and everything has changed all at once. Mariam and I have sort of settled into the same people we were when we were teenagers — except now we are sort of acting like the parents. My mom is completely distraught over my dad. My dad is learning things all over again just like a preschooler would. He's even learning to talk again. But on the other hand, they treat us like we're in junior high school."

"That must be awkward," Sadie says sympathetically as she starts to paint her fingernails.

"You have no idea, jigger, jig, jig. Everybody is acting like we're a couple or that we should have been and I just didn't get the memo. Some people seem to think you had a secret crush on me all along — and I was simply too oblivious to figure it out."

Sadie chokes back a snort of laughter. "Is that what you think?"

"Jigger, jig, jig, no! At first, I was arguing with everyone and telling them they were flat out wrong. Then everyone seemed to be coming to the same conclusion and I began to second-guess myself and wonder if I was the only one who didn't see the situation as it truly was. So, I finally figured I should man up and ask you if I've completely misread the situation for years and years, jigger, jig, jig."

"No, you didn't misread anything. We just decided to be friends instead of lovers. We were too busy trying to survive high school. We didn't have time for all the romance jazz and the head-games which come with a relationship. I have always figured we got the best end of the deal. We got all the benefits of having a relationship without all the weird drama of being in a traditional boyfriend/girlfriend deal, right?"

I nod. "Just for argument's sake, let's say you're right. Where do we go from here?

Sadie chews on her bottom lip like she does when she's thinking through a problem. She's quiet for several minutes before she finally replies. "Wow, Elijah!" she says as she sucks in a deep breath. "I usually have an answer for this kind of thing, but I don't know. I really don't."

"What do you mean you don't know? Jigger, jig, jig, you always have the answers. What am I supposed to do now?" I ask, only half kidding.

"You know me well enough to know it's only an illusion. I don't know half as much as people expect me to know. By the way, you started this conversation saying you totally screwed up. This doesn't sound like a screw up. It only sounds like you're confused. So, what gives?" Sadie asks as she blows on her fingernails to dry the polish.

I groan as I rake my fingers through my hair, making it stand on end. "Oh … geez … I don't even want to tell you this part, jigger, jig, jig."

"Come on, I'm sure it wasn't completely catastrophic," she cajoles. "We have no secrets from each other — I held your hand when you had your wisdom teeth out, remember?"

"Jigger, jig, jig, yeah, I remember. I still feel the need to apologize for puking all over you."

"See? Whatever you have to tell me can't be that bad."

"I guess you have a point. So, I took your advice —

"

"You'll have to be more specific, I give you lots of advice."

"I asked Mindy out," I explain.

"Mindy Whitaker?" Sadie's voice squeaks with excitement.

After I nod, Sadie gets up from her chair and starts to dance in front of her desk. "Took you long enough! Wait ... you can't tease me like that — I need details!"

"I guess you can blame Mariam for my dilemma. Like I said, it's a little like being a teenager again. I swear my sister can talk me into doing almost anything. So, she was teasing me after we saw Aidan in concert. She noticed I only had eyes for Mindy, so she basically dared me to talk to Mindy after the concert. I totally blew her off thinking I would never get a chance to see Mindy again — like ever. But then, Mariam basically ran into Gabriel after the concert."

"Ran into him?" Sadie asks with equal degrees of hopefulness and skepticism.

"Yeah, Gabriel said to tell you 'Hi'. My sister was backing up the aisle after the concert and literally ran right into him. Jigger, jig, jig, it turned out to be Mindy's eighteenth birthday party and they were having a get together for her backstage. Gabriel recognized me right away and so he invited Mariam and me to go backstage. So, we did. Long story short, Mindy wanted to jet, so we went and got a bite to eat and ended up talking for a couple hours. It was totally cool."

"That doesn't sound like you screwed up," Sadie remarks. "Actually, it sounds pretty awesome."

"It was totally epic. I couldn't believe we had so much

to talk about and so much in common. You know how you told me Mindy has some sort of psychic gift?"

Sadie nods. "Yeah. Sometimes, Mindy is downright spooky."

"Jigger, jig, jig, turns out there are days she struggles with it like I struggle with my Tourette's. I've just never met anybody who feels the same way about their life. It's weird, some days I wouldn't change my life for anything because Tourette's made me the kind of person I am. I have a lot of time to sit around and observe people because they tend to avoid interacting with me. I think the whole thing has made me a better writer. Other days, I would give anything to be completely normal so I would fit in with all my friends, jigger, jig, jig. Before I met you and Mindy, I'd never met anyone who can honestly say they know what it's like to be in my shoes." My hand flies up and strikes the side of my face.

"What's the problem? The whole situation sounds wonderful." Sadie winces as she sees the blow.

"The problem is I listened to Mariam, jigger, jig, jig."

"I thought you said the date went great," Sadie asks with a completely befuddled expression.

"We had a phenomenal time, jigger, jig, jig. Probably the best time I've ever had with anyone — who wasn't you — but then I had to go there," I confess as I turn bright red.

Sadie leans in toward her webcam. "Go where?"

"You know me, jigger, jig, jig, I'm terrible at conversation and I'm even worse at flirting. I tried to flirt."

"You can't be any worse than some guys I run across. I'm sure Mindy thought you were fine. What did you say?"

I take a deep breath and let it out before I confess, "I told her I can probably keep her occupied."

For a moment, Sadie merely blinks at me. "Umm ... Wow! Yeah ... That's not the smoothest line you've ever said. How did Mindy react to it?"

I shrug. "As far as I can tell, she didn't even notice my blunder. She texted me earlier today but I don't know how to respond. So, I haven't written anything back."

Sadie grimaces. "Oh, I don't think I would recommend the avoidance strategy. You probably should say something to her. You want to go out with her again, right?"

"Of course I do!" I insist. "I had a great time, even though it was a spur-of-the-moment date."

"Okay, now we're getting somewhere. Maybe spur-of-the moment dates that you don't spend a lot of time obsessing over are the key to your success. Just try not to over think it. Mindy is tons of fun. She's remarkably adaptable. She'll have a great time regardless of what you guys do. She's pretty unusual. She won't be impressed with the regular, traditional perks of dating like most normal college-aged women. She thinks on a whole different level. Go with your gut and have fun. If anyone needs a break, it's probably Mindy. Think outside the box. You're a creative person — you'll be great this."

"Jigger, jig, jig, you want me to plot out our dates like it's a book?"

"No! I want you to go against your OCD tendencies and let your creativity fly free. Take Mindy along for the fun of it."

"I don't know if I can do it, Sadie. You know me. I

tend to live life small and safe within my own comfort zone."

"That's why dating Mindy is such a great thing for you. If anyone can persuade you to throw caution to the wind and tempt fate, it's Mindy. Besides, having her around is like being brave with training wheels."

I open my mouth to correct Sadie's assumption but think better of it. After all, it's not my secret to share.

CHAPTER NINE

MINDY

"MINDY, I DON'T WANT you to think I don't appreciate your help around here. I do. Still, I can't help but wonder if there aren't more important things you could be doing with your time."

I wipe away tears as I struggle to take the cellophane wrap off the spool of ribbon before I put it on the display rack.

My grandma walks over and gives me a hug as she murmurs in my ear, "Come now, Mouse, I know helping me with inventory isn't the most exciting task in the world, but it shouldn't reduce you to tears. What's really going on?"

She lets me go and peeks her head into the storeroom. "Denny, I need you to watch the front of the shop. Mindy and I will be out in the greenhouses for a bit."

My papa comes out of the storeroom and wipes his hands on his apron. When he looks at me, he kisses me on the cheek. "Aww, you look a little wilted." He runs over to the bloom cooler and hands each of us a bottle of water. "You two take as long as you need."

My grandma puts her arm around my waist and escorts me to the back of the Flower Pedal'r. On the side of the greenhouse is a bench my Papa made with my dad and Uncle Tyler. I sit down and take several gulps of my water before I'm brave enough to meet Grummy's gaze. "So, where do you want to start?"

"That's a great question. I don't know. My whole life is a mess right now."

"Why don't you start with what's making you cry today?"

"Do you want the big thing or the stupid thing?"

"Why don't you try the stupid thing first? It'll get you warmed up for the big thing."

"Okay, don't say I didn't warn you. This is dumb."

My grandma raises an eyebrow. "I'll consider myself forewarned. You do remember I am a member of the Girlfriend Posse. We don't do dumb. Every issue is treated with respect."

"I understand — but still, I feel foolish about this."

"I'm sure whatever is bothering you isn't trivial."

"Okay, maybe it's not trivial, but it feels juvenile. So, I went out with this guy, Elijah. I've liked him for a long time. I thought he liked me too. I sent him a text message the other day and so far it's been crickets. Like nothing —"

"Men are funny about that kind of thing. Sometimes they have rules we don't even know about — like they can't contact you for a week or something. Maybe it's his job or family obligations. Have you tried again?"

I shake my head slightly as my cheeks flush with embarrassment. "I was afraid to because I didn't want to seem too pushy. The time we spent together seems too good to be true. It was like he could pull thoughts right out of my brain. I've never talked to anyone who is so in tune with me. I'm almost afraid I dreamed the whole thing up."

"Well, it seems like something special is going on between the two of you. If it were me, I'd probably give your young man another chance or two. Maybe he is shy and doesn't know what to say."

As I listen to my grandma's theories, I smile. "You're probably right. His family is going through a terrible time right now. He's probably busy helping his dad. It might be his shyness too. He's come out of his shell a lot since I met him a few years ago, but I think he's still pretty reserved. He reminds me a lot of Gabriel. I suspect he is a lot more comfortable behind the computer than he is out in public."

"When we get back into the shop, why don't you make his mother a bouquet of flowers? I bet she would appreciate it."

"That's a great idea. I'll text Elijah's sister and ask what his mom's name is so I can send a card along with the flowers."

"Plus it will give you a great reason to check in with your gentleman to see if everything is okay."

I chuckle. "Oh Grummy! You are so devious."

My grandma places her hand dramatically in front of her chest. "Who me? I'm not devious! I'm merely creatively resourceful. Now that we have those problems solved, are you ready to talk about the big stuff?"

I take a long swig of my water and lean back against the bench. "I don't know if I'll ever be ready to talk about the big stuff but I suppose I might as well start."

"You know anything you tell me won't make me love you any less, right?"

"I know. That's why I feel safe with you."

"So, what can I help you with, Mouse?"

"It's so ironic. I used to ask people how I can help them all the time too. Now it seems I can't. You know my roommate died, right?"

"Yes, your father mentioned it the other day. Such a sad thing to happen to a promising young woman."

"What if it's my fault?" I whisper hoarsely.

"What do you mean? I thought your dad said you were in your dorm room when it happened."

"I don't mean it literally. I was back in our room talking to Aunt Tara. I don't know what happened to Melanie. I suppose that's my whole point. Why didn't I stay with her? I was supposed to be her wing woman. I should've just stopped her from going to the stupid party in the first place."

"Oh honey, you can't blame yourself for Melanie's choices. They aren't your fault."

"What good is my so-called gift if I can't prevent bad things from happening?"

"I don't know the answer to that because I'm not in your shoes. I can tell you every parent and grandparent in the world feels your pain. We want to shield our kids and grandkids from every bump in the road. But we can't because everyone has to make their own mistakes. I know before your Aunt Donda was sober, I held my breath every time she left the house. I wasn't sure if she would ever come back. Heck, she was even a danger to herself in the house. She was harming herself in her own bedroom. Even with all of my experience, I couldn't keep her safe."

"College is nothing like I thought it would be. I thought I would be best friends with my roommate. I figured we'd study together and take the same sort of classes. I never counted on my roommate being pretty much the opposite of me."

"I'm sorry it's been so disappointing for you," My grandma says as she reaches out and gathers me into a hug.

"It's not just that I couldn't get along with Melanie. I questioned whether I should be at college at all. I mean, I understand my values are a bit different from everyone else's because of all the things I've been through in my life. Still, I figured that if I stayed true to myself people would eventually understand me." I shrug and wipe tears from my eyes. "But it never seemed to work out that way. All I seem to do is let people down. Now someone is dead because my gift is on the fritz."

"I think maybe you're looking at all of this wrong."

I stiffen at Grummy's criticism.

"Take a moment to hear me out. I've never been in your shoes, so I don't know this for sure. But, what if your gift isn't intended to save everyone? Maybe that's not the way it works."

"Why would God even give me this kind of gift if I can't help everyone? Right now, my gift is more like a curse! Maybe my Nana was right. Maybe I am evil at the core."

"Oh child, you know that's never been true. Even when you were tiny, you gave me the courage to take the steps I needed to leave the only truly evil man I've ever known. I know evil and it's not you. You don't have an evil bone in your body. I'm the last person to try to explain to you how God or fate works. I beat cancer while one of the nicest women I've ever met lost her battle. She fought every bit as hard as I did and her family loved her as much as you guys love me. Yet, she didn't make it. I can't pretend to understand why that happens. Just like I'll never understand your gift, I don't understand how fate works. But I'm grateful you have your gift."

"But that's just it, Grummy. I can't truthfully say I'm gifted at much of anything anymore. I'm just Mindy."

"Being you is more than enough for anyone who matters."

———◆———

Wiping my sweaty hands on the back of my jeans, I nervously ask Elijah, "Are you sure this is all right for a date? I wasn't really expecting to go anywhere special today. Aunt Madison asked me to come help her organize the tack in her barn." I awkwardly climb into his low-slung car and fasten my seatbelt.

Elijah glances over at my sweatshirt with kittens and puppies, which has one of my favorite quotes from James Herriot's *All Creatures Great and Small*. He smiles. "Jigger, jig, jig, I figured we probably had a lot in common. I just didn't know how much. Jigger, jig, jig you couldn't have chosen a more perfect outfit for today."

I tighten the ponytail holder at the end of my braid and look down at my well-worn sweatshirt and jeans with a not-so-artful hole in the knee. "I guess I'll have to take your word for it."

"By the way, jigger, jig, jig, I love that saying. In my opinion, animals are more capable of feeling loyalty and gratitude. They are the definition of love and soul. Human beings are vastly inferior jigger, jig, jig."

I snicker at his grand pronouncement. Pointing at my sweatshirt I reply, "Does it look like I disagree? Were you able to bring your pets with you from California?"

Elijah flinches. "Jigger, jig, jig, no, I lost Popeye last year. He got cancer in his jaw. It wasn't treatable."

"Oh, I'm so sorry. My dad lost his golden retriever a few months ago too. What kind of dog was Popeye?"

"Beats me, jigger, jigger, jig, jig. Whoever lived in my condo before me apparently left him behind just like the mounds of garbage they forgot to take to the dump. The vet thinks he probably had some bull dog and some Labrador and maybe even a little poodle. Jigger, jig, jig, he was one strange looking dog — but he adored me with every fiber of his being. It's almost as if he could tell I had saved his life."

"I do think they know. Even Uncle Tyler's horses understand what he did for them."

"I miss my slobbering mutt. He was my most patient writing partner, jigger, jig, jig."

I nod. "I totally get it. Lucky was my study buddy until I left for college. I never got used to doing homework without having him around."

"Then jigger, jig, jig today ought to be good for your soul." Elijah pulls his car over to the side of the dirt road and opens a heavy wooden gate. If the road gets any rougher, I'm not sure his sports car can handle it. My skepticism must be showing on my face because Elijah raises an eyebrow as he addresses my unspoken concern.

"Jigger, jig, jig don't worry, I'll take care of you. It's not far."

He carefully maneuvers up a gravel driveway. I gasp when I see the beautiful log cabin perched on a beautiful hilltop. "Wow! That looks like it belongs on the cover of a fancy magazine."

Elijah grins. "I'm sure Betty Sue probably has a photo album full of them somewhere."

Before I can answer, someone comes up to Elijah's car window and taps on it, scaring me half to death. Elijah quickly rolls down his window. An older gentleman sticks his head in. When he sees me, he does a double take.

"Young man, when you told me you were bringing someone with you today, you didn't tell me it was going to be somebody famous."

My face grows hot. "I don't think I'm all that famous. My uncle Aidan is the famous one. I'm simply along for the ride."

"Nonsense! Don't you go telling my granddaughter your line of malarkey. She stood in line at the mall for three hours so you could sign her T-shirt."

My jaw goes slack. "For real? When was this?"

"Oh, sometime last summer. You were doing a fundraiser for the place that finds missing kids. Lexi was just happy to be there."

"Thank you so much for attending. I'm sorry she had to wait so long Mr. —" I let my speech trail off hoping he'll provide his name.

"Jigger, jig, jig I'm sorry, this is my friend Chester Franklin. Chester, as you've already guessed, this is Mindy

Whitaker. We've been friends for a long time. She helped me with one of my projects during high school."

Chester leans his head down into the car and in a stage whisper asks Elijah, "Son, I thought you told me you were bringing a date — although for the life of me I can't figure out why you would choose to bring a woman here if you're sweet on her."

Elijah flushes bright red and shakes his head. "If we ever get out of the car, jigger, jig, jig, I think you'll see Mindy will fit in just fine."

Chester gallantly steps out of the way and waves his arm in a wide arc to invite Elijah and me to join him as he starts to walk up his porch steps. Elijah walks around the car and helps me out. He places his hand at the small of my back and escorts me up. We pause at the front door and he offers me a heavy canvas apron. When I raise an eyebrow in question, he explains, "Betty Sue and Chester's place can get a little messy, jigger, jig, jig."

I let out a surprised laugh as I point at my torn jeans. "I was planning to muck out barns in this fetching ensemble. I think I'll survive."

An older woman with bright red curls streaked with gray at the temples throws open the door. "Oh Elijah, I'm so glad you're here. I need another set of hands or two." She does a subtle double take when she sees me there. "I wish I had time for a proper introduction but I don't. I'm Betty Sue. All I can say is I hope you like dogs."

"I do — very much."

"Big ones or little ones?" she asks as she steps away from the doorway and lets us in.

"Pretty much all of them. I like tiny ones and huge ones, young ones and old ones — cute ones and ones people think are not so cute. It matters not to me."

Betty Sue looks up at Elijah. "I see you picked a keeper. Good job! One of my regular helpers got a terrible case of tonsillitis. You know Avery left for college, so I'm shorthanded," she explains as she strides down the hall. As we follow her, the noise level increases.

We enter what would be considered the family room at my house and I count about a dozen dogs. "Wow! This is quite a collection."

"People know Chester and I have a soft spot for the dogs no one else wants. We started out as normal pet owners. But as word got around that we were skilled at helping animals, we became a formal rescue group."

"I see you've got a few new babies in since the last time I was here." Elijah says as he peers over the side of a large dishpan sitting under a heating lamp.

"We do. It was the saddest thing. The mama had an undelivered puppy and passed away unexpectedly. Tigger, Roo, Piglet, and Pooh got left behind. At least we're up to two hours between feedings now. It's not quite as crazy as it was in the beginning."

Betty Sue turns to me. "I'll give you Roo. She's pretty good at eating. She's a little messy, but she's more enthusiastic than the others. I think she'll eat for you just fine."

I walk over to the sink and wash my hands. I grab a couple of large washcloths from the stack sitting on the counter and place one in my lap after I perch on the edge of a long bench sitting in front of the bay window.

"Looks like your friend has done this a time or two," Chester says as he hands me a small bottle which looks almost like a bottle I used to have when I pretended to feed my dolls as a kid. When he sees my sweatshirt, he grins. "Hey, Betty Sue — did you get a gander at this gal's sweatshirt? She really is a kindred spirit!"

His wife walks over with one of the tiniest dogs I've ever seen in my life. She carefully hands Roo over. The puppy barely fills the palm of my hand. Betty Sue takes a moment to read my shirt. She smiles softly. "Well, isn't that something? Have you ever done this before, sweetie?"

I shake my head. "Not with something this small. I have helped my aunt with her foals."

"It's pretty much the same concept. The puppies are a little easier to handle I would imagine. Just try to make sure they don't get too much milk at once. We don't want them to aspirate it into their lungs."

Roo squirms in my hands and I find it difficult to balance the bottle. Elijah walks over and abruptly sits down behind me and places his arms around me as he steadies the puppy. He takes a washcloth from my lap and swaddles the puppy. "This makes them a little more manageable, jigger, jig, jig. Otherwise they can be like holding onto Jell-O. They calm down a little more if you rest them on your lap. Jigger, jig, jig, they like to be close to our bodies — just like human babies."

As I put my hands over Elijah's to move Roo, he clears his throat. "Jigger, jig, jig, it looks like she's settling down, I'm going to go help with Tigger now."

When Elijah pulls away and gets up, I instantly feel the loss of his warmth and subtle spicy scent. I can't remember the last time I enjoyed being so close to another person. Before I can think about the odd sensation too much, a vision hits my psyche so hard I physically sway before I shout, "Chester! Duck!"

Chester crouches instinctively at my warning a few seconds before the glass shatters in the china cupboard. He looks up at the broken dishes and back at me in amazement. "You want to tell me what in the tarnation just happened?" he demands. He reaches up and swipes at a trail of blood trickling down his face as he brushes off several small shards of glass.

My hands are shaking as I try to focus on feeding the puppy with a few drops of formula left in the bottle. "Honestly, I'm not sure. Sometimes — but not always — I can see a little of what will happen in the future. Usually, it's little snippets here and there. Based on what's happened in the past, my guess is it might be a gunshot, but I don't know."

"I told Earl it was a mistake to get his grandsons BB guns for Christmas. Those kids don't have any ounce of common sense."

I jump when Elijah places his hand on my back. He startles as he struggles to balance the little brown puppy on his shoulder. Elijah comes around the bench and sits down beside me and places Tigger in his lap. He takes a couple of seconds to settle the puppy. He is so incredibly gentle he reminds me of my dad and my uncle when they work with the horses.

Without warning, a wave of emotion hits me and a tear leaks out of the corner of my eye. I quickly swipe it away. Elijah leans down and asks, "Jigger, jig, jig, are you okay?"

I nod. "I think so. I wasn't expecting my abilities to reappear so suddenly."

Betty Sue looks startled. "You mean this doesn't

happen all the time?"

I solemnly shake my head. "It used to, but not so much anymore. After I wasn't able to stop something tragic from happening, my abilities seemed to disappear."

Betty Sue pulls a paper towel from the roll by the sink and walks over and hands it to me. "You poor thing! That must be incredibly frustrating. I am so glad things worked out today. I don't know what I would've done if something would've happened to my Chester."

Chester walks over to us with a hunk of metal captured between the teeth of a pair of needle nose pliers. "You can say that again. If I don't miss my guess, this is at least a .22. It could have done some serious damage. We're just lucky we had the window open or we would've been replacing a windowpane as well."

I blush as I look at Elijah. "I'm sorry I wasn't paying attention to where we were going when you were driving. Are we still in Uncle Tyler's jurisdiction?"

Elijah nods. "Jigger, jig, jig, as far as I know, we're still within the boundaries of the county, jigger, jig, jig."

I groan and hide my face behind my hands. "Oh, good gravy! Uncle Tyler is gonna lock me in jail for my own safety. I was supposed to be safer at home than at college — so much for that theory."

Chester narrows his eyes at me. "You havin' some sort of trouble with a crazy fan or something?"

His question draws me up short as I remember the crazy mess Tasha was in a couple years ago, but I shake my head. "No, I don't think so."

"If that's not it, what is it?" Chester presses.

"My college roommate died under mysterious

circumstances and my family thought it would be safer for me to move back home for a while until they decide her official cause of death. "

"What do you think she died from?" Chester asks sharply.

"Keep in mind it's been a long time since I've been around this kind of stuff because my adoptive parents rescued me before I was seven. But, from what I remember of my birth family, I think it had something to do with drugs or alcohol."

"Oh honey —" Betty Sue breathes softly. "You're not mixed up and all that stuff, are you?"

"No ma'am," I insist emphatically. "Jeff and Kiera gave my sister and me a second chance. I wouldn't spit in their faces like that."

Chester holds up the set of pliers holding the misshapen bullet "Looks like we got a serious situation here. Maybe you should call your uncle."

I gently hand the puppy over to Betty Sue as I pick my purse up from the floor. Before I can dig out my phone, it rings. When I retrieve it and see the number, I answer, "Wow, Uncle Tyler, I thought I was the one who's supposed to be psychic."

When I hear Uncle Tyler's answer, everything goes black. The last thing I remember is Elijah uttering a word which would make my Grandpa cringe and reaching out to catch me.

Chapter Ten

Elijah

I TRY TO BREATHE as I ease Mindy down to the floor. My body wants to fly into a huge tic storm as adrenaline flies through my system. I hear a voice coming from her phone. I grimace when I see a crack across her screen. I caught her, but I couldn't save her phone too. I hope she's not too upset.

After I pull off my sweatshirt and put it under her head, I reach over and push the speakerphone button. "Tyler?" I guess. "Jigger, jig, jig, this is Elijah."

"Not that it's not nice to talk to you, Elijah, but wasn't I talking to my niece?"

"Jigger, jig, jig, I don't know what happened, but she seems to have passed out or something —" I explain as I brush the back of my hand against Mindy's forehead and lean in closer so I can feel her breath on my cheek. "Jigger, jig, jig, she seems to be breathing fine, and she's not overheated."

I hear Mindy's uncle breath out a sigh of relief. "What was Mindy doing right before she passed out?"

"Jigger, jig, jig, we were getting ready to call you when you called us. I'm visiting a friend of mine who rescues dogs and there was a near miss with a bullet."

"That doesn't really sound like Mindy. I can't imagine she'd be messing around with guns— especially after what happened with Logan and Katie," Tyler responds, his voice sounding like a growl.

"No sir, jigger, jig, jig. They weren't our guns. Chester and Betty Sue Franklin's house was shot up."

I hear shuffling on Tyler's end of the phone. "Was Mindy hit? Do I need to dispatch an ambulance?" Tyler asks with alarm. "You got an address?

"Jigger, jig, jig, 1345 Wood Ashes Lane." I answer reflexively. "Mindy was fine after the shooting — just a little shook up. No one here was badly hurt. There was only, jigger, jig, jig, a little superficial damage from flying glass. She didn't pass out until she was talking on the phone to you. I'm not sure what you guys were talking about, jigger, jig, jig. Maybe something upset her."

Tyler groans. "Oh shoot! In all the craziness, I forgot to tell you. Your sister is trying to reach you. There must be something wrong with your phone. I was just telling Mindy you should probably call your family."

"Oh, okay, jigger, jig, jig. I don't know why that would cause her to pass out."

Betty Sue approaches with a wet washcloth and wipes Mindy's face. Mindy's delicate blonde eyelashes flutter against her pale cheeks.

"Did anything strange happen before the gunshot incident?" Tyler asks.

"Strange by everyone else's standards — jigger, jig, jig, or strange by Mindy's standards?"

"So, you know?"

"I do. I also know she's been struggling with her precognition skills for a while. Even so, she said she had a vision in time to tell Chester to duck."

Tyler sighs. "That explains a lot. Her episodes can take a bunch out of her. When she was tiny, she used to have to take a nap for several hours after an intense episode. I don't remember her passing out, but she might have. Hang tight, I'm about fifteen minutes out."

Crouching down beside Mindy, I will her to open her eyes as I carefully study her chest to make sure it's still moving. She abruptly opens her eyes and struggles to sit up. I've been concentrating so hard on her minuscule movements, her abrupt change in demeanor startles me.

"What happened? Was there another shot?" she asks as I kneel behind her to support her weight.

Betty Sue hustles around to clear a collection of throw pillows off of an overstuffed leather couch and Chester brings Mindy a can of root beer. "I'm sorry, this is all I have handy — but I thought you might want something to drink."

I help Mindy to her feet and walk over to the couch. I help her sit down, pull an Afghan off the arm of the couch, and tuck it around her. Much to my surprise, she pulls me down to sit next to her. I place my arm along the back of the couch and around her shoulders. She snuggles next to my side. Mindy glances up at Chester. "Actually, root beer is one of my favorite. My grandpa got me started on it. It's his favorite too." Mindy turns to me. "What happened? Why was I on the floor?" She examines herself briefly. "I don't seem to be hurt."

"Jigger, jig, jig, I'm not sure. One minute you were telling me that you were afraid your family would lock you in your room if you got into anymore close scrapes. You were about to call your uncle, jigger, jig, jig, but he called first."

A horrified expression crosses Mindy's face as she gasps. "Roo! What happened to Roo?"

Betty Sue smiles softly. "You were right Elijah. Mindy truly is a kindred spirit." She points over at the large dishpan. "All the puppies are safe and sound napping under the heat lamp."

I pull Mindy's phone out of the pocket of my sweat jacket. "I'm afraid this is the only real casualty. It didn't make it through in one piece. But I was able to talk to your uncle. He's on his way."

Mindy carefully takes the phone from my hands as she examines it. "This still works?"

I nod. "Jigger, jig, jig, it seems to — but I haven't tried to make any outgoing calls. Your uncle was still on the phone when you passed out."

Mindy turns pale again. "You need to try to call your family. You have to tell your dad not to leave the house. It's very important."

Before I can reach for Mindy's phone, Chester holds his cell phone out. "Your dad's number is in my contacts. I haven't known your gal for very long, but she probably saved my life this afternoon. If she tells you to do somethin', I think you should."

"Jigger, jig, jig, thank you, I'll call right now."

Out of the blue, my hand flies up and smacks the

side of my face harder than usual. Mindy reaches up and grabs it. She squeezes my hand tightly. Then, in a move Sadie has done a million times, Mindy reaches up with her other hand and pulls my heavy sleeve down over both of our hands and calmly lays our joined hands in her lap as if nothing happened.

I attempt to stop my hand from shaking as I hold Chester's phone up to my ear. I don't even know what I'm going to say to my family. How do I explain what Mindy knows? I mean I sort of understand because I've seen her in action a couple of times. I know everyone who loves and respects Mindy fully believes in her gift, but I have no idea how to explain it to someone who isn't part of Mindy's life.

I'm surprised when my mom answers my dad's phone. "Jigger, jig, jig, is Dad all right?"

"As far as I know he is, but your sister got a call from that accident expert and some lawyer. They took off like they were running from Satan himself. Your dad didn't even stop for lunch, so I'm not sure what's going on."

"Jigger, jig, jig, I don't know either. But I have reason to believe it might be safer if Dad stuck around home. I don't know much more right now. Just tell jigger, jig, jig Mariam to be extremely careful, okay? I'm trying to get more information and when I know more, you'll be the first to know. I love you, Mom."

"Elijah Fischer, you cannot call me with one of your fanciful stories and scare me like that!" my mom scolds.

"I'm sorry, Mom. I wish this was all just a scene from a scary novel, but I'm afraid it's so much more."

Tyler shines a small flashlight into Mindy's eyes as he squats down in front of her and watches her reaction. She flinches and sticks her tongue out at him. "Oh, for Pete's sake! I'm fine. I told you Elijah caught me. I don't even have as much as a tiny scrape."

"In my world, 'fine' people don't just pass out for no apparent reason. Are you eating okay? Are you still stressed out over what happened down in California? I bet you're not sleeping, are you?"

"Okay, first … you know who you're married to. She is best friends with my mom and you know who my grandma is — what are the chances I'm not eating well? I thought you were some hotshot Sheriff. You're not using your deductive reasoning very well. Of course, I'm worried about what happened in California … but it's not enough to make me pass out. For as long as you've known me, you've known I can't sleep worth beans." Mindy holds her wrist up under his nose. "In addition to feeding me more goodies from Joy and Tiers than any one person should ever eat in a lifetime, your lovely wife makes me this perfume out of vanilla and essential oils from lavender which is supposed to help me sleep. You know Aunt Heather makes the best perfumes and soaps. She's trying to help me solve my sleeping issues."

"So why do you think you passed out?" Mindy's uncle presses.

Mindy shrugs. "I don't know. It's been a couple years since I've been able to make any sense out of my precognitive stuff and all of a sudden, I had two bursts of activity. Maybe it was that."

"Min, I know you get chatty when you're stressed, but can we focus here? Could you see who fired the shot?"

I can feel Mindy tremble next to me. I squeeze her hand. "Jigger, jig, jig, are you up to this? Maybe Sheriff Colton could do this another time. I don't want this to wear you out."

Mindy shoots me a grateful smile. "I appreciate your concern, but Uncle Tyler needs this information." She pivots back to him as she answers, "No, I only saw them climb out of the back of a pickup."

"Them?" Tyler asks with concern. "As in more than one — besides the driver?"

Mindy starts to tremble in earnest. "I'm sorry Uncle Tyler I don't know any more. It … it's… not clear. I couldn't tell what they were wearing, the color of the truck, or anything. I only saw the gun." A tear slides down her face.

Instinctively, I pull Mindy closer and shield her from Tyler's questions. "Jigger, jig, jig, it's okay. Any information you give law enforcement is more than they had before. Nobody expects you to have it all."

Tyler runs his hand through his hair and down his face in frustration. "I'm sorry, Mouse. I know better. I've been friends with you and Tara for more than a decade. I guess I tend to take your gifts for granted. I know it's not like a surveillance camera. Still, I forget occasionally because you guys are so spooky good."

Mindy sits up and takes a drink of the soda Chester gave her earlier. I watch as she takes a deep breath and composes herself. "It's all right, Uncle Tyler. Sometimes I frustrate myself too — especially when I can't make all the pieces make sense."

"Mindy, don't put so much pressure on yourself. You've given us a place to start. You know, a lot of people have home surveillance systems now. Maybe somebody caught something on camera." Tyler observes.

"He's right you know, honey," interjects Betty Sue. "Before you said something, I would've assumed it was Earl's bratty hellions he calls grandsons — but they're not old enough to drive. Now, I'm pretty sure it's not them."

"I don't know where you left things off with Aidan, but I think maybe he should reinstate your protection through Logan and his team."

Mindy stiffens against me. "Uncle Tyler, we don't even know if this is related to me. It could be random. I'm not sure I'm going back on tour with Uncle Aidan. I might go back to school. It would be unfair to ask him to protect me if I'm not even part of the band."

I reach up and rub Mindy's back between her shoulder blades. "Mindy, call me crazy, jigger, jig, jig — but I was there at that concert when your uncle celebrated your birthday. I have a hunch if he catches even a hint that you had a close call today, he'll assign an army of people to you to make sure it doesn't happen again. Jigger, jig, jig, I don't think he cares how much it costs to keep you safe."

Tyler lets out a guffaw of laughter as he looks at me and asks, "How long did you say you've been hanging out with Mindy? You've got her family — real or honorary — nailed to a T."

"We've been friends since I was in high school and she's always talked about her friends and family as if they're one and the same."

"That's because they are," Mindy insists. "You're right. Aidan would have an apoplexy if he knew a bullet was anywhere close to my head. He almost stopped touring after the incident with Logan and Katie, when Tasha and Jude were in the car."

"Weren't you in the car with them too?" I ask. "Maybe he was worried about you too."

Mindy rolls her shoulder. "He probably was. Although back then, I was really a nobody with the band. Uncle Aidan was simply being nice and giving me a chance to get a feel for the business."

Tyler shakes his head. "Mindy, you know that's not true. Aidan is bombarded with people who are begging for a chance to get their shot at the brass ring every single day. If he didn't think you had the talent to make it, he would've never given you a shot. Don't undersell yourself. Even if you decide not to go back on tour with Aidan, I think you should give him a call. After the weirdness that went on with Tasha, you never know. It could be a really big deal."

Mindy looks pensive for a moment, but then looks determined.

"All right, I'll call him. But probably for different reasons than you expect."

"What do you mean?" Tyler asks with obvious trepidation.

"It has to do with the second thing I saw today. It was a vision which knocked the wind out of me psychically and made me pass out."

Tyler pulls a little pad of paper out of his breast pocket and a pen from behind his ear as he gets ready to write down whatever she says. He crosses one leg over the other to form a makeshift desk from his legs. "Okay, ready. I know your stories don't always have a beginning a middle and an end. Start wherever you feel comfortable."

"Well, this particular story has a beginning. My vision started as soon as you told me Elijah's phone was broken and he needed to call his dad. I don't know what to make of all this. As strange as this sounds, I think Mr. Fischer was hurt before he was hit by a car. I wish I could tell you more. The pictures are weird and don't make any sense, but that's what's coming to me. I think Mr. Fischer is in danger."

As Mindy is revealing all of this, Tyler narrows his gaze at me. "Elijah, you don't look all that surprised to hear this. What's up?"

I shrug. "Jigger, jig, jig, some of Dad's coworkers have been calling Mariam and me. We've heard several versions of what happened and not everybody's jigger, jig, jig story matches up. That's why Mariam asked you for the phone number of the accident reconstruction expert, jigger, jig, jig."

"Do you think your dad might be a target?"

"Jigger, jig, jig, he thought so," I confirm.

"The car you're driving has Oregon plates. Any chance it belonged to your dad before he was injured?"

I nod. "It was his pride and joy. Jigger, jig, jig, he restored it himself."

Mindy grimaces. "We just made your life a lot more complicated, didn't we, Uncle Tyler?"

Tyler attempts to smile. "You know me. I love puzzles. I'll call your Aunt Heather and tell her I'll be late for supper."

Mindy lays her head against my shoulder. I lean down and whisper, "Jigger, jig, jig, just so you know, this isn't how I planned for our date to go."

"Believe it or not, I don't think it's going so badly. You kept me safe in the middle of a crisis and you kept me calm when I was falling apart. I don't think I can ask for much more," she says as she leans over and brushes a kiss across my cheek.

CHAPTER ELEVEN

MINDY

I PACE BACK AND forth in front of Uncle Aidan's office indecisively. Finally, he opens the door and waves me in. "If you're trying to decide whether to tell me what happened the other day, don't bother. I already know."

I groan in frustration. "Doesn't Uncle Tyler have any sort of professional ethics?"

Aidan smirks at me. "He does. You're assuming I heard about the incident from him. I did not. The Franklins are quite influential in this county. They have a lot of friends and word gets around quickly."

My jaw goes slack. "It does?"

Aidan nods. "Indeed."

"All of it?" I ask, my stomach sinking to my toes. I've never made a huge secret of my abilities among my friends and family. But I'd rather not have them be exploited through the tabloids. I've seen what they've done to Aidan, Tara, Tasha, and Jude.

"I think she told an abbreviated version of the story."

I sink down into the leather chair in Aidan's office.

"Oh thank goodness. There are parts of my life right now I do not want to explain. Like how do I rationalize how I could save Chester's life, but not Melanie's? That would be a nightmare! I don't even understand why my gift works that way."

"I know your dad has told you this a million times, but you are not responsible for what happens in the world around you."

"I know that in my head. Still, sometimes my head and my heart don't agree."

"So, let me guess — that's why you're wearing grooves in the carpet outside my office?"

I lean forward and bury my face in my hands as I admit, "Yes, I don't know what else to do."

"Mouse, I told you once, I'll do anything you ever need to make you safe and happy. Just name it."

"Do you remember Elijah Fischer?"

Aidan grins at me. "Boy, do I ever! That guy will change the world one day. As I recall, you were kinda sweet on him, weren't you?"

"Am. I *am* sweet on him. He's still a great guy even after all the fame. His dad is hurt and I have reason to believe it wasn't an accident. I think Mr. Fischer may still be in danger. I'm afraid Uncle Tyler doesn't have enough resources to assign him surveillance or anything. I was hoping that since we aren't touring over the Thanksgiving holidays maybe the Fischer family could borrow a couple of Logan's guys," I explain tentatively.

"Consider it done."

I regard my honorary uncle with wide-eyed shock.

He chuckles at my expression. "What? Did you

expect a different answer? This guy means a lot to you. You're going to be hanging around him and his family. It only makes sense for me to protect him. Besides, it would be really bad karma if I knew something bad might happen to someone and I had the power to prevent it, but I didn't." A chill seems to go up Aidan's spine. "I don't want any part of that bad juju. If you or Tara give me a warning, I've been around the two of you long enough to take it totally seriously."

I slump back in the chair as I confess, "This would probably be a good time for me to tell you my gift is a bit on the fritz. This whole thing might not even be real. My visions may not be as cohesive as they usually once were. I might be reading them all wrong."

"Or, you might be reading them right on the money. I know from what Tara tells me, sometimes things are fuzzy in the beginning and toward the end they come together to form a solid picture."

This time, it's my turn to shudder. "If the bits and pieces I've seen come together to form a solid picture, it will be one of the ugliest things I've ever seen. I hope to heavens, I'm not right. That would be horrific."

"You said Mr. Fischer was hurt pretty badly in the accident, correct?"

"That's my understanding," I answer with a sigh.

"I recently hired an ex-military guy with the perfect background. His name is Josiah Greenberg. He happens to be an ex-medic with experience as a trauma nurse and a sharpshooter. You don't get that combination very often."

"Where did you find him?" I ask. "Never mind. Between Tyler and Trevor, you probably had your bases covered."

Aidan grins smugly. "Nope, I just flat out lucked out with this one. Tristan was planning to recruit him for Identity Bank West, but he was so interested in the music business Jameson and Tristan decided it would make more sense for him to work directly for me."

"Are you sure he doesn't secretly want to be a star?"

Aidan shrugs nonchalantly. "What if he does? That strategy seemed to work out okay for Jude, didn't it?"

I swallow hard. "I feel bad saying this because I don't even know if I plan to stay with the tour. Having a bullet whiz by my head and miss me by mere inches makes me more sure than ever I want someone focused on watching the principal and not watching their latest single climb up the charts."

"I understand your point. I don't think it'll be a problem with Josiah. The guy has been interviewed by Tristan, Jameson, Logan, Katie and me. We were all incredibly impressed with his dedication to his country and to his profession. If he's a little star struck by musicians, I don't blame him. Silent Beats is an impressive organization. We are a popular group of musicians. It's not as if no one has ever heard of us."

I blush. "Okay, that might be true of you guys, but I'm only a background musician."

"You might have started out that way, but your fan base is quickly growing. We learned the hard way with Tasha, not all adoration from fans is a good thing. I'll have Katie step up your protection detail too. It's actually the perfect cover. She'll be able to train Josiah on the protocol here at Silent Beats at the same time she's providing backup and additional protection for you."

"It all seems like a lot. I wish it wasn't necessary."

"I wish it wasn't needed either kiddo, but that's simply not the world we live in these days." Aidan walks over and kisses me on the forehead. "Speaking of the world we live in, I've got to go pick up Maddie from school. Why don't you swing by in a couple of hours with Elijah and see what you guys think of Josiah?"

<hr />

"Jigger, jig, jig, don't get me wrong, I love being with you — but I promised my mom I would hang with Dad today. She's had a really long day. She's incredibly worried about what Mariam found out."

"I talked to your mom earlier today when I was trying to track you down. It's all good. She just told me to make sure you get a new phone. She said your dad is sleeping because of all the running around he did this afternoon."

"Jigger, jig, jig, I didn't realize you and my mom were such good friends."

"Are you kidding? I'm like one of your biggest fans. So, how could your mom dislike me?"

Elijah dips a nacho in cheese sauce before he asks pointedly, "So why are we just sitting around? We have stuff to do."

"We're waiting for Uncle Aidan and Logan," I explain.

Elijah rolls his eyes at me as he involuntarily slaps the side of his face. "Jigger, jig, jig, I might be older now, but I still think your uncle is one of the coolest dudes around. Jigger, jig, jig I have puppy poop dripping down my sweatshirt," he says with a sigh. "I'm not exactly prepared to meet a rock star."

"Come on, you've gone rock climbing with Uncle Aidan before. Puppy poop will raise you several notches in his eyes. He's all about the gross and unexpected — especially if you were helping someone else in the process."

"Jigger, jig, jig, I'm not sure I buy your argument, but let's just say I do," he responds skeptically. "That doesn't explain why we're here."

"Since we don't know which one of us is actually in danger, I figured we could use some help. It seems like your dad is in danger and he needs some special help." I shrug. "So… I found some."

Elijah slumps back against the booth. He is quiet for a few moments before he asks, "Just like that? Jigger, jig, jig, you simply snapped your fingers and solved all my problems? Without even asking me?"

Puzzled by the bitterness in his voice, I respond, "Umm … I am asking you — that's why we're meeting with Aidan and Logan. I'm just trying to be helpful I don't want anything to happen to your dad. My uncle, and a guy who helps protect me every day have an answer for you — it's kinda what we do in my world. Is that a problem?"

I can see Elijah grit his teeth and sit on his hands as he tries not to tic. "Jigger, jig, jig, jigger, jig, jig, it's just that a lot of people think I'm not smart enough to make my own decisions because I do things like talk funny and hit myself or count random things — like the number of times my pencil touches the paper, jigger, jig, jig."

My eyes widen in surprise as I absorb his words. "You think I believe that about you?" I gesture toward myself as I push up my glasses. "As the saying goes, 'I see dead people' and a bunch of other bizarre stuff no one else sees. Do I really look like I'm in a position to judge you or anyone else?"

Elijah vehemently shakes his head. "Jigger, jig, jig, no! I'm sorry, jigger, jig, jig. I'm just totally stressed out. I don't even know what I'm saying. You're one of a handful of people who has never been that way with me."

A wave of energy hits me and I have to close my eyes. "They're here. Something has Uncle Aidan tied in knots."

Elijah looks around the restaurant and starts to ask, "How do you —"

I raise an eyebrow and smirk.

Elijah shakes his head wryly as he picks up his large mug of coffee. "Obviously, I haven't had enough of this."

Aidan comes around the corner and comments, "There isn't enough caffeine on the planet to get me through the kind of day I'm having." He pins me with a laser like gaze. "Please tell me this gets better?"

"It does," I assure him solemnly. "Maddie will find her footing, I swear."

"What am I supposed to do? Some little punk took her backpack and called her a retard on the bus!"

"I'm sorry, Uncle Aidan, but it'll probably happen thousands of times before she's done with school."

Elijah nods. "Sometimes when my parents tried to help, it made it worse — especially if the kids knew they went to the teachers."

My uncle rakes his hands through his long, curly red hair as he admits, "You would think I would know what to do since the kids were terrible to me during my whole childhood. There was no way I could compete with Rory. He was like the perfect child. I was a carrot top with braces and an unhealthy obsession with Broadway tunes. It was even worse after the meningitis."

"Yeah, and look at you now. You've got a couple Grammy awards under your belt," Elijah points out. "I didn't learn this skill until I became friends with Sadie — but things didn't get better for me until I decided what my boundaries were. Rather than fight with the bullies or run away from them, my best strategy was to learn what made me strong."

"The same was true for me. Once I found music, it was easier for me to fit in. It became my strength. Maddie will find what makes her strong too," I assure Aidan as I walk over and give him a hug.

He signs, "I love you the same."

When Aidan finds his voice, he says, "We didn't actually come here to talk about my problems." He looks directly at Elijah. "I understand Mindy thinks your dad is in trouble."

Elijah clears his throat before he frowns. "Jigger, jig, jig, she's mentioned it."

Aidan laughs out loud. "I don't know if you know this, but my wife, Tara has the same gift as Mindy. We've been together since Tara was just a little older than Maddie. One thing I've learned along the way is that when these women speak, you need to listen with a very open mind. They are very rarely wrong."

"It's not that I think Mindy's wrong, I just worry because it's not her responsibility to fix my life, jigger, jig, jig."

"Oh, I see. You just haven't been around as much.

We tend to take responsibility for each other a lot. It's kind of a group thing. I have a problem that you can help me solve."

Elijah looks skeptical. "Jigger, jig, jig, I do?"

Aidan nods as he points to Josiah. "I recruited this guy all the way from Georgia before we found out Maddie needs a follow-up surgery on her hip. That means we won't do another large-scale tour until February. Unfortunately, he moved all the way out to Oregon because I promised him a job as part of the protection team."

Logan picks up the story. "I'll be doing some short-term gigs with Joe Summers and Declan. So, Katie is planning to stay behind and train Josiah on the way we do things around here at Silent Beats. My wife says she's nicer than me. There's probably some truth to that — but she prefers hands-on learning protocols. So, we'd like to lend Josiah and Katie to your family until we're ready to go on tour."

"Jigger, jig, jig, jigger, jig, jig, I'm not sure I follow. You want to let us 'borrow' thousands of dollars' worth of private security services because you don't want the new guy to get bored?" Elijah asks incredulously.

"Well, there's a little more to it than that. Josiah is transitioning his skills in the military to the world of security services. Tristan ran him through a couple of courses at his training academy before he decided Josiah would be a better fit at Silent Beats."

Josiah clears his throat abruptly. "Does anyone here mind if Josiah speaks for himself?"

"By all means," Logan says as he gestures toward Josiah. "We encourage that around here. Although, you probably couldn't tell that from the conversation you just witnessed."

Josiah grins. "I'm not worried. I've hung around you guys long enough to know you all carry on like my grandma used to with her friends at church bingo night. If I have something important to say, I'll say it."

"You sound like me, jigger, jig, jig." Elijah grins shyly.

"I've also hung around with these guys long enough to know that if they say there's a threat, there *is one*. I can help with that. I used to be in competitive shooting when I was in high school. But, I also was a medic in the military and then I went back to school and got more training as a nurse after I got out."

"So, Aidan O'Brien is cool and all, jigger, jig, jig, but it's not the same as being a nurse, why come to work here?" Elijah presses.

Josiah shrugs. "It's a fair question. Honestly, I got tired of feeling powerless when people died on my watch despite everything I did to stop it from happening. It didn't matter how smart I was or what techniques I learned, death always seemed to be a step ahead of me. It gets old after a while."

I raise an eyebrow. "Providing personal protection isn't exactly a safe line of work," I challenge. "People do die."

"They do. On the other hand, I am a very, very good shot."

"So why not just take a few months off and lay on a beach somewhere and chill? It sounds like you've earned it." Elijah asks.

"I'm not wired that way. I need to be doing something. If I can be helping someone who needs me, that's what I want to be doing. I understand your family has been facing some challenges recently," Josiah explains.

"That's putting it mildly. If Mindy is correct, those challenges aren't over yet."

"I know it's a hard decision because you just met me a few minutes ago, but if you need some help, I'm qualified to give it to you," Josiah offers.

Elijah sends me a panicked look.

Logan sees it. "Don't worry, you don't have to decide tonight. I just wanted to give you guys these." He opens his ever-present satchel and pulls out two boxes.

When I see the familiar logo, I have to catch my breath. "Oh, wow! Tasha told me about the time you did this for her —" I try to cover my amazement.

"Jigger, jig, jig, are you serious? This is a brand-new phone," Elijah interjects.

Aidan smiles. "I am aware. Folks around Silent Beats go through them so fast I practically buy them in bulk. For a bunch of people who handle expensive musical instruments for a living, my crew is remarkably hard on phones."

"Jigger, jig, jig I don't even know what to say," Elijah stammers.

"Generally, 'Thank you' works," Aidan quips. "Besides, Dorothy would kill me if she knew your dad was hurt and I left you without a phone. She raised me with better manners than that."

"I think your manners are just fine Uncle Aidan. Thank you so much for this. Mrs. Fischer will be grateful." I reach out and touch Josiah's shoulder. "Give us a little while to wrap our minds around what's happening and clue Elijah's family in on everything. I'm not sure they even understand the danger. We'll be in touch. Thank you for your help."

Elijah steps up and shakes Josiah's hand. "Jigger, jig, jig, I wish I could say it better, but I can't, so what she said."

◆ ●

After I pull my Volkswagen bug up to Elijah's parents place, and place it in park I glance over toward Elijah. He looks like he's about to be sick.

"Okay, I know it was a close call with the bicyclist who pulled out in front of me, but I'm a pretty good driver. I didn't hit him or anything," I say, trying to lighten the mood.

Elijah abruptly gets out of my car and walks around the front of it. He opens my door and helps me out. Silently, he puts his hands on my shoulders and draws me close. He brushes a kiss across my lips.

"Oh …" I whisper softly.

Elijah buries his face in his hands. When he looks up he says, "Jigger, jig, jig, sorry, jigger, jig, jig. I shouldn't have done that."

"I don't have any complaints. Honestly, I've wanted you to do that for a long time."

Elijah looks bewildered. "Really?"

I nod and lean in and kiss him again. "Yes, even when I thought you were Sadie's boyfriend, I had a huge crush on you. You should kiss me more often."

Elijah draws in a deep, shuddering breath. "Maybe I

will, jigger, jig, jig. Right now, I have to figure out what to say to my family. Jigger, jig, jig, how do I make any of this make any sense?" he asks as his hand flies up and strikes the side of his face.

I capture his hand and lace my fingers through his and stick our hands in the pocket of my oversized jacket.

He continues, "I feel like I'm living in the middle of a crazy, surreal reality show. Jigger, jig, jig, the thing I can't figure out is if I'm the only one who's clueless or if everyone else is just reading from a different script."

"Interesting. That's kind of how I felt the whole time I was at college. I had this whole vision of what it would be like and it was nothing like I expected at all," I confess. I'm amazed how naturally we fit together as we walk up the steps to his parent's house. "The new ramp looks nice."

Elijah shrugs. "Jigger, jig, jig, my dad hates it. He says it ruins the aesthetic of their house. I should warn you, he doesn't have a very positive attitude about much of anything these days. He might hate you at first — especially when he hears what we have to say. Jigger, jig, jig, try not to take it personally."

"Don't stress. I am used to having to explain my weirdness to people. This is nothing new. If your parents don't understand, that's not unusual either. Josiah and Logan will be by in a few minutes to explain their end of things too. They had to go pick up Katelyn."

Elijah shakes his head. "I still can't believe they even offered to do all that for us. You have the nicest friends and family I have ever met."

"Yeah, Becca and I definitely won the adoption lottery."

"Do you ever wonder what it would've been like if things would've gone a different direction, jigger, jig, jig?"

"I don't have to wonder. That alternate scenario is only a nightmare away."

Elijah takes his hand out of my pocket and puts it around my waist as he hugs me closer and whispers against my temple, "Min, jigger, jig, jig I'm sorry. That's something no one should have to remember."

"It's okay. It doesn't happen very often anymore. Usually only when I don't get enough sleep or something super stressful happens."

"So, my presence in your life isn't helping, is it? Jigger, jig, jig, your time with me has been nothing but stressful. You were shot at, jigger, jig, jig."

"I won't lie. That was pretty stressful, but it wasn't your fault and it sure as heck isn't the whole story." I pull Elijah over to a porch swing and sit down. Grasping both of his hands, I study his face. "I don't think you understand what you've done for me. You spent hours listening to me ramble on about my brother and sister, my parents, and my nightmarish experience at college."

"I didn't mind. You had pretty broad shoulders that night too," Elijah insists.

"I know but you went above and beyond the call of duty. You did more than rescue me from a party I didn't ask for. You listened to me tell you how I made a fool out of myself at a college party I had no business going to, but you weren't judgmental. When you knew I was stressed out about what direction I wanted to take my life, you didn't put me in a situation where I had to dress up and pretend to be something I wasn't — instead you let me play with puppies."

Elijah grins. "To be fair, I love playing with puppies too, so it wasn't much of a sacrifice."

I smile back. "Still, you sensed that I'm reluctant to trust very many people. So, you didn't put me in a situation where I had to perform and act older than I am. You simply let me be me — part wary little kid, part old soul who hasn't found a comfortable spot on this planet. It was the best time I've had in forever."

Elijah grimaces. "And then you got shot at, jigger, jig, jig."

"So did you — but that wasn't our fault. They weren't aiming at us, or maybe they were. It's too early to tell. But you didn't plan for that to happen. It just did. Most things that happen in my life aren't planned. Some are good and some are bad. It's simply fate. I'm so glad you're part of my life."

"Jigger, jig, jig, are you really? I think things are about to get a lot more complicated. I don't know. Maybe you don't need me to make your life more difficult than it already is."

"I think it's too late for that. Maybe our fates were decided a long time ago. Perhaps it was settled years ago when I first saw you or maybe before we were born. Who knows?"

Before Elijah can answer, the front door opens and his mom sticks her head out. "I tried to give you a little privacy but your father is champing at the bit. He wants to know what's taking you so long to come in the house."

"Jigger, jig, jig, sorry Mom. Mindy and I were just talking."

"It looked pretty intense to be just talking. Besides, if you want to convince your dad that's all it was, you might want to wipe the lipstick off your face."

CHAPTER TWELVE

ELIJAH

GLANCING AROUND THE LIVING room, I take a few deep breaths. The last time I was this nervous I was preparing to announce my decision to drop out of college. I don't think this will be quite that difficult, but it might be. I place my hand on the small of Mindy's back and escort her to what used to be the den. We've turned it into a bedroom for my dad since he can no longer climb the stairs. Before I can make introductions, my dad addresses Mindy, "You look older than I thought you would," he whispers hoarsely.

His speech has made a remarkable recovery in the last couple of weeks, but in this moment, I kind of wish it hadn't. But Mindy seems to take it in stride as she giggles. "You are not the first person to say that. I guess it comes from having a rough start in life. I've always seemed to be older than my chronological age." She reaches out to shake my dad's hand. She's not even put off by his awkward backwards handshake. He is unable to use his dominant hand. "Hi, I'm Mindy Whitaker."

My mom steps forward. "It's so nice to meet you. I

am Roxanne and this is my husband Seth."

"Mariam says danger. True?" my dad croaks as he looks directly at Mindy.

Mindy nods solemnly.

"How do you know, dear?" my mom asks. "You weren't there when the accident happened, were you?"

"No ma'am. I was down in California. I go to college down there … or, at least I did, until there was an incident with my roommate."

"What kind of incident?" my mom asks.

"It seems the authorities believe she may have taken some drugs or had too much to drink."

"Our son has enough to cope with. He doesn't need more garbage in his life. If that's your scene, you can leave Elijah the heck alone," my mom warns.

"Jigger, jig, jig, Mom!" I chastise.

"Elijah, that's all right. She doesn't know my whole story. Drugs and alcohol are definitely not my scene. My sister and I were terribly abused because of addiction. I don't touch the stuff. You'd be hard-pressed to get me to take so much as an aspirin. Melanie's decisions were her own. I tried to talk her out of her risky choices, but she didn't listen."

"Musician?" my dad whispers.

"Yes, it's true I am a musician. But at least where I work, the stereotypes aren't true. My uncle is my boss — well he's not really my uncle, but he's best friends with my dad and he's been my honorary uncle for what seems like forever. His wife has been friends with my mom since college. Everyone who works there is like family. I'm only a backup singer. The woman I sing with, Tasha, is like a big sister. If Uncle Aidan finds people at Silent Beats who are abusing, he doesn't tolerate it."

My dad smiles tightly. "Good. Gunshot?"

Mindy walks over and pulls up a chair beside my dad's bed. "That is a more difficult question to answer. Do you ever have a strong sense of déjà vu?, Mr. Fischer? Like you could swear you've done something or said something the exact same way before?" Mindy asks.

My dad nods.

"Do you ever have a hunch you know what's going to happen even when other people disagree? When you try to explain your feelings to other people, do you sometimes find it difficult to choose the perfect words, but somewhere deep inside you know you're right?"

"Heck yeah," my dad whispers as he points to the hospital bed. "Probably why I'm here."

"That's kind of what my gift is like. It's like those premonitions regular people get, except they're magnified many times over. Sometimes they're crystal clear and I know exactly what's going to happen to someone. It's like reading the script from a television show or a movie. Other times, it's only a teeny-tiny sliver. I'll see only a glimpse and it will be totally out of context — or the scenes will be all mixed up."

My mom closes her eyes and shakes her head as if to block out Mindy's words. "I don't believe in that kind of thing."

"Mom, I was there. I saw her gift in action. If she hadn't told Chester to move, the bullet would've hit him, jigger, jig, jig. Even though it was from a small caliber weapon, it still could have done some serious damage."

Mindy shrugs. "Still, I wish I could've done more."

"What about me?" my dad asks with a pained expression.

"Seth, I wish I had better news for you. But the images are making even less sense in your case. I see lots of rage, a bunch of hardhats, someone striking you with a piece of equipment of some sort before you were hit by a car. Then, I see a bunch of executives in a meeting talking about how to make sure none of the information is made public."

"What does any of that mumbo-jumbo mean? Dad, what if she's right? What does it mean for your job?" Mariam asks as she watches the conversation with morbid fascination.

"I don't know. What if this gal is working for the driver's insurance company on the sly and trying to talk us out of suing?" my dad asks stubbornly.

Mindy stares down my dad. "I know you don't have any reason to believe me. I can't prove my gift one way or another. It's not like a parlor game — I can't simply demonstrate it on command. It's a matter of trust and faith. The person who provides security for me and his wife are pulling up front as I speak. My uncle is with them if you would like to talk to them. If the threat I see coming materializes, you're going to need protection. My Uncle Aidan has offered some members of his personal protection team. Whether or not you believe me, you might want to listen to your daughter and the expert she consulted. If you love your wife and children, I beg you to take her findings seriously."

<hr/>

For several moments, I quietly hold Mindy in my arms as

I rest against her car. I've been trying to figure out a good way to say goodbye for at least ten minutes and I can't seem to find the words. I knew my parents wouldn't take the news about the potential threat against them well. Even so, I didn't expect them to come right out and call Mindy a liar.

I gently kiss her forehead and whisper against her temple, "Jigger, jig, jig, I'm so sorry. They had no right to say that stuff about you."

Mindy puts her arms around my neck and places a soft kiss on my lips. "Elijah, it's not your fault. People have all sorts of different reactions when they meet me. Your parent's attitude was pretty common." She holds up her scarred hand. The moonlight highlights the rough texture of her scars. "I've had much worse. My grandmother tried to boil me alive because she believed I harbored evil spirits."

"I have a hard time believing there are people in this world who are so deranged, jigger, jig, jig. Honestly, I expected better of my parents."

"I think we should cut them a little slack. Your dad recently suffered a severe head injury. His brain is probably a little scrambled still," Mindy counters.

"Okay, that's true enough, jigger, jig, jig. My mom knows better though. Jigger, jig, jig, she knows that you've been part of my life for years."

Mindy's eyes widen. "I have?"

It's a good thing it's dark outside and Mindy can't see me flush dark red.

"Jigger, jig, jig, that didn't come out quite right."

"Welcome to my world. Most of what I say doesn't come out quite right."

"I mean, from the moment I met you, you made an impression on me, jigger, jig, jig. I remember telling my mom how much I liked you."

Mindy smirks. "Did you happen to mention I was still in junior high school?"

"Jigger, jig, jig, that might not have come up until Mariam mentioned your birthday party."

"Let's face it, a lot of people are going to think our age difference is a little weird."

"That's stupid, jigger, jig, jig. I'm only four-and-a-half years older than you."

Mindy steps forward and leans her cheek against my chest. "I think people need to root against happiness. I watched people make snide remarks about my parents when they thought I couldn't hear. If they found out my dad was a lawyer, they wondered why he would settle for a woman in a wheelchair. Other people assume my mom was supporting a black man with her job as a social worker. No one could guess that they were simply lucky enough to fall in love at first sight."

"That's disgusting! Why is it any of their business?"

Mindy shrugs before she pulls away. "I don't know. I've never figured that out. People have a funny way of deciding what to care about."

"Jigger, jig, jig, I hope my family decides it's none of their business soon."

Mindy smiles up at me. "I wouldn't hold your breath. My grandma says it doesn't matter how old her kids are, she'll always care who's in their lives. I think it's probably the same with your mom. I'll just have to gain your parent's trust, and that takes time. After all, we just met, and I had to tell them that your dad's life is in danger. It wasn't the best beginning."

"Jigger, jig, jig, I think they already knew something like that was coming. Mariam and my dad met with Claudia Featherstone, the accident reconstruction expert your uncle recommended. There are real discrepancies between, jigger, jig, jig, jigger, jig, jig the story the company is telling and the stories the witnesses are telling. Apparently, my dad's injuries are inconsistent with the official report. Ms. Featherstone wants to look into it further. She has advised my dad to hire a private attorney."

"Oh, your poor mom; she must be completely at her wit's end."

"She is. She's finding it incredibly difficult to take care of Dad even with us kids around to help. Jigger, jig, jig, I'm glad Josiah convinced her to bring him on board."

"I'm not sure it was so much Josiah as it was Kate. I've always known she was tough as nails, but I didn't realize she was such an effective salesperson. Your poor parents didn't stand a chance."

"Jigger, jig, jig, either way, everyone who matters to me will be safer with them around. So, it works for me."

Mindy stands up on her tiptoes and kisses my lips before she pulls away and says, "I'm glad I matter to you."

"Not as glad as I am that I matter to you. Jigger, jig, jig, thank you for taking care of my family."

The porch lights flicker on and off. Mindy looks up at them and giggles.

"Well, I guess that's my cue to go." Mindy hugs me before she gets in her car. She rolls down her window and says, "By the way, all this is no problem. It's just what I do —especially for people I care about."

I take a moment to collect myself as I watch her taillights disappear down my parent's driveway. Who knew a trip home would change my life so dramatically. I know Mindy thinks that I'm exaggerating when I tell her how much I thought about her all those years ago when we met — but I'm not. I found her intriguing then, but she's downright fascinating now.

———◆———

As soon as I get through the front door and close it behind me, my sister comes out of nowhere and starts jumping up and down in front of my face. "Oh my gosh! You are serious about her! I only dared you to go out with Mindy because I thought you would be too scared to try! You know, the strange stuff we challenged each other to do when we were younger? I never thought you'd go through with it and I sure as heck never thought you'd ask her out again."

"Jigger, jig, jig, will you hold still so we can have a rational conversation like two adults?"

My sister snorts. "Yeah, like you're even into adults. Seems you prefer kids these days."

"Shut up! You have no idea what you're even talking about. Mindy went through more stuff before the first grade than most people should ever have to endure in a whole lifetime. She might only be eighteen, but she's smarter and more together than I could ever hope to be."

"You shut up!" Mariam counters. "At the moment, she's a college dropout who's riding on her uncle's coattails to become famous. At least you got famous for doing your own thing."

"Hey! Jigger, jig, jig, that's unfair. I thought you were a fan," I argue.

"I was — until she started hanging out with my little brother and filling your head with all this psychic, telepathic crap. You don't know if she's up to some weird scheme. You heard her — her roommate died. What if she's mixed up in all that?"

"Mariam, she's not. She wasn't even there, jigger, jig, jig. You sound worse than Mom and Dad. What's up with calling her a hack? When you were at the concert, you thought she was amazing."

Mariam walks over to the couch and flops down. "Okay, here's the real truth. I don't want to like her. I don't want Mindy to be in our lives at all. I want to pretend I've never met her. Because if I don't know her, then I don't have to pay attention to what she said is going on with Dad. If I can ignore her, then we don't have to have bodyguards hanging out at our house to watch over him. If we don't have to have bodyguards, we can go to temple, to the grocery store, see a movie, go to therapy or wherever else we want to go without looking over our shoulder. But now, because she had a 'vision', we can't do any of those things. That's why I want to act like she doesn't exist and that you guys aren't already halfway in love and the cutest couple I've ever seen. Can't we pretend none of this ever happened?"

"Jigger, jig, jig, sure. I'd like that too," I answer sharply, unable to hide my pain. "Don't you think I wish I could turn back time to a couple weeks before the accident so we could talk Dad into retiring before he ever went on this last job? I wish he had taken Mom on a cruise for their anniversary, jigger, jig, jig. But, that's not the way real life works. You don't get to wish away the

144

past. We can't make it so the accident didn't happen and you can't undo Mindy and me. Whatever is happening between us is a thing. A thing I like very much."

"How can you be so sure? Everything has been crazy and upside down in our lives right now. How do you know what you're feeling is real?"

"Jigger, jig, jig, I don't know for sure. I just know Mindy sees me. She doesn't care about the Tourette's syndrome. She takes time to listen to what I have to say. She hears what I mean and listens to what I don't say too. She listens to my hopes and fears, jigger, jig, jig. She goes out of her way to make my life better. Mindy is amazing in so many ways and I can't believe she likes me too."

Mariam looks dubious.

"Don't you think she's a bit odd?"

"How can you say that? She got her friends and family to rally around ours to provide Dad with top-notch security services and she helped save our friend from a potentially serious bullet wound and she loves animals. She even helped Mom cook dinner tonight. What else do you want from her?"

"I don't know! I just find her a little spooky and weird," my sister admits.

"Well, a lot of people think I'm a little spooky and weird too, but that doesn't keep you from loving me. So, please try a little harder with Mindy. She means a lot to me."

My sister frowns and chews on her fingernail. "Okay, you're right. Maybe I jumped to too many conclusions. She did step up for Dad. I'll try to give her a chance, but if she hurts you, I won't be happy."

Chapter Thirteen

Mindy

MY DAD STOICALLY STIRS his coffee as he pretends to read the legal brief in front of him. I know he's not really paying attention to it because he keeps looking up at me every few seconds. "Go ahead, I'm listening," I finally say as I take a sip of my coffee which is more creamer than actual coffee.

"Haven't seen much of you around lately."

"Umm … I've been helping Elijah proofread his latest novel," I stammer awkwardly.

"Huh," my dad answers with a knowing twinkle in his eye. "I think your papa would say you're courting the young man, if I don't miss my guess."

I shrug in what I hope is a casual manner. "It would be stupid of me to deny that there is a fair amount of that going on — but I'm trying not to scare Elijah off. He can be a little on the shy side."

"Wouldn't it be easier to date him if Katie wasn't glued to your every move?"

"Probably," I answer succinctly.

"You want to tell me what's going on? Or do I have to put you under cross-examination? Is this related to Melanie's death? Have you received threats or something?"

I shake my head. "You know how my gift has been glitching recently. Katie's presence in my life is more of a precaution than anything else. It's really complicated but essentially we're using Katie as a tool to help make sure that Elijah's dad, Seth, has protection. If she keeps me safer in the process, that's just an added bonus."

"Why is Seth in danger?"

"I'm not entirely certain. I have a feeling it has to do with his job. He was trying to stand up and tell people they were taking too many shortcuts to save money. It's his job to inspect bridges and other road construction sites to make sure they meet proper technical specifications. I have a feeling his accident wasn't really an accident but rather an attempt to shut him up. Something tells me the attempt against his life was only just the beginning. Since Uncle Aidan isn't planning to use the newest security guy he hired until after Maddie has her surgery, he's loaned them to Elijah's family members to watch over his dad."

"Wow! I hope they know what a valuable gift full-time protection is. I remember helping Aidan look into the cost of security before Tara faced down her attacker in court. Aidan was afraid Warren Jones' parole might be granted and wanted to have some personal protection lined up for her in case he was paroled. It was outrageously expensive, even all those years ago. I can't imagine what it would cost these days."

"Uncle Aidan doesn't seem to care about the cost. That's why he's having Katie train Josiah in Silent Beats protocol while they are guarding Seth. As far as letting the Fischer family know what it actually costs, I'd rather not. They are having a hard enough time asking for help since Mr. Fischer's accident. I don't want to give them any excuse to turn down the help they've already accepted."

"Makes perfect sense to me. Are you convinced Mr. Fischer is in danger?" my dad asks with a look of concern.

"Dad, if a fraction of what I see is true, it's a wonder he's not already dead."

My dad looks at his watch and grimaces. "I wish I had more time to talk. Unfortunately, I have a meeting this morning." He stands up and kisses me on the forehead. "I know Katie is watching your back, but be careful, please. I love you until. Don't forget that Mouse."

My eyes tear up. "I love you too, Dad. Don't let the bad guys win today."

I chew on the end of my pencil as I study the manuscript. I reread the passage several times as a question forms. Finally, I find the words to articulate it. "In this scene, was Cody showing Jasmine more of who he really was on the inside, or was he still pretending to be the person he had always been in front of Scott and his friends? Which version was Jasmine attracted to?"

"Jigger, jig, jig, I don't know. I'm not sure Jasmine ever met the old version of Cody before he started changing."

"Maybe it's just the way my brain works, but I wonder something. They seem perfect together now, but would Jasmine have even given him the time of day before he started figuring out who he was and what he stood for?"

"Wow, that's a great question. I should have asked that. Maybe I'll do a follow-up interview before I finalize the book. So, keep track of your questions and I'll see about asking them some cleanup questions."

My cell phone rings and I reflexively answer it. "Hello?"

"Mindy Jo Whitaker?" the voice on the other end asks.

"This is she," I answer.

"Hello, this is Officer Brannon. Did I catch you at a bad time?"

Initially, I shake my head before I collect my wits and verbally respond, "No this is a perfect time. How can I help you?"

"For the record, this conversation is being recorded as evidence in the investigation into the death of Melanie Lake, do you object?"

"No, of course not. Do what you need to do. I have nothing to hide."

"I just need to clarify some of your previous statements, if that's all right with you?"

"I guess so," I answer wondering what my dad would say.

"When we talked last, you told me you had purchased no alcohol or drugs for Melanie, is that correct?"

"That's right. I've never bought any drugs or alcohol for anyone. I just turned eighteen."

"You'd be surprised how many people don't care about the law."

"I'm not one of those people."

"We have evidence which suggests otherwise, Ms. Whitaker."

I draw in a deep breath and whisper, "That's impossible."

Elijah regards me with concern etched on his face. He slides a note across the bed where I've been sitting cross-legged. It reads, "Are you okay? Do you need me to call your dad?"

I take the pencil from behind by ear and scribble. "I'm fine. I'll let you know."

"Oh, it's possible all right," Officer Brannon continues. "We found a receipt which directly ties you to an alcohol bottle in Ms. Blake's possession on the night she died."

"You have to be mistaken. I didn't buy Melanie any alcohol. Ever."

"The receipt says otherwise. It ties directly back to your bank account. We've confirmed it with bank records."

A sick feeling hits my stomach as I realize what happened.

"My car was broken into and my purse was stolen right after I moved into the dorms."

"With all due respect, sounds like a convenient excuse to me."

"Trust me, there was nothing convenient about it. I was hundreds of miles away from home and had only been at school for a few days. Trying to prove who you are is a pain in the butt when you're at home, but when you're away at school, it's even tougher."

"I don't suppose you have any proof of this?"

I can't help myself — I laugh out loud. "Maybe we didn't talk about this before. But my dad is a lawyer and my mom is a social worker. If there's one thing I was trained to do, it's document. I reported the break-in to campus police, the local police, my insurance company and my employer because when I tour with him, I have a bodyguard."

"Don't you think that was a little overkill for a few missing CDs and a missing purse?"

The hairs on the back of my neck stand up. "Wait a second! I didn't tell you about the CDs. So, you knew all about my police report when you tried to make me feel bad. So, you already knew I took pictures of the break-in and provided them to the campus police and the police department, my insurance company and the bank. I also canceled all of my credit cards, bank cards and got new school identification and a new driver's license. There wasn't anything else I could do. I was a victim of crime too — not like Melanie, but still something bad happened to me. Newsflash: I'm not the bad guy here."

"I never said you were Ms. Whitaker," Officer Brannon replies.

"Perhaps not in so many words, but you implied it with your questioning. I've turned that night over in my head so many times. I don't know what I could've done differently. Maybe if I would have stuck closer to Melanie's side and watched her like a hawk, I could have intervened, but I don't know. Maybe I should have tried harder to talk her out of going to the party. I knew there would be alcohol there. I'm not stupid — I'm just young. I tried to get her to drink something else like pop or water, but she wouldn't listen. It was so important for her to be popular, she couldn't see anything else. Still, I wish I could have seen what was coming and stopped it from happening."

"I appreciate your candor Ms. Whitaker. I'll have to independently verify aspects of your account of course. I will be sending you a few forms to the email address you provided. If you still have those pictures on your computer, please send them to me. It will aid in the investigation and help rule you out as a suspect. I can't guarantee you won't have to come back to be re-interviewed in person but documentation will help."

"I'd really like to know where you found my bank receipt. It could tell me who broke into my car. I know it might not mean a lot to some people. One of those CDs which was taken was my very first hit. It was the first one off the presses so to speak. It doesn't have a lot of monetary value, but it has tons of sentimental value."

Officer Brannon's voice gentles. "I'm sorry. I can relate. After I graduated from high school my place was broken into and someone stole the baseball I won the state championship with. I was royally ticked off. I worked my butt off to earn that thing. I will always have the memories, but I was honored when the coach gave me the ball."

"Yeah, the break-in was a rude introduction to college life. But I guess it was merely prep for what was coming."

"I'm sorry your experience down here has been so negative. I hope you'll come back and give us another shot."

"I don't know if I can. It seems like I might be needed here. But, I haven't taken the idea completely off the table."

"I'll be in touch Ms. Whitaker, you have a nice rest of your day. Thank you for taking the time to speak to me."

"It's not a problem. Really. If I could do more, I would. Melanie should not have had to die to be popular. No one should."

"I couldn't agree more Mindy," Officer Brannon says as he hangs up the phone.

My hands are shaking as I click the end button on my phone. Elijah puts his computer down on the desk and rushes over to my side. He slides onto the bed next to me and props himself up against the headboard. He pulls me up beside him and puts his arm around me. "Jigger, jig, jig, jigger, jig, jig are you okay?" he asks with a panicked expression. "What happened? From the part I could hear, the whole conversation sounded insane, jigger, jig, jig."

"It was more than a little crazy. It seems being the victim of a crime put me in the crosshairs of the investigation."

"What do you mean?"

"My bank card was stolen and I guess whoever took it used it to buy alcohol. Alcohol which contributed to Melanie's death. I need to find a way to prove I wasn't the one who bought it."

"Jigger, jig, jig, should be easy enough, right? You have to provide ID when you buy booze."

I sink deeper into his side and he places his other arm around me and hugs me tighter. "They stole my ID too."

"Did you have a fake ID? 'Cause you're not twenty-one."

I abruptly sit up and give Elijah an incredulous look. "Yeah ... because that would really work when my dad is a lawyer and my uncle is a sheriff. Of course, I didn't have bogus ID! I still had my dorky picture when I got my driver's license when I was sixteen. It was a terrible picture. I had a zit roughly the size of a large pizza on my chin."

Elijah chuckles. "Jigger, jig, jig. Sounds like mine. I lost my contact lens, so I had to wear my glasses. I felt like I was back in junior high school."

"I guess that was the upside of having my wallet stolen. I got new ID pictures which were marginally better than the old ones. Oh man! I probably need to call my dad and Uncle Tyler and let them know what's going on."

"I've got a better idea. We've been at this for hours. I'm tired and hungry. The words are swimming on the page. Let's invite them out for lunch and tell them in person."

As Katie expertly maneuvers the large SUV into the last remaining parking spot at the busy truck stop, Elijah turns to me. "You weren't kidding when you said this is your family's favorite hangout. I figured your dad might choose someplace a little fancier."

I shrug. "Nope. He has to do fancy for work. When he has a choice, he wants meatloaf and mashed potatoes."

Elijah places his arm around my waist as we walk into the restaurant. Uncle Tyler and Dad have a table waiting for us. There is a spot for Katie too, but she begs off. "I actually have a lunch date with Logan. We'll be over here if you need us."

Tyler reaches out to shake Elijah's hand, "Nice to see you again."

My dad carefully scrutinizes Elijah. "My daughter has been smiling an awful lot more now that you are in her life. I hope it stays that way."

The muscle in Elijah's cheek twitches for a few moments before he says, "I do too, Sir. Jigger, jig, jig, I've been smiling a lot more recently too. Jigger, jig, jig, Mindy is responsible for that."

"Sounds like a good thing. Remember, I used to be a terrible stutterer. So, don't worry about being nervous around me. I know how it is," my dad assures Elijah.

"Thank you, I appreciate that, jigger, jig, jig," he responds shyly.

Uncle Tyler leans forward as he puts the menu down.

"Not that I object to good food, because you know I could eat twenty-four/seven but I'm dying to find out why you called a mini family meeting — usually you call the Girlfriend Posse for this kind of thing."

"Uncle Tyler, no disrespect to the Girlfriend Posse. I love them to pieces but this is a little bigger than needing a prom dress, or needing a wedding planned in just a few days. I need the professionals here."

My dad puts down his cup of coffee and pins me with a serious glare. "Is everything all right, Princess?"

"I don't know Dad. It should be, but I'm a little scared. That's why I called you guys."

"What happened?" Uncle Tyler asks.

"Well, remember when my car was broken into? Apparently, whoever took my wallet used my card to buy alcohol. Melanie drank the aforementioned alcohol and died."

"Do you think Melanie broke into your car?" My dad asks.

"I hope not! That would've been a terribly scummy thing to do. I drove her to her job."

My uncle is the first one to put the puzzle pieces together. "So, somehow they've tied your bank card to the alcohol she drank and they think you purchased it for her?"

I nod. "But I didn't. You guys know how I feel about this. I would never buy that crap for anyone. You know what it did to my parents. I think it's poison."

Tyler sighs. "Unfortunately, the LEOs down there don't know that — and they can't just take your word for it. The evidence is probably leading them to an entirely different conclusion."

I slump back against the booth. "Does that mean I'm doomed? I swear I never bought anything like that for Melanie or for anyone else."

"Relax Mouse, I'm sure there are surveillance records around. I know for a fact there is a camera above the entrance to your dorm room," my dad insists.

"He's right. You live in a college town. The liquor stores around there card carefully I'm sure."

"But they took my ID too, Uncle Tyler," I lament.

"Out-of-state ID which clearly identifies you as a minor."

"Obviously whoever used your ID wasn't you. The clerk should've been alert to that. And if they didn't use your ID, it's not your problem," my dad argues.

"Do you really think it'll be that easy?" I try not to sound overly hopeful.

"I've been in this business too long to ever assume anything is going to be easy. But, it should be pretty straightforward. I'll give Tristan a call and see if Identity Bank can use some back channels to help secure any surveillance tape which might be involved."

"In the meantime, you should ask Logan to back up all of those pictures you took of the car break-in and send them to the police department. Since he is involved with your protection detail, they might give it a little more weight than if it came from you or me."

Tyler stands up from his seat and walks over and puts his arm around my shoulder. "Chin up, Mouse. I know it seems overwhelming right now. Believe it or not, us law enforcement types don't try to jump to the wrong conclusions. It's simply a matter of sorting through the information we've got until we come to the right one.

"Jigger, jig, jig what if they don't come to the right conclusion?" Elijah asks quietly.

"That's where people like me come in. One of the advantages to working on the prosecution side of things is I get to see the very best defense lawyers in action. If it comes to that, I'll call in the best help I can find."

My eyes tear up. "Daddy, please tell me you don't think it will come to that."

"I practice law in Oregon. I'm not terribly familiar

with the laws in California. But generally, the prosecutors would have to make a huge leap to hold you responsible for Melanie's choice to drink — especially since you were not holding a party or serving her drinks at an establishment like a bar."

"Dad! I didn't encourage her to drink at all. In fact, I tried to stop her. I mean yeah, I went to the party with her but I didn't give her any alcohol and I tried to tell her she needed to slow down," I reply.

"When they took you in for questioning, they tested your BAC, correct?" Tyler asks.

I nod. "They didn't quite believe the result when it was 0.0, so they used another machine and tested me again."

"Perfect! That works in your favor. It reinforces your account of what happened and shows you were telling the truth," my dad says with a smile.

I shoot my dad a blank look. "Why would I lie? Melanie is dead. I want to find out what happened to her."

"I wish all of my witnesses were as forthcoming as you," my uncle says. "Seriously Mindy, try not to worry. You have the truth on your side."

I sigh before I take a drink of my milkshake.

"Hopefully, it will be enough. I've seen some ugly things in my life. I know enough to know the good guys don't always win."

CHAPTER FOURTEEN

ELIJAH

OVER THE TOP OF his newspaper, my dad shoots me a frustrated glance. "Why are you still here? I thought you hired me a babysitter." He gestures over toward Josiah with his head. "Shouldn't you be writing?"

"Jigger, jig, jig, I guess I could be. My editor is reviewing a bunch of rewrites, so I'm in an awkward spot in my project right now. I'm not sure whether I want to start a new one quite yet. Besides, I moved up here to be with you. Don't you like having me around, jigger, jig, jig?"

"To be honest, I'm a little tired of you hovering over me. You're worse than your mom. I'm sick of this whole thing. Can't go to work. Can't do anything except go to physical therapy. Can't even remodel the house or work on the yard," my dad says, as he runs out of breath.

"I'm sorry Dad, I wish I could help you heal faster, but that's not jigger, jig, jig under my control."

"Nothing is under control these days."

The door from the kitchen swings open abruptly and

my mom rushes into the room. Her eyes are red and her hands are trembling as she shoves a letter in front of me. "Please tell me I'm wrong and this doesn't say what I think it says."

I quickly scan the letter and then, when the words sink in, I start over and read it again to make sure I understood it correctly.

I sigh and reach over and grab a tissue off my dad's bedside table. As I hand it to my mom, I confirm, "I'm sorry Mom, jigger, jig, jig, I don't think you misunderstood. This doesn't look good. Do you mind if I call a friend who is a lawyer?"

My dad scowls at me. "Does anyone want to tell me what the heck is going on?"

I hold the letter up to show Dad. "This is a letter from our insurance company. Jigger, jig, jig, it seems that the insurance company who covers the guy who hit you is saying your injuries are not his fault and they are withholding payment until a comprehensive forensic investigation can be done by their experts, jigger, jig, jig."

My mom straightens to her full height. "The jerk's car ran over Seth as sure as I live and breathe. I saw the tire marks on the clothes they cut off of him in the ER. That insurance company is trying to cheat and lie. What a bunch of crooks!"

My dad slumps back in his hospital bed. "No, Roxanne. This is what Mariam was trying to tell you the other day." My dad coughs as he tries to catch his breath. His speech is better now, but it still wears him out. "Something doesn't add up. I wish I could remember what happened that day."

"Mindy says —" I try to interject.

My mom holds up her hand. "I know she means well, but her ideas could be as pretend as the stories in your books. I don't think we should rely on anything she says."

Josiah leans forward on the couch as he addresses my mom. "With all due respect ma'am, I'm not sure that's true. Both the FBI and the military have programs which utilize people with telepathic abilities to more efficiently find missing soldiers or solve cases. I don't think we know everything there is to know about the human brain. I don't know Ms. Whitaker very well, but everyone around her seems to respect her abilities. If what she says is consistent with all the other information about what happened to your husband, I'm not sure you can afford to discount it."

"What if I don't want it to be true?" my mom whispers, sounding defeated.

"Well, that's a whole different issue altogether. We all have things in our past we wish weren't true. Even so, wishing them away doesn't change reality."

My mom swallows hard. "Call your friend. Obviously, we will need all the help we can get."

———⬤———

My mom is fascinating. Once she decided to bring in outside help, she pulled out all the stops. She not only invited Mindy's dad — although at this point I don't think she's made the connection about who I've consulted — but his wife as well. My dad suggested that Ms. Featherstone and Josiah be invited to our meeting too.

I figured for convenience we'd just have the meeting at my parents' house, but my parents wouldn't hear of it. They wanted to entertain the lawyer at one of the town's finest restaurants. So, Josiah and I went shopping to find my dad some dress clothes which would accommodate his cast and the brace on his arm. As we nervously wait for everyone else to arrive at the meeting, my mom looks around the table. "Aren't we missing a chair?"

"Jigger, jig, jig, no, when I made the reservations, I told them to remove the chair. We won't need it."

"I thought you said everyone was coming," my mom replies in a puzzled voice.

"Everyone is coming. Dad isn't the only person in a wheelchair, jigger, jig, jig."

"I don't want this to be a pity party," my dad protests.

I can't hide my eye roll. "Jigger, jig, jig, that's not what this is about. Mom told me to invite Jeff's wife. So, I did."

"You didn't warn us," my mom complains.

I raise an eyebrow. "Does it make a difference, jigger, jig, jig?"

My dad looks half-broken as he awaits her response.

My mom is silent for a few moments before she concedes, "You're right. Seth is the same man inside I've always loved. The rest of it is just going to take some time to get used to — but our love hasn't changed."

"I'm glad to hear that, because here they come." I gesture toward the door.

"You didn't say Mindy was coming," my mom challenges.

"Oh, I'm sorry, I forgot to mention it. I thought it made sense to invite her since the attorney involved is her father."

"Is her father really an attorney or is this something

she made up too?"

"Mother! That was uncalled for," Mariam chastises. "At least hear the man out."

Mindy's mom wheels up to the table. She is carrying a small bouquet of flowers. She hands them to my mom. "Thank you so much for inviting us to dinner. I just love this place. My name is Kiera Whitaker. This is my husband Jeff. It's nice to meet you. I hope you like flowers. My mother-in-law owns a floral shop, and she just got these in. I thought they were perfect for fall."

My mom seems a little stunned. "Your hair is gorgeous," she stammers as she looks at Kiera.

Kiera pats her hair self-consciously. "Oh, thank you. I swear if Jeff didn't braid it for me, I would cut it all off. It drives me crazy."

My mom looks up at Jeff. "I've seen you on television. You're the guy who put that crazy man away who kept driving drunk with his kids in the car. I could swear he almost hit me with his car on the freeway one time. It about took ten years off my life."

Jeff nods toward my mom. "Thank you, I'm glad our team was able to make our community a little safer. I'm happy to report those kids go to school with our son and they are doing much better now."

A tall, dark-haired woman walks up behind Jeff and puts her hand on his shoulder. He turns and acknowledges her, "Claudia, have you met my wife, Kiera?"

"No, I don't think I've had the pleasure. It's nice to meet you."

"This is Claudia Featherstone. She does accident reconstruction. She is one of the best in the business."

Jeff turns toward me. He points next to me where Mindy is observing the interactions quietly. "This young lady is my daughter Mindy Whitaker."

Claudia smiles. "Perhaps I shouldn't say this here, but I am a huge fan. You play the acoustic guitar with such grace."

Jeff grins. "Hey, I don't mind. You can say nice things about my daughter any day of the week."

"If you don't mind me asking Mr. Whitaker, how much experience do you have as an attorney?" my mom asks

"Close to twelve years now," he answers.

"As you can see, things have not gone well recently for my dad," my sister explains. "Now, the driver of the car that hit him while he was working says it's not his fault. So, I think we need an attorney." She slides the letter over to Jeff.

He takes a moment to read it. "It would seem they've come across evidence which makes them question whether their client is culpable in the accident."

Ms. Featherstone nods. "That's consistent with our preliminary investigation. From everything we've gathered, it looks as if something happened to Seth before he was hit by the car. Now, I'm not saying he wasn't hit by the vehicle, but our preliminary investigation indicates something catastrophic happened to him before the vehicle was involved."

My mom gasps. "What? What happened to him?" she demands. "He was simply doing his job. How could he have gotten hurt if he wasn't hit by the car yet?"

"I'm sorry Mrs. Fischer, we're still trying to find the answers to those questions. Unfortunately, the people who have those answers are not being very forthcoming. I believe it is in your best interest to hire the most qualified attorney you can afford. We might actually have to go to trial to find the answers in this case," Ms. Featherstone asserts.

My mom turns to Jeff with wide eyes. "Can you take the case? I know you're tough. I've seen you take on husbands who beat their wives and that drug dealer who was selling to schoolchildren, and, of course, the drunk driver."

Jeff looks at my mom with a sad expression. "I wish I could. People who hurt other people are exactly the kind of creeps I want off the street the most. Unfortunately, I can't. I represent the state. I am a prosecutor. You need someone who specializes in personal injury. The best attorney I know in this field is Max Dixon of Dixon, Applegate and Sorensen. I'll have my paralegal send you the contact information. I'll call ahead and tell them I've made the referral."

"I don't know if we can do all this," my mom admits with a shaky voice.

Kiera puts a reassuring hand on my mom's forearm. "Sometimes, you don't know how strong you are until you have to go through something. I know my dad didn't know a thing about the system until he had to navigate through it with me. Then he became my biggest champion."

"I'm so worried we're going to do something wrong and make things worse," Mom replies.

"I wouldn't worry too much about that. You got a lot of great people around you. My daughter tells me Aidan O'Brien and Tyler Colton are already in your corner. I've heard my husband talk about how phenomenal Claudia Featherstone is at her job. If Aidan and Logan hired this gentleman over here to be on their team, you are in fabulous hands. It might take a while to get answers, but they will come," Kiera insists with a smile.

My dad looks directly at Kiera. "I don't mean to be rude, but how much faith do you have in your daughter's predictions?"

Kiera's eyes widen. "Oh my … they're a little disconcerting, aren't they? It's hard to believe in something you can't see or experience yourself. When Mindy first came into our lives, I didn't quite know what to make of them. But, experience has taught me that she has never, ever been wrong. You definitely need to pay attention to whatever she's told you."

"I was afraid you were going to say something along those lines," my dad says with a grimace. He glances over at Mindy. "I'm sorry. I didn't mean for that to sound so rude."

"It's not a problem, Mr. Fischer, I'm used to people having that kind of reaction to the things I say. I don't take it personally. I know I give people the creeps," Mindy replies with a sad smile.

I squeeze her hand under the table. "Jigger, jig, jig, you don't give me the creeps. I like you."

CHAPTER FIFTEEN

MINDY

"So sorry I'm late, we had to get gas in the SUV," I greet Claudia Featherstone breathlessly as I slide into the chair at Aunt Heather's bakery. I nod toward Elijah. "Is it all right if he is here?"

"That depends on you," Claudia answers with a furrowed brow. "Will you be able to be honest in front of him or will you want to spare his feelings?"

"You've worked with my Aunt Tara before, right?"

"I have." Claudia confirms.

"Then you know we operate under some guidelines. The situation with Seth falls within those. I'd like to say what I'm going to tell you won't be influenced by Elijah's presence, but I can't promise you that with one hundred percent certainty. Elijah means a lot to me and I would probably instinctively try to protect him from pain even if I don't mean to censor my words."

"Jigger, jig, jig, I told you before, I'm tough. I can handle it, jigger, jig, jig," Elijah insists.

I reach out and lace my fingers through his. "You

might be able to cope with me telling you what I see, but I might not be able to process your emotions after you hear my vision. Remember, I not only see snippets of scenes playing out in front of me, I can also see people's emotional reaction to the things I say."

"What do you mean jigger, jig, jig? Do you mean you might pass out again?"

"Elijah, I honestly don't know. The closer I am to the person my visions pertain to, the harder it is for me to control my visions and my reactions to them."

"Jigger, jig, jig, are you saying I'm bad for you?" Elijah asks with a horrified look.

"Elijah, I don't know if Mindy is saying that at all. I think she's feeling like her loyalties are torn here. If she is brutally honest with me, it's going to hurt you and you'll naturally react. Your reaction will cause her pain which will hurt you even more. She's really in a no-win situation. She's not being cautious because she doesn't trust you with the information, she simply doesn't want to hurt you any more."

"So, what you want me to do, jigger, jig, jig?" Elijah asks me. His disappointment is spelled out clearly on his face.

"I know you want me to help your dad and you want to be here for me. I get that. I totally do. But I need to be brutally honest with Claudia. In order for me to do that effectively, you can't be here right now. I'm sorry." I brush my hand against his cheek. "Why don't you go take your mom out for breakfast or something?"

"If I leave, I take away your protection. Jigger, jig, jig, Katie has to drive the SUV," Elijah argues.

I look around the empty shop. "Joy and Tiers isn't

even open yet. Aunt Heather just let us meet here because it was convenient for Claudia. Besides, she has a hotline to Uncle Tyler. If she so much as said boo, he'd have the whole force here in seconds flat," I answer. "I don't think anyone is stalking the bakery on the off chance I might be stopping by."

"Jigger, jig, jig we didn't expect to get shot at when we were playing with puppies either," Elijah replies pointedly, as he gets up to leave.

"Touché," I whisper as I stand up with him. I place my arms around his neck and whisper in his ear. "Please try to understand I'm doing this because I care about you — not because I don't."

"I'm trying to understand, jigger, jig, jig — but like so much about you, I don't really. It seems like we would be stronger as a team. Isn't that the way it usually works?"

"Probably for most normal couples, but I've never been normal and you're kinda my first boyfriend, so I'm not sure how 'normal' works either."

Elijah rests his forehead against mine and sighs. "Jigger, jig, jig, I thought things were going pretty well between us and we had things sorted." He swallows hard. "Now, I just don't know, jigger, jig, jig."

Elijah turns around and leaves without another word as Katie follows him. I've never felt so alone in my life.

After I sink back into my chair and wipe away tears, Claudia clears her throat. "I'm going to go wash my hands. I managed to get ink on them. I swear I'm not safe around ink pens."

"Thank you, do you want more coffee?"

"Sure, I like a little coffee with my caffeine," Claudia jokes.

"You sound like my uncle. Aunt Heather makes an extra strong batch for him. I'll have her pour some for you."

"Sounds good," Claudia replies as she places her purse over her shoulder and walks toward the back of the shop. As soon as she leaves, my aunt pokes her head around the corner and walks toward the table.

"Is everything okay? Elijah didn't look very happy when he left."

I can't contain the sob which escapes. Aunt Heather gasps, runs over, and pulls me up into an embrace. "Whatever it is, it'll all work out in the end," she whispers as she brushes my hair out of my face.

"I don't think so Aunt Heather. I've always known my gift would be too much for a relationship to handle. I think this might be the beginning of the end. I don't even know how to fully explain to Elijah what I mean. If he's not in my head, he can't possibly grasp what it means to be me. I don't have the words to tell him why he can't help me through this."

"Is this your first spat with Elijah?" Aunt Heather hands me a napkin to dry my eyes.

I shrug. "I'm helping him edit his work. Sometimes we have creative differences, but this is the first time we've argued over anything major. Sometimes he tends to be overprotective — and you know me. I'm bossy to the 'nth degree."

Aunt Heather holds up her hand for me to high-five. "Here's to bossy women. May we live long and rule the world. But, our toughness can be hard on the guys around us. It takes a little more negotiation and compromise to be in a relationship with women like us. It's hard because your relationship is just brand-new."

"I know. What if Elijah decides there's not enough between us worth saving?"

"I wouldn't panic just yet. You guys just haven't figured out how to best communicate. There'll be some rough spots. That's true of every couple. You've watched parents go through it and most recently you watched Tara and Aidan go through it when they were dealing with the loss of Adriana."

"Our relationship might not be there yet. Elijah hasn't told me he loves me or anything."

"I saw your young man's face when he was leaving. That wasn't the face of someone who didn't care about you. Just because you guys haven't said any formal words between you, doesn't mean the feelings aren't there."

"I know what I feel, but I'm not sure if Elijah is on the same page. In fact, I'm not even sure it would be a good idea for Elijah to feel the same way about me as I do about him. I'm not an easy person to love."

Aunt Heather puts her arm around me. "You and I are just going to have to agree to disagree. I think you are one of the easiest people to love that I've ever met. Something tells me Elijah feels much the same way. Do me a favor — don't talk yourself out of love before you guys have a chance to actually fall in love."

———————•●•———————

Claudia Featherstone studies me carefully as we finish eating the strawberry filled crepes my Aunt Heather made after my meltdown. They've always been one of my favorite foods. Most kids are spoiled by pancakes on a

Sunday morning, but Aunt Heather always likes to kick it up a notch.

"Are you ready to get to work or would it be better to reschedule?" she asks quietly.

I take a drink of my chai tea then swallow hard. "No, I need to do this. Seth needs my help. I'll have to sort out the stuff with Elijah later."

"Your first love will always be the most enduring and complicated love story you'll ever have in your whole life."

"It sounds like there's a story there," I comment.

Claudia looks wistful. "There is, but it was a lifetime ago and it's ancient history."

"Someday, you and I should compare notes over a slab of Aunt Heather's decadent triple chocolate cake. It's her fix to everyone's heartache. Or conversely, it makes a great celebration cake depending on your mood."

Claudia laughs out loud. "Yeah, I could see how it could be versatile like that." She takes a sip of coffee. "I suppose we should get to the tough stuff. Do you mind if I take you back to the morning of Mr. Fischer's accident?"

I shake my head. "I don't mind — but I have to wonder what they think of all this. If Roxanne and I talk about anything other than Elijah's writing, she looks at me as if I'm some sort of bug crawling across her clean kitchen floor. The look she gives me reminds me of the one my grandma used to give me right before she would give me a long sermon about how evil I was and how she needed to do something terrible to me to cast out my evil spirits."

"I'm sorry you feel that way. It's true, Roxanne is

openly skeptical about your abilities. It's possible she was raised in an environment where she was taught people like you represented evil. It wouldn't be the first time I've encountered people who believe things like that about those who are different from them."

I roll my eyes. "Trust me, I have heard just about every excuse for hate there is."

Claudia nods tightly. "Me too. Still, Seth seems open to the possibility, even if he is skeptical. Mariam is simply afraid her little brother will get hurt. I don't see her resistance is anything more than a big sister being protective over a little brother bringing a new girl around. She seemed all about getting any clues however we can. She simply wants to figure out what happened to her dad."

"What does Seth say about the morning of his accident?"

"Regrettably, he has no memory of that morning or of several days before the accident. His head trauma was pretty severe."

"Does he understand what you're asking me to do and the complications it might bring to the investigation?"

"I believe he knows. Elijah did a good job of explaining to him that you don't control what you see and that you don't always see the full picture. We explained that the knowledge you bring us is only a small piece of the puzzle and that the rest of the investigation will help fill in the rest of the picture."

"And he's still on board?" I press.

Claudia nods. "He is.

I grimace. "This case is scary for me. I always feel a

sense of responsibility to try to interpret what I see, but in this case, it feels monumentally important. I haven't felt this conflicted about my gift since I knew my aunt was going to miscarry her daughter and there wasn't anything I could do about it. I could feel Adriana's heart stop. It was like a part of me died too."

"I'm so sorry, Mindy. If this is going to harm you, I don't want you to do this. I solve cases every day without using extrasensory powers. I can work Mr. Fischer's case without imposing on you."

"No, that's not what I mean … exactly. I can help you. I *need* to help you. There's a reason I got my gift back when I was around Elijah. I believe it was so I could help solve the mystery around Seth's accident. To spit in the face of my gift when I just got it back would be tempting fate in a way I'm totally not comfortable with. I know it's a big risk, but there's a reason God gave me this gift, I need to use it responsibly. It's just that sometimes it's hard," I finish, letting my speech trail off.

"I can't even imagine. I thought my job was hard. I take measurements and hard cold facts and turn them into 3D renderings and video reproductions of what we think happened in homicides and accidents. Sometimes they are terrifyingly realistic — too realistic for me to sleep well at night. Even so, it's what I have to do to make sure justice is done and other families can sleep well knowing the truth was told to the best of my ability."

"So, you know what it's like to tell the truth even when it's painful and you know you're going to hurt people in the process?"

"More than I care to admit," Claudia says. "Families always want the evidence to favor the facts as they see them. The hardest situation is when I'm hired by one side of the case but when I start to investigate and prepare materials for a trial, my work points in the other direction."

"What happens then?"

"Usually, there are a lot of very awkward conversations. In most jurisdictions, I am required to turn my findings over to the other side as part of discovery."

"I'm afraid that if what I see really happened, there will be a lot more than just a few awkward conversations. Seth and Roxanne's whole life might just blow apart in front of them. You know, it's funny. When I was a little girl, I used to be so excited to share what I could see. My papa used to call me the town crier. Now, I'd really rather not because it'll destroy everything Seth thought was true about his life."

Claudia reaches out and grabs my hands. "I know this is hard — but so is not knowing. As it stands right now one man faces the possibility of being falsely accused of causing all of Seth's injuries and someone else may be getting away with attempted murder. In my book, that's just not right."

"You're right, it's not." I squeeze her hands one more time before I let go and take a large gulp of my chai tea. I take a deep breath and try to shake off all of my nerves.

"The day of the accident, Seth is exceptionally nervous. It's not nervous in a way you'd expect — like my nerves before I go on stage. This is more like he's got a bad feeling in the pit of his stomach. I see him staying up extremely late the night before going over paperwork and looking at specifications. Something isn't right with the tensile strength of the building materials they used or the design or something. It's pretty fuzzy. It seems like he tried to bring it up with several people during earlier inspections and his concerns were tossed aside and overruled. He's agonizing over something."

I'm quiet for a moment as more images fill my brain. As another piece of the puzzle starts to make sense, I breathe a sigh of relief. "Okay, that makes a little more sense," I mumble to myself. Louder I say, "Ferreting out the discrepancies became a bit of an obsession for Seth — but Roxanne didn't want him to do this. She's been encouraging him to play it safe until his retirement because she's heard horror stories of people losing their whole retirement at the very last minute because they weren't covered by whistleblower laws."

"Wow, so what happened that morning?" Claudia asks, clearly riveted by the story.

"Even though Seth was up late doing research, he couldn't sleep before the big inspection on the bridge. Seth got up early and was puttering around the kitchen when he noticed Roxanne's day planner out on the kitchen table. That's when he realized the next weekend was their anniversary. Impulsively, he decided he would do something special for her every day the week before their anniversary like he used to when they first started dating. So, he asked her to go out to dinner at a fancy place. She laughed him off and said she didn't have time to get herself ready in the middle of the week."

"Poor Roxanne, she probably feels terrible now," Claudia comments.

"She does. I wonder if that's why she didn't want to believe in my abilities? Maybe she didn't want me to know that they were arguing over his job?"

"Could be I suppose. Although it seems relatively

benign."

"Yeah, but when things go wrong, people blame themselves for the silliest things."

"That's true. I had a wife blame herself for changing the radio station in her husband's car. She thought maybe changing from country to pop made it so he couldn't concentrate on the road and caused the accident."

"We have a few passionate fans who might argue music is just that powerful."

"So, what happened when Seth got to work?"

"I don't see much about this. It seems like he went into a meeting where he tried to show them the information he found about the tensile strength of the bridge. They basically told him if he valued his job he would do what was expected of him."

"Who is they?" Claudia presses.

"This is where my gift is really frustrating. I can't see any faces. I can only feel emotions in this one. Betrayal, anger, disappointment. Resolve. Defiance."

"What's the next scene you see?"

"Seth is going around the construction project on the bridge showing people where the deficits are. At first, people think he's like some sort of prank because this inspection is merely a formality. He's just supposed to sign off on the paperwork so they can finish construction on the bridge. It quickly becomes evident he's not playing and the mood changes. People are starting to get ticked off. The chatter is that Seth Fischer is pulling one last power play before he retires."

I stop and take a sip of tea. This next part is difficult.

"Somebody yells an anti-Semitic slur at Seth and he

spins around to respond as he drops his clipboard — you know one of those metal ones you can keep lots of papers in?"

Claudia nods.

"The noise of it hitting the asphalt seems to jar Seth out of his angry haze and he bends down to pick it up. At that point someone hits him over the head with something very heavy and hard. I sense a moment of recognition and resignation from Seth. I feel like he knows who hit him and was crushed by the realization. But, as soon as Seth lost consciousness, I drop out of the scene. Sometimes, I can identify strongly enough with another person on the scene to continue to see what happened, but in this case, I can't. I'm sorry."

"What you've told me is exceptionally helpful. If you think of anything else, please let me know."

"There is one more thing," I add tentatively. "There are a bunch of well-dressed people who meet in a conference room somewhere to talk about what happens if Seth ever gets well enough to come back to work and tell everything he knows about the project. There are ongoing discussions about how to stop him from ever coming back. This is the kind of stuff that keeps me awake at night."

"Have you ever worked with a sketch artist before?"

"Once, a long time ago. But I was just a little kid. I thought she was kind of magical. Unfortunately, the sketch wasn't magical enough to catch the bad guy, but I still thought she was amazing."

"Maybe we'll have better luck this time. I think it's worth a shot."

"I'm willing to do whatever it takes to keep Seth and

Roxanne safe. I could see things a lot more clearly this time. I wonder if it would be better for everyone if I stepped back from Elijah for a while until whoever did this to his dad is caught. Maybe I would have more psychic clarity if Elijah and I weren't together."

"Didn't you tell me you lost your gift for a while and it only came back because Elijah was in your life?"

"That's true too. I don't know what the right answer is. I just want everyone I love to be safe and happy."

Chapter Sixteen

Elijah

I let myself into the back door of my parents' house and startle my mom as she's doing dishes. When she turns around, I notice there are tears streaming down her face. "What's wrong? Jigger, jig, jig, where's Dad?" I glance around the house with alarm .

"That stubborn old fool is at therapy with Josiah."

I chuckle. "Uh-oh, what did Dad do now?"

My mom stuffs her hands in the pockets of her colorful apron after she tucks a dishtowel in the tie at her waist. "Well, I was planning to go with him. Before he got out of the rehab unit, the nurses told me it was really important for him to have family around to cheer him on during his rehabilitation process. But he told me today that it was actually harder for him when I'm there because he doesn't push himself as hard because he doesn't want to hurt me."

I straddle a kitchen chair like I used to when I was a teenager. "Jigger, jig, jig, hurt you?" I repeat with a raised eyebrow.

My mom throws her hands up in the air in frustration. She dabs at her eyes with the dish towel. "That's what he said. He can tell I'm upset when he's in pain so he holds back when I'm around. Can you believe he told me to stay home?"

The irony strikes me as funny. I came home planning to have this same conversation with my mom. Agitated, I run my hand through my hair. "Actually, you know what, after today I can believe it, jigger, jig, jig. You want to go grab a cup of coffee or a bite to eat?"

My mom looks up at the clock on the wall. "Weren't you going somewhere this morning? I thought you had a meeting with Mindy?"

"Jigger, jig, jig, I did. But I was summarily ejected from my meeting — sort of like you were dismissed from yours, jigger, jig, jig."

"What do you mean?" my mom demands.

I spring up and stride toward the kitchen counter. "It's a long story, jigger, jig, jig." I grab a cup of coffee from the drip coffee maker which is probably older than I am. "Are you sure you don't want to grab something?"

"Oh, heavens no. I've already eaten. I can scramble you a couple of eggs and make you some toast."

"Mom, I can cook that stuff, jigger, jig, jig," I offer as I shrug off my coat and hang it on the hook by the back door.

"Oh no you don't. I've seen your definition of a clean kitchen. Let's just say it's not the same as mine. I just got this place put back in order."

"We can go up to the truck stop. Mindy and I have eaten there. Jigger, jig, jig, the food is great."

"No need to pay someone else to cook. I need you to feed the outside cats. By the time you're done, your breakfast will be on the table."

Reluctantly, I put my coat back on and go feed the cats. I make a mental note to go buy more food as I empty out the rest of the bag. A group of cats comes running when the cat food hits the bowl. To my surprise, Tommy is still hanging around. The scruffy black cat has been a fixture around my parents' house since I started elementary school. I'm amazed when he lets me pet him like old times.

After I finish feeding the cats, I walk into the kitchen with a grin on my face.

"What turned your frown upside down?"

"Tommy still thinks he's my pet."

"Son, I think you're the only creature around here who refuses to acknowledge Tommy is in fact your cat. He always has been since the moment you rescued him from under our porch. You simply refuse to accept that it's possible to be both a dog and a cat person."

"Jigger, jig, jig, okay fine. He is my cat — but I am surprised he's still around."

"He's far too stubborn to die."

I sigh. "It seems like stubborn is the theme of the day today, jigger, jig, jig."

My mom's lip turns up with distaste. "You were going to tell me why you are here and not on a date with your beloved."

"I'm not sure I'm ready to call Mindy my beloved quite yet."

"Baloney. I see how you watch her when she leaves

the room. It is like your father watches me even to this day."

I shrug. "I won't argue with you. I feel things for Mindy I've never felt for anyone else."

"I wish you would've felt those things for Sadie. She is so good to you."

"Mom, that's not fair. Mindy is good to me too."

My mom raises an eyebrow. "Really? If things are so great between you then why are you sitting at my breakfast table eating my food instead of having a romantic meal with your girlfriend?"

My hand flies up and hits the side of my face before I get it under control. "Jigger, jig, jig, I'm not sure what exactly happened. One minute we were preparing to meet with the accident reconstruction expert and the next minute Mindy was telling me she didn't feel comfortable being honest in front of me because she was afraid of causing me pain."

My mom chokes on her coffee. "You're kidding me. Do they script this stuff?"

"As far as I know, jigger, jig, jig, Mindy and Dad haven't had a chance to talk recently which makes all of this even more spooky."

My mom clicks her tongue at me. "All that stuff she does makes me very uncomfortable. There's something dark about it, you know what I mean? If she has all that power she claims to have, where does it come from?" My mom shudders and then fans herself as if she's trying to wave away bad energy.

Even though I've sometimes wondered the same thing, hearing my mom say the words out loud makes me want to jump to Mindy's defense.

"I don't know, okay!" I say, raising my voice. "Jigger, jig, jig, I have no idea where her gift comes from. I don't think she knows either. All I know is that Mindy has a set of extremely complicated rules about when she uses her gift to help people, jigger, jig, jig."

"What kind of rules?" my mom asks.

"You know, like she doesn't play the lottery, bet on sports games or predict the gender of people's babies. She only tells people the outcome of things if it's a matter of life and death. Jigger, jig, jig, she doesn't want to change fate. She's a real stickler about that."

"How do you know she doesn't simply manufacture all her predictions like you make up all your stories?"

"I guess I have no way to prove it. I've just seen her in action. I was there when she told Chester to duck and seconds later there was a bullet through his grandmother's china cupboard."

"Maybe it was an elaborate set up?" my mom challenges.

"How in the world would she have pulled that off, jigger, jig, jig?" I reply. "She'd never met Chester or Betty Sue before. Do you think she had a sniper on standby in case we played with puppies on my very random date choice?"

My mom is quiet for a few moments. "You're right. That sounds ridiculous. But, so does the fact that she can tell the future or see things she was never present for. Doesn't that all sound crazy to you? I mean this lady Mariam hired — she's supposed to be some nationally renowned expert — but she's still relying on the word of some girl who's barely older than a child to tell her something she sees in her imagination? It doesn't even make any sense!" my mom says in a huff.

"I know, Mom. I'm trying to understand it myself. I think it's one of those things that if you don't experience it, you can never fully understand it."

"Well, if I were in your shoes I would be very bothered by the fact that she wants to do it in secret without you present. It just seems like she's trying to pull the wool over your eyes. You know, I watch those crime shows on TV. That's how con artists work."

I want to stand up and argue with my mom from the top of my lungs. But there's a tiny voice in the back of my head that wonders if maybe, just maybe, she might be right. I don't understand all there is to know about Mindy. If she keeps pushing me away, maybe I never will.

I place the cat food in the grocery cart with more force than necessary because the longer I think about the conversation with my mom the angrier I get at myself. I know I should have unequivocally stood up for Mindy and told my mom she had no idea what she was talking about. Why do I always have to over think things and let doubt creep in? I know Mindy is only trying to help.

Why couldn't I just say that?

I thought the last few years had taught me a little something about standing up for myself and those I care about. I guess not. A profound sense of shame and defeat washes over me. It's a good thing Sadie isn't around because she would have kicked my butt into next Tuesday if she could've heard my conversation with my mom.

Impulsively I reach up to grab a couple of cat toys

with feathers and catnip and throw them into the cart. Out of the corner of my eye, I see someone try to maneuver around me in the narrow aisle. As I start to move out of the way, I realize it's Jeff Whitaker.

"Elijah? Elijah Fischer, right?" He reaches out to shake my hand.

"Yes, sir, jigger, jig, jig it's good to see you," I answer awkwardly. I look at the items in his cart and see several types of chai tea. "Jigger, jig, jig, Mindy get thirsty?"

Jeff flinches. "She had an exceptionally tough reading this morning. She's exhausted and psychically drained. I thought these might make her feel better."

"Darn it, jigger, jig, jig, I knew I should've never left," I reply as both hands start to tic and fly around my face.

Jeff leads me to the front of the store as we check out in the express lane. "Your car this way?" he asks as we walk out into the parking lot. After we put our groceries away, he points to a bagel shop next to the grocery store. "It's not Joy and Tiers, but it's a decent little place. Do you have a moment?"

I shrug. It's not as if I need to be with my parents every second of every day. When Josiah got back with my dad, my mom practically shoved me out the door. I have a feeling they don't want me back anytime soon. "Sure."

When we enter the bagel shop, he looks over at me and asks, "Regular or decaf?"

"Jigger, jig, jig, I'm staring down rewrites. Better make it fully caffeinated."

"Want a bagel?" he asks pointing to a tray of bagels. "Mindy says the double chocolate chip ones are the bomb."

"No thanks, I'm good."

"So, you said you were with Mindy this morning — why did she come home alone?"

"Jigger, jig, jig, it definitely wasn't my plan. Mindy told me she wouldn't be able to do-whatever it is she does as well if I was around. She sent me away, jigger, jig, jig."

Jeff studies me intently. "I see. You just let her do that?"

My eyes widen. "With all due respect, I don't think it was my place to stop Mindy from her mission. It seems like it's an almost sacred thing — jigger, jig, jig, like fate. I'm not sure anyone can change Mindy's mind once she's set on something."

Jeff lets out a low chuckle. "I see you have my daughter pegged quite perfectly. Her mother is very much the same way."

I lean forward in my chair as I regard him somberly. "I was there the last time. Jigger, jig, jig, things didn't go well. I was afraid it would happen again. But she didn't want or need my help. Turns out, I guess I was right, jigger, jig, jig. What am I supposed to do with that? She needed me — but she still wouldn't allow me to be there."

"You have to understand — most women are overprotective of the men in their lives. They don't want to see us harmed. What makes a relationship with Mindy even harder is she is hypersensitive to our pain."

"Jigger, jig, jig, you mean she does this to you too?"

"Oh, absolutely! Sending her away to college was one of the hardest decisions her mom and I have ever made. We were afraid she would revert back to the way she was when we first adopted her. It took her months, if not years, to trust us enough to reveal her gift. Even then, if she perceived someone was having a negative reaction to her precognitive skills, she would hide them to avoid hurting people."

"So, is Mindy right, jigger, jig, jig? Should I step aside to make things easier for her?"

Jeff places his large hand on my shoulder. "Son, that's one of the toughest calls you'll ever have to make. Sometimes Mindy will need extra space — there's no doubt. Her gift simply demands it. It's those other times, the times between when her gift has demanded everything she's got to give and more. Those are the times you'll have to soothe her and refill her reserve; the times you love her with your whole heart and soul and fill her up with happiness and light."

"Jigger, jig, jig, you make it sound so easy," I openly scoff as I cross my arms in front of me.

Jeff shakes his head. "It isn't at all. No, that's not exactly right." A bemused smile crosses his face. "Falling in love with Mindy is probably the easiest thing you will ever do. Understanding what she's been through and what she goes through every single day of her life is the most difficult challenge you will ever face. But I can tell you it's so worth it."

The muscles in my face twitch uncontrollably and I have to sit on my hand to control the tic. "Jigger, jig, jig, I have to be honest with you. I'm not exactly sure where things stand between Mindy and me. Everything is up in the air in my life right now. Jigger, jig, jig we know my dad's life has been threatened. There is evidence which suggests someone tried to kill him. We don't know if jigger, jig, jig that means the rest of us are in danger too. Mindy was standing right beside me when a bullet went whizzing by my head jigger, jig, jig. I don't know what it all means for us. I don't want to put her in danger, jigger, jig, jig."

"I don't think you get to blame yourself for all that. Besides, you know Mindy is in her own tough spot. For all you know, some of that drama could be related to the death of her roommate," Mr. Whitaker insists.

My brows furrow as I concede, "I suppose you're right. That's what she was trying to figure out this morning, but she didn't want to tell me what she was planning to tell Ms. Featherstone."

Jeff flinches. "I can imagine not. What Claudia does can get downright gruesome. I understand why Mindy wouldn't want you to see the raw, unfiltered visions of what she sees."

The muscles in my face twitch uncontrollably as I confess, "This is all so confusing. Jigger, jig, jig, I don't want to make the wrong decision. Lives are at stake."

Jeff takes a sip of his coffee. "I want you to stop thinking so hard and tell me one thing. How does being around my daughter make you feel?"

Slowly, a smile creeps across my lips. "Happy. Settled. Contented. Whole."

Jeff grins at me. "There you have it. Call me old-fashioned, but I'd call that love."

"Jigger, jig, jig, with the way we left things, I'm not sure we're there yet," I protest.

Jeff guides me out of my seat and over to the bakery counter. "There's only one way to find out — although, I strongly suggest bringing a bribe. She really likes the chocolate bagels. If you want bonus points, I would bring some black cherry cream cheese," he suggests with a wink.

"Jigger, jig, jig, it's better than any plan I've been able to come up with all day," I admit. "I've got to let my sister and my parents know my plans have changed and then I'll be over. Jigger, jig, jig, thanks for the coffee and everything else. I appreciate it."

"Hey, it's no problem. I once fell head over heels in love with a beautiful woman. In those days, it seemed that the only thing life threw at us were obstacles, but we learned to pull together and face them as a team. Hopefully you and Mindy will learn a play or two from us."

"I hope so too, sir. Mindy says your love story started a legacy."

CHAPTER SEVENTEEN

MINDY

MY HEAD IS POUNDING. I don't know if it's because Seth means something to me personally, or because of the violent nature of the threats against him, but my session with Claudia left me feeling like I'd volunteered to be the bad guy in one of Aunt Tara's self-defense classes. I feel mentally bruised.

My dad walks through the family room. He tosses me a bottle of something. "For old time's sake, Aunt Heather made a fresh batch of your favorite shower scrub." He walks over and hands me a little thermos. "I made you some of your favorite chai tea too."

I get off the couch and stand on my tiptoes and kiss him on the cheek. "This is perfect. I'll shower later. Thanks."

My dad looks vaguely uncomfortable. "You probably want to do it sooner rather than later. I may have arranged for you to have company."

"Dad! Do I look like I'm ready for company?" I growl as tears sting the corner of my eyes. "I know you don't completely understand me, but you should get it by now. I can't entertain anybody like this."

My dad reaches out and hugs me. "I know Princess. But, this isn't just anyone. It'll be all right. If it isn't, please let me know, okay?"

"I can make no promises that I'll even be nice. I am exhausted to the bone."

"I'm sure everyone will understand." My dad wipes away a tear with his thumb and kisses my forehead.

When I walk around the corner, I pause in the doorway and watch Charlie interact with Elijah. He has drawings spread out all over the kitchen table. "Okay, this one is next. See, he is making a basket in this picture."

"Oh, I see. Very nice, jigger, jig, jig. I like the way you used color to indicate the crowd."

"You talk funny," Charlie comments abruptly.

Elijah shrugs. "Jigger, jig, jig, I know. It's called a verbal tic. I can't help it. I have something called Tourette's syndrome. It's like my brain takes a little detour. The harder I try not to do it, the more it happens, jigger, jig, jig."

"Does it mean you're dumb?"

I cringe. I hope Elijah doesn't take offense at Charlie's intrusive questions. Charlie can be frighteningly blunt. He is openly curious about everything, and at six years old he hasn't learned that some topics can be sensitive.

Elijah laughs out loud. "No, jigger, jig, jig, I'm not

dumb. Although sometimes people seem to think I am. Every once in a while, I make funny faces and my hands will fly up and hit me in the face for no good reason, jigger, jig, jig. Those are also tics. Jigger, jig, jig, since people don't understand why I do those things, some folks automatically assume it's because I must not be very smart."

I clear my throat as I enter the room. "But that's not true. Elijah Fischer is a famous best-selling author. One of his books has even been turned into a movie."

Charlie's eyes widen as he regards Elijah with awe. "A movie? Can I watch? Is it on YouTube? Does that mean people like you even though you're different?"

Elijah's lips form a thin line and I know he is remembering his difficult past. I'm anxious to see how he explains it all to Charlie.

"Jigger, jig, jig, my movie isn't for kids your age, I'm sorry," Elijah replies. "When you get older, we can watch it together and I'll tell you the inside scoop."

"What about the other thing?" Charlie presses. "I bet everybody likes you now 'cause movies make you famous, and famous people have lotsa friends."

"Not everyone likes me, jigger, jig, jig. I used to be upset if people picked on me or didn't like me. Your sister and my best friend, Sadie, taught me the number of people who claim to like me doesn't really matter. Jigger, jig, jig, my true friends like me despite my weirdness."

"Can I tell you a secret?" Charlie asks in a not-so-quiet whisper.

Elijah leans forward with a concerned expression. "Absolutely. Jigger, jig, jig, my lips are sealed."

"I need friends like yours. People think I look funny

because I'm black and I have red hair and freckles."

"Oh … I see," Elijah answers sympathetically. "We'll work on giving them something else to notice. That's what helped me. Jigger, jig, jig, I discovered something I was really good at. In my case, it was writing. What do you like to do?"

Charlie rolls his eyes before he points to the table. "Duh! My teachers say I'm really great at drawing."

"I agree." Elijah picks up a couple of the drawings. Jigger, jig, jig, if I write a story, could you illustrate it for me?

"Illi … what?" Charlie asks, stumbling over the word.

"Illustrate. It means I want you to draw pictures to help my words make sense, jigger, jig, jig."

"Would it be a book for kids or only grown-ups?"

"Jigger, jig, jig, I know another little girl who is having trouble making friends. I was thinking about writing a book about friendship for her. This would definitely be a book for kids. I wondered if maybe you would like to help me by drawing the pictures?"

A skeptical look crosses Charlie's face. "Do you mean like a real book at the library or just something my mom hangs on the refrigerator?"

Elijah grins and winks at me. "I don't know how my agent will feel about this. But with any luck, this would be in libraries and bookstores everywhere. It would be much bigger than your mom's refrigerator."

"Wow! You mean my teacher might even read it to the class?"

"It might take a little while to pull it all together, so maybe in a year or so — but your teacher could eventually read it to a class," Elijah responds with an amused smile.

Charlie reaches out to shake Elijah's hand in a move I've seen my dad do countless times. "Well, I think we've got a deal." Charlie scrambles off his chair and runs out of the kitchen.

"Where are you going?" I yell after my brother.

"Weren't you paying attention?" he answers over his shoulder. "I have important work to do!"

———————•◀——————

Elijah tucks a soft fleece blanket around me. He hands me a fresh chai tea and sits next to me on the porch swing as he slowly rocks it with his foot.

He pulls something out of his backpack. I smile when I see it's from one of my favorite bagel places. "Your dad said this was one of your favorites."

"Just how deep does this conspiracy go?" I probe when I open the box.

"Only as deep as my trip to the store to get cat food. I was worried about you jigger, jig, jig, so I pumped your dad for information about you when I ran into him. Jigger, jig, jig, he told me about the bagels when I asked him if there was any way I could help you feel better."

"Okay, that sounds innocent enough — but with my dad you never know. He is a masterful manipulator."

"I definitely got that sense. Jigger, jig, jig, I'm glad he intervened though. I felt bad about the way I left this morning. I definitely didn't make it easier for you."

I sigh and snuggle deeper into his chest.

"Elijah, that's what I've been trying to tell you. Nothing about us is going to be easy. Ever."

195

"I don't know if it's easy for any couple, jigger, jig, jig," Elijah protests. "Even before my dad's accident, my parents had their ups and downs. Jigger, jig, jig, my sister is always on again/off again with her boyfriends. These days, she seems more off again than on."

I chew on my bottom lip for a bit while I try to organize my thoughts. Finally, I just give up trying to make sense of it all. I sit up straighter and face him. "I don't even know where this falls in my set of rules. I don't think I'm changing anyone's fate by sharing this because it pertains to me."

Elijah sets my chai tea down into the little cup holder built in the arms of the porch swing. He grasps both of my hands between his. "Mindy look, jigger, jig, jig. I want to make this clear. You don't ever have to tell me another prediction again if you don't want to. That's not why I love you."

His words make whatever little speech I had planned vanish from my brain as if it was never there.

"What? What did you say?" I stammer.

"Jigger, jig, jig, I know I'm making a big mess out of this — but I want you to understand. Although I don't understand what you do or how you do it, I see the huge toll it takes on you. The help you have given my family can't be measured. It may very well save my dad's life and bring the people who assaulted him to justice, jigger, jig, jig. Even though all that is true, you need to know that if you never made another prediction or gave us another clue, I would still love you for just being you."

I burst into tears — not the cute little girly kind you see on Instagram, but big, ugly sobs.

"Oh no! I blew it, jigger, jig, jig, didn't I? I shouldn't

have gone there yet. I guess you weren't ready for me to say those words jigger, jig, jig."

I feel Elijah's hand start to move so I change my grip and hang onto his hand to prevent him from hitting the side of his face.

"Elijah! Listen. I was trying to tell you something before. It seems you and me together are something that's never happened to me before. In a way, we might be tempting fate."

"What do you mean?" Elijah asks, as he takes one of the napkins from the bagel sack and wipes away my tears.

"One of my gifts, which has come naturally since I was a small child, is the ability to see which couples belong together. I see them whether I want to or not."

"Jigger, jig, jig, that must get a little annoying. Like you see them in the line at the DMV or when you go shopping at your local convenience store, jigger, jig, jig?"

"Yeah," I confirm. "It gives a whole new level of insight into high school drama in the hallways."

"Can you filter it out?"

"For the most part, I've learned to ignore it."

"Jigger, jig, jig, I promised I wouldn't ask for another prediction from you. I didn't say I wouldn't be curious about what you see for the future of us."

"That's what I've been trying to tell you all night. It's part of the reason your announcement took me off guard. My whole life I've been mentally pairing people off. It's as natural for me as breathing. Yet when it comes to myself, there has never been anyone in the picture. All I've ever been able to see is a big abyss of loneliness."

"What does that mean for us?" Elijah asks with

trepidation.

"I don't know. I never expected to have you in my life and I didn't expect to fall in love with you. In a million years, I never dreamed you'd fall in love with me. Maybe our love is enough to change my fate."

It's as if time stands still for a moment. Elijah swallows hard as he looks at me intently. "Say it again, please."

"Elijah Fischer, I love you."

"Mindy Jo Whitaker, I love you too." Elijah whispers before he kisses me gently. "Tonight, love is enough. We'll worry about fate another day."

Chapter Eighteen

Elijah

"I THOUGHT YOU WERE meeting with a new publishing company?" Mariam yells as the drummer pounds out a solo during the sound check.

"Jigger, jig, jig, I was. But they were more than happy to reschedule when I offered them tickets to tonight's performance."

"Didn't Mindy tell us she was done singing for a while?"

I shrug. "That was the plan, but then Jude and Tasha got strep throat or something. Jigger, jig, jig, Mindy and Joe Summers are covering the gig."

My sister elbows me. "Joe Summers is massively cute. Aren't you afraid Mindy will fall in love with her co-star? It happens in Hollywood all the time."

"Whose side are you on? Jigger, jig, jig, I've met Joe. He's a teacher who specializes in teaching autistic kids. He's totally cool. He would not poach my girlfriend, jigger, jig, jig."

"I was just asking!" Mariam exclaims. "I want to see

how committed you are to Mindy. As you know, I've dated a few total losers who couldn't decide whether they were actually dating me or not."

"Well, that's not me, jigger, jig, jig."

"What are you going to do if she goes back to school?"

"Jigger, jig, jig, Mindy and I haven't really talked about it, but Dad and Mom don't really seem to need me around much. I can work anywhere I've got a computer and a phone."

"So … that's it? You're choosing Mindy over your family? You guys have only been dating a few months."

"What does time have to do with it? I've known her for years. Jigger, jig, jig, Mom married Dad six weeks after they met."

"You don't even know if Mindy's planning to go back to school," my sister challenges.

"So, what? Did you forget I'm a college dropout too, jigger, jig, jig? I'm doing all right for myself. Last I checked, Mindy's single is still at the top of the charts and she's got a huge fan base out there. Jigger, jig, jig, she's a remarkable songwriter, and she's got a ton of credits to her name, and not just on the Silent Beats label."

"Geez! Don't get so defensive," Mariam snaps. "I just want to make sure you guys have realistic plans."

"We're doing the best we can. Everything is up in the air, jigger, jig, jig," I answer impatiently. "Speaking of plans, how are your life plans going? I don't think you have any room to talk, jigger, jig, jig."

"I don't. That's what makes this so unfair. Why do you get to be all in love and happy when my life is a colossal mess with no light at the end of the tunnel? I've done everything I'm supposed to, but it didn't matter."

"Who knows, jigger, jig, jig? The fact that I reconnected with Mindy after all these years was a weird twist of fate. Maybe something equally miraculous is just around the corner for you. You never can tell, jigger, jig, jig. You can't give up hope," I squeeze my sister's hand like I used to when we went to scary movies together as kids. I know she doesn't mean anything by her comments. She's just scared.

The house lights go down and it's dark for a moment before Mindy appears under a soft spotlight in the center of the stage. Suddenly from offstage Aidan's voice erupts over the sound system, "Sometimes nothing goes according to plan. You just have to wing it and let the magic happen. Ladies and gentlemen, Mindy Whitaker —"

After the thunderous round of applause dies down, Mindy starts to play the classic Ben E. King song *Stand By Me* on her acoustic guitar. Joe Summers joins her on the guitar during the second verse and Declan joins in during the chorus. It's hauntingly beautiful with acoustic guitars. They transition immediately to John Lennon's *Imagine*.

Even though the venue is sold out, it is so quiet you could hear a pin drop. I look over at Mariam and tears are rolling down her face.

Mariam catches me watching her. She turns and says, "I was wrong. Your woman has some sort of magic. She may be young, but her soul is old."

I take a moment to kiss Mindy after the last customer leaves the back section of the restaurant. "There aren't enough words in the English language to tell you how awesome you were tonight. I felt like you were singing directly to me."

Mindy smiles up at me over her mug of hot chocolate. Her mug is so huge it could double as one of the mixing bowls my mom uses to make homemade cookies. "You're a silly man. Don't you know? I always sing my love songs straight to you." She takes a sip of hot chocolate and hides her grin.

I am at a complete loss of words so I change the subject. "Jigger, jig, jig, Aidan isn't going to like me very much," I comment as I wipe a dollop of whipped cream off of Mindy's nose.

Mindy slides her shoes off and stretches out on the red vinyl booth in the corner. Fortunately, the truck stop is quiet tonight and the owners put us back in a quiet area so we can have at least an illusion of privacy. We are here often enough these days; they almost treat us like family.

"Why do you say that?" she asks as she stretches out her wrist muscles.

"This is the second time I've taken you away from a backstage party. He probably thinks I'm some weird stalker or kidnapper or something."

"Don't be silly!" she says as she chokes back a giggle. "Uncle Aidan knows you love me. Besides, this time I stayed and signed autographs for all the VIP folks. I even gave Howard an interview for his rag magazine."

"Who's Howard?"

"Oh, technically, he's Tasha's uncle — but we didn't know that until a couple of years ago. He works as a tabloid reporter."

"Aidan lets him hang around you guys?" I ask incredulously. "I'm surprised Logan doesn't give him the boot."

Mindy shrugs. "Mostly, he's a pretty nice guy. He usually runs positive pieces about us and he's a lot more polite than most of them. Sometimes it's helpful to have him around because he can tell us what's going on out there. He's given us more than one scoop when things were about to get nasty."

"So, you guys give him exclusive stories in exchange for inside information? Jigger, jig, jig, isn't that a little slimy?"

Mindy frowns at me. "I don't think you understand. Since you're so quick to assume we're up to no good, let me tell you what happened. Another less-than-reputable tabloid contacted Aidan today because they had gotten word Tasha and Jude would not be performing. They threatened to run a story that Tasha and Jude broke up and that Tasha's cancer was back and Silent Beats refused to cover the cost of her cancer treatment."

"Jigger, jig, jig, what garbage! How can they make up lies like that?"

"I have been around this business a long time and I've never quite figured that out. We got permission from Jude and Tasha to tell Howard the real story. So, Howard took pictures at tonight's concert. He's pairing them with pictures of their positive strep test and a statement from their doctor indicating Tasha only has strep throat and not cancer. It's ridiculous that they even have to answer this sort of thing — but there you have it. That's why I gave an interview to Howard. He's running the story in tomorrow's edition."

"Jigger, jig, jig, geez, I sound like my sister. I'm sorry I jumped to all the wrong conclusions."

"It's all right. I didn't do a very good job of explaining things at first," Mindy answers with a sigh. "What'd I do to upset Mariam this time?"

"I'm not exactly sure. As near as I can tell, she's upset because we're in love and she's not, jigger, jig, jig."

Mindy looks pained. "I can't say I blame her. I've been in her shoes. It's terrible to be the odd one out."

"It is. Jigger, jig, jig, but for once, we are the ones in love. I plan to celebrate our love each and every day."

Mindy rests her head on my shoulder. She draws in a deep breath and lets it out. "That's the best news I've heard all day. Since we're celebrating, can I start with pie?"

"Jigger, jig, jig, works for me," I answer with a grin.

<hr/>

"Elijah, will you roll this out for me? My arthritis is bothering me," my mom asks as she rubs her shoulder.

"I can do that Mrs. Fischer," Mindy offers.

"Are you sure you know what you're doing?" my mom asks skeptically.

"I've helped make cinnamon rolls a time or two in my life," Mindy answers diplomatically.

"Okay, Elijah looks busy playing cards."

Actually, I'm not. Dad and Josiah are playing Rummy.

They seem to be in the middle of an ongoing match, so I'm simply watching them play. But, I'm not going to argue with my mom — especially if this gives her a chance to bond with Mindy.

Mindy walks over and hands me her bangle bracelets and oversized sweater before she kisses me and goes back into the kitchen to wash her hands.

I know I'm supposed to be hanging out with the guys, but I can't help myself. I'm compelled to watch Mindy as she gracefully rolls out the yeast dough and sprinkles it with cinnamon and sugar. "Roxanne, do you want raisins and pecans in both batches?"

My mom glances over at Mindy in total shock. "You have those rolled out already?"

Mindy shrugs. "I've had a little practice. I grew up helping my mom, my aunt, and my grandma cook."

"I can see that. Let's use pecans. Mariam isn't fond of raisins. Since his accident, Seth has a hard time chewing, so we should do one batch without."

"Makes perfect sense." Mindy puts pecans in one batch and then rolls them up. When she finishes, she asks, "Where can I find your sewing kit?"

"Why do you need my sewing kit?"

"I need some thread to cut these," Mindy explains.

"Don't you just use a knife?"

"I find it's easier to use thread. It's a trick I was taught. It helps avoid squished rolls."

"Elijah, your woman seems to know her stuff and she says she needs thread. Can you get her a spool from my mending kit?"

I run into the laundry room and grab a spool of

thread from my mom's kit and take it back to Mindy. I'm curious how she plans to use the thread.

Mindy cuts about a ten-inch piece of thread off of the spool. She slides it under the log of cinnamon roll dough and crosses it at the top of the roll, about an inch from the edge, and pulls it tight. It neatly slices a piece of the roll off and she places it in the pan my mom provided. She quickly does a couple more. My mom is watching with rapt attention. "Where did you learn to do that? That's neat."

Mindy shrugs. "My Aunt Heather owns Joy and Tiers. She went to a fancy culinary school before she opened the bakery. She taught me all sorts of cool little cooking tricks while I was growing up."

"Can I try?" my mom asks tentatively.

"Absolutely." Mindy steps back and snips a new piece of thread from the spool for my mom.

My mom arranges it under the log and crosses it like she saw Mindy do. "Like this?" she asks.

Mindy nods. "Uh-huh. Now just pull the end of the strings until they cut all the way through."

My mom grins like a child. "This is kind of fun. It's much better than smooshing them with a knife. You're welcome to come cook with me anytime. Do you have any other secrets?"

"The next time you make cinnamon rolls, I might have to share my secret recipe for orange rolls."

"Those sound divine," my mom compliments as she continues to slice up the cinnamon rolls.

My attention is diverted when Katie abruptly gets up and confers with Josiah. Their expressions are intense.

Katie walks over and touches Mindy on the shoulder. She whispers something in Mindy's ear. Mindy pales and immediately sits down in one of my mom's kitchen chairs.

"I'm sorry Mrs. Fischer. I need to go. I promise I'll come back and we'll cook some more. I had fun." Mindy looks up at Katie. "Should Elijah come with me or stay here with Josiah?"

"Since he was with you that night, Logan might want to talk with him. He'd better come with us," Katie answers, as she texts something on her phone.

My dad looks at Mindy with alarm. "Are you having one of your visions again?"

"Not this time. This is something different. Uncle Aidan received a threat against my life on his fan page. Logan and Katie want us to meet with the security team at Identity Bank West to see if there are any holes in the system."

"I'm sorry to hear that. But do you think it's a good idea to drag Elijah into the middle of all that?" my dad asks.

I whirl around on my dad. My hand flies up and smacks the side of my face before I can stop it. "Jigger, jig, jig, that is incredibly unfair. Mindy isn't dragging me into anything, jigger, jig, jig. I'm standing by her side because I want to be here. I love her. Why do people find that so hard to believe?"

"It's just that you're so young," my mom interjects.

"Mom! I'm twenty-two. You and dad got married right after you graduated from high school."

She spins her well-worn wedding ring around her finger. "I know. We were young too."

"Are you saying you would've made a different choice?" I challenge.

My mom shakes her head. "No, I don't mean that. I just mean slow down. What's the rush? Your life is crazy right now."

Kate sticks her phone in her pocket and tightens her ponytail. "I know you're having a serious conversation, but we need to get going." She looks at me. "Are you going or are you staying here?"

"I'm going. The way I see it, both people I love have threats against their lives. I'm in danger either way."

My dad tilts his head as he considers what I've said. "The boy has a point."

Josiah pats his side-arm. "I wouldn't worry about it too much, Seth. Katie and I know what we're doing. Actually, I haven't met anyone who works for Aidan or Tristan who doesn't. Whoever is feebleminded enough to go after you guys has no idea who they're up against."

CHAPTER NINETEEN

MINDY

ELIJAH'S HAND DOESN'T MOVE from the small of my back as he escorts me into a large conference room at Identity Bank West. I'm grateful for his quiet, steady presence beside me. I'd like to say I'm calm and collected because I've got Katie watching over me — but with all the weird stuff going on in our lives, I have to admit I'm a little unnerved.

Although Tristan's influence is clear in the technology rich environment of the conference room, this building is nothing like you would expect. The traditional log cabin blends into the rural environment and looks like a cozy bed-and-breakfast or serene country store rather than a cutting-edge company which specializes in personal protection and computer safety.

Nervously, I make my way to the seats which have clearly been reserved for us. Elijah sits on one side of me and Katie on the other. After I sit down, Tristan's image appears on a large screen in front of me. In a startled voice, I stammer, "Umm … hi … Tristan. If you want to see me, all you have to do is come to a concert."

He chuckles. "I know, Mouse. Rogue is in love with your new single. We plan to see your show real soon. For once, my wife is impressed by my inside access to stars."

I blush. "I'm not really the star. Uncle Aidan is."

Tristan makes a face at me. "Funny. I don't remember hearing his voice on that song … and I hear your song a lot."

Elijah looks at me and raises an eyebrow. "Jigger, jig, jig, see? What did I tell you? I'm not the only one who feels that way."

Uncle Aidan looks up at the screen. "Tristan, it seems someone isn't happy with the amount of attention Mindy is getting. Did you get a chance to trace the IP address of the threat?"

Tristan glances toward the end of the conference table. "Toby, you're the newest member of the team. Do you want to introduce yourself?"

A guy who looks about my age clears his throat. "Hey, my name is Toby Payne. I'm a computer programmer."

"Don't let Toby's boyish good looks fool you. He is one of my most experienced programmers. I was lucky to get him before one of the big-name companies got a hold of him."

"*Pfft…* as if I would've worked for one of them," Toby scoffs. "Anyway, in answer to your question, it looks like whoever posted the threat used a couple of layers of virtual private networks and probably set up some anonymous burner accounts."

Elijah scowls. "Great! So, basically we still know nothing."

Katie shakes her head. "I don't agree. I think it tells us a lot. Whoever posted this message is invested in making their point. This wasn't simply a casual one off."

Jameson nods. "Obviously, they took some time to cover their tracks."

"Logan, you've done a risk assessment of everyone on the roster at Silent Beats, correct?"

My eyes widen and my jaw goes slack. "You did?"

The conference room door opens abruptly, startling us all. Jude and Tasha try to enter inconspicuously. "Sorry we're late. I had a final exam," Tasha explains as she dumps her backpack at her feet.

Logan nods. "The situation with Tasha's mother made it clear we needed to adjust the way we evaluated threats. We did a top-to-bottom assessment of our whole organization."

"There is more than a little crazy in my life at the moment. Did you update your assessment to include all the stuff going on in California?" I ask with a weary sigh.

Logan shuffles a stack of files and opens one. After a few moments, he refers to a list. "It looks like we've identified a few areas of risk for you."

I grip Elijah's hand tighter and draw in a deep breath. He leans over and brushes a kiss against my temple. "Jigger, jig, jig, it's all right. It's better to know what the bogeyman might look like than to be in the dark."

"Elijah is right," Katie says gently. "I know this is hard to hear, but it helps prepare the team."

"Okay. Let's hear the roster of my enemies," I concede.

"I don't know if I would call them your enemies —

these are more like people we need to watch for. We identified people we thought might have pre-existing grudges against you or your fame."

"Got it." I swallow hard. Hearing Logan put it in such stark terms is disconcerting.

"The first group of people we identified is your birth family," Logan says, as he consults the list.

I let out a startled breath as I hold up my scarred hand. "I definitely would put them in the enemy camp. They've already injured me once. Then again, I haven't heard from them in a dozen years. You would think if they had it in for me, they'd actually have to care."

Tasha winces. "Jealousy is a powerful motivator."

Elijah looks at Toby. "Do you have any evidence to support identifying her birth family as the suspects, jigger, jig, jig?"

Toby shakes his head. "I don't."

"Last I heard they were on the run chasing drugs. I have no idea where they ended up. I have no idea whether they're alive or dead," Mindy answers as she crosses her arms protectively in front of herself.

Katie writes a number two on her list. "Who's next?"

"The suspect who tried to abduct Mindy and Becca while she was escaping from her birth parents was never located."

Mindy shakes her head. "I don't think it's him. I believe that was a crime of opportunity. I think he was into little girls."

Katie nods. "I've studied guys like him. I think Mindy's assessment is dead-on. If Mindy could outsmart him at six with her little sister in her arms, I doubt he has the brains to pull this off." Katie scratches him off her list.

"What about the mess in California?" Elijah asks.

Logan shuffles through his file.

"I checked with one of my contacts at the CBI. Seems the surveillance tapes came through." He pulls a surveillance picture out of the stack of papers and pushes it across the table at me. "Anybody you know?"

I draw in a surprised breath. "That's Jodi Humphreys and her roommate." I rub my eyes and look again. I can't believe what I'm seeing. "I thought Christina was my friend. She was my lab partner."

Logan looks sympathetic as he passes pictures down to me. "Mindy Mouse, I wouldn't jump to any conclusions just yet. Look at this frame. If Christina is the one with short dark hair, she looks as shocked as you are by Jodi's actions. In this next picture, she looks like she's about to say something to the clerk, but Jodi is literally pulling her out of the store."

I slump back against my chair. "This is all surreal. I mean, I knew Jodi wasn't my biggest fan. She thought I was young and stupid. She resented the fact that I was admitted to college at all. One of her friends was denied admission and somehow Jodi figured it was all my fault because I got her friend's spot."

Tasha shakes her head. "I'm sorry. That sucks."

"Jodi made a big show of being sympathetic toward Melanie because she was 'stuck' being my roommate. Jodi was the one who promised Melanie she had all these connections at the sorority and guaranteed she would help her through pledge week. Melanie fell for it. She was willing to do just about anything to be popular."

Uncle Aidan shakes his head. "How sad. You would've made a much better friend."

"Jigger, jig, jig, I don't want to sound insensitive, but do these tapes mean they are not investigating Mindy anymore for Melanie's death?" Elijah presses.

Logan looks through the file again. "I don't think the coroner has officially ruled the death an accident, but my contact at the CBI seems to think that's the direction they are headed. Apparently, Ms. Lake's issues with drugs and alcohol were long-term started well before college. It's likely she simply died of alcohol poisoning combined with drug intoxication."

I sit forward and take a drink from the bottle of water Jameson provided for us all. "I need a moment for this all to sink in. I was beginning to think I was going to end up being charged with a crime I didn't commit. Every time I was questioned, it started looking worse and worse for me. It didn't seem to matter that I didn't have anything to do with what happened to Melanie. It was like watching a nightmare come to life."

Katie gets up and hugs me from behind. "Wrong place, wrong time. It occurs to the best of us. I'm sorry it happened to you and your friend. At least now you can start to put your life back together."

Jude puts his hand up in the air, "I hate to be a party pooper, but is it possible this Jodi person still has it in for Mindy?"

Tristan rejoins the conversation, "That's a good question. What do you think, Mindy?"

I shrug. "Jodi definitely dislikes me enough. But, I doubt if she has the technical skills to pull it off. I had to help her figure out how to sign on to the school's Wi-Fi and she couldn't set up her printer in the dorm room."

"Jigger, jig, jig, you said she had a boyfriend, right?" Elijah asks.

"At least one," I answer with a snicker.

Toby makes a note. "She could have outsourced. We should leave her on the list of suspects."

"Is there anyone else? I'm starting to feel like I have more enemies than friends."

"I'm afraid there's one obvious suspect we haven't talked about," Tasha says in a resigned voice.

"Seriously?" I ask.

"If you think about it, my mom makes the perfect suspect. You know she's always been obsessed with my career and over-the-top jealous. The threat didn't come until you took over my slot on stage. We didn't tell my mom that Jude and I were sick. Howard's publication has blocked my mom's account from their website. She might not even know why I wasn't on stage. She probably saw the pictures on Twitter of you and Joe on stage and drew her own conclusions."

Uncle Aidan rubs his temples. "What is it going to take for Nadine to give it up? You don't even tour with me full-time anymore."

Tasha sighs. "I don't know. I've essentially run away from home. But, that doesn't seem to be enough. I just want to be able to start my life with Jude and pretend she doesn't even exist."

"So, why don't you?" I ask.

"Why don't I what?"

"Why don't you and Jude get married? You guys have been engaged like forever."

"Just throw a wedding?" Tasha asks incredulously. "Who would come?"

I gesture around the table. "Everybody!"

"How can I plan a wedding? I'm swamped with school and I can barely get in recording time as it is."

"Do you trust me?" I ask. "Is it all right if Uncle Aidan and Aunt Tara walk you down the aisle?"

Tasha's eyes tear up. "Yes, and yes! Aidan and Tara have been amazing to me. I would be honored if they stood in for my family." Tasha's expression turns sad. "There's no way I want my mom there, but I miss my Nana."

Aidan rubs his hands together as he looks over at Logan. "Hear that? We've just been issued a challenge. The Girlfriend Posse hasn't had a complicated mission in a while. This will be fun."

Logan looks down at himself. "Don't know about you buddy, but I don't think we meet the membership qualifications of the Girlfriend Posse."

"Nonsense. During a mission this big, if your significant other is part of the Girlfriend Posse, so are you. Saddle up. We've got a wedding to plan. If I say so myself, my daughter is going to make the cutest flower girl you ever did see."

Tasha pulls on Jude's sleeve. "Can you believe it? We are finally going to get married. I have a feeling if we have any requests, we should probably let people know."

Jude chuckles. "Sorry to break it to you, but I think that train left the station about five minutes ago. I'm just going to let the professionals handle this while I stand back and watch with awe."

"Good point. The Girlfriend Posse has a reputation of putting on flawless weddings. I'd hate to muck up their plans."

Toby clears his throat. "I know I'm the new guy here, and I hate to break up the festivities — but if Tasha's mom is behind the threat against Mindy, how are we going to catch her?"

Tristan looks directly at me. "Mindy the next steps are up to you. We have no definitive proof that Mrs. Keeley is behind the threats. But she is the most viable suspect. The plan I am proposing would involve some risk to you. I won't pursue it unless you're totally on board."

Elijah sits straighter in his chair. "Jigger, jig, jig, if it's risky for Mindy, why propose it at all?"

"I understand your concern. However, I didn't say it was risk we couldn't manage," Tristan answers.

"I'd like to hear the plan," I announce. Elijah turns toward me and gives me an exasperated look.

Tristan clears his throat. "Aidan, would it be possible for you to release a single featuring just Mindy?"

"Sure. It's before Christmas, we could release a Christmas single. Can you explain why?"

"Toby and I have been developing some new software to help law enforcement officers break identity theft rings. I think it might help in this situation. I'm hoping whoever is helping Tasha's mom will log in to the announcement of the single which I plan to do live from our website. Toby can help me track it back. Hopefully we'll find the real IP address of the person who issued the threat."

"How would we ever generate enough media interest

in a single that quickly?" I ask.

Tasha raises an eyebrow. "Ahh … you've forgotten about my social media phenom, Haley. She is amazing. Hey, there's an idea. Why don't we donate the proceeds to St. Jude's Hospital? That would be a double whammy for my mom."

Jude snickers. "Oh, that's right. She's annoyed by my name — not to mention the fact that little kids get cancer and inconvenience their parents."

"Jigger, jig, jig, I'm sorry. I don't want to be rude or anything, but your mom sounds like a horrible human being," Elijah says as he blushes.

Tasha laughs out loud. "Don't be sorry. My mother is rather horrible. She doesn't even bother to apologize for being awful. In fact, she's amazingly proud of it."

Logan taps his pencil on his tablet. "We should work Howard into this too. I bet he'd would love a chance for a bit of revenge on his former sister-in-law."

"Good plan," Uncle Aidan responds. "What do you say Mindy Mouse? Are you on board with the plan to catch Nadine in the act?"

"I guess I'll be at the recording studio bright and early in the morning. I haven't performed much Christmas music since I was in choir. I guess I'll be hitting YouTube tonight to see what translates well to acoustic guitar. I have to say I can't believe we're doing this. I keep trying to tell you I'm not the star of the family."

Uncle Aidan winks at me. "I guess that remains to be seen."

Recording Booth C at Silent Beats looks like a music a store threw up all over it — but at least I've finally settled on a song. This may not be Uncle Aidan's fanciest recording studio, but it's my favorite. If I didn't know better, I'd swear he decorated it with me in mind. There is a hammock chair hanging from the ceiling and there are special lights designed to look like candles. With all the soundproofing on the walls, we are not allowed to use real candles in here, of course. But the fake ones are close enough.

I glance down at Elijah who is sitting in an oversized beanbag chair typing furiously on his laptop. "What do you think? Which is your favorite? I'm torn between *Away in a Manger* and *Silver Bells*."

Elijah pulls the earbuds out of his ears and looks at me blankly. "I asked you which Christmas song was your favorite?" I repeat.

"Mindy … jigger, jig, jig, I don't have a favorite Christmas song. We're Jewish."

I cover my mouth with my hand. "Oh my Gosh! Sometimes I'm just so clueless. I can't believe I never figured that out. To most people, your name should be a big clue. So, your family doesn't celebrate Christmas? Do you celebrate Hanukkah?"

Elijah shrugs. "My mom used to make a bigger deal about it when Mariam and I were little. Now, they don't do much, jigger, jig, jig."

"It's coming up soon, right?"

Elijah types something into his computer. "It starts

Mary Crawford

the weekend after next."

"I'd like to do something nice for your parents. Do you think they'd mind?"

"You don't have to. My mom wouldn't expect it."

"That's exactly why I want to."

Elijah sets his laptop on the ground and walks over to give me a kiss. "You are way too sweet. I'm so glad you chose me."

Just then Joe Summers walks into the recording studio. "The light wasn't on, so I figured you guys weren't recording. But I thought you'd be rehearsing at least — I mean rehearsing music, that is."

Elijah blushes bright red to the roots of his hair. "Jigger, jig, jig, I was just leaving. I'll let you guys work," He packs his computer into his backpack and turns to leave. With his hand on the doorknob, he turns to us. "I still think this idea borders on insanity. I don't like the idea of you being dangled like bait in front of anybody. I hope everybody knows what they're doing. I just found what it means to be happy. I would be devastated if I lost you."

Joe smiles at Elijah. "I hear what you're saying. I wouldn't worry about Mindy. Between Logan, Jameson and Tristan, she'll have more eyes on her than the President of the United States. She'll be fine. We're just trying to give Mindy and Tasha some peace of mind. Nadine Keeley needs to be held accountable for her actions for a change."

"After watching Tasha yesterday, I can't disagree with that. I just wish we didn't have to make Mindy a target."

I stand up and walk over to Elijah and hug him tightly. "You forgot something. No one is making me do

220

anything. I volunteered for this. It's the only way Tasha and Jude get to be free."

Elijah pulls away and kisses me on the forehead. "Like I said, you're amazing."

My eyes follow Elijah's progress as he leaves the room and closes the door behind him. Joe chuckles. "Oh Baby, you are so far gone for that boy."

I turn and grin. "I know. Isn't it great?"

Joe shakes his head. "I don't know if I remember being so young and in love."

He sits down on the beanbag chair. He balances his guitar on his knee. "I can't wait to hear what you've decided to cover — or, did you decide to do one of your originals?"

"No, I don't think I'm confident enough to do that on my own yet. Since this is a fundraiser on Haley's behalf, I decided to keep it simple. I'm planning to cover *Silver Bells*."

"Sounds great. That one should have wide appeal. You want to have Aidan play piano on it or should we just go with acoustics?"

"I don't know. We could ask him. Better yet, we could do it both ways in the jam session and run it by folks and see which version they prefer."

"I know Aidan doesn't need any rehearsal. But it's been a while since I've done any Christmas music. I could use a few run-throughs. Do you mind?" Joe asks me as he tunes his guitar.

I roll my eyes at him. "Why do you think I'm here before breakfast? I like to practice until my fingers bleed, remember? Just because this is a ruse, it doesn't mean I don't want to put my best work out there."

"That right there is the reason why you're at Silent Beats. It has nothing to do with the fact that Aidan considers you his niece. You are a kick-butt artist and you are one of the hardest workers around here. This may have come about through unfortunate circumstances, but I hope it's the break you need to send you through the stratosphere."

I cough lightly to clear my throat as I blink back tears. "It seems I'm not the only ridiculously nice person around here. Thanks for the vote of confidence, Joe. It means a lot."

CHAPTER TWENTY

ELIJAH

I CLOSE THE LIFT to the back of the SUV after I place my dad's scooter it. After I climb into the middle row of seats with Mindy, my dad turns around from the front seat. "I appreciate you swinging by and picking Josiah and me up. The repair shop said it was a bad sensor in my lift. It shouldn't be a big deal. It's just a hassle."

"No sweat. We had to come to Salem anyway to look at invitations for Tasha's wedding."

My dad pauses for a moment and listens to the music playing in the SUV. "This is pretty. I've always liked this kind of music. Who is this singing?"

Mindy and I start speaking at the same time. "Jigger, jig, jig, Dad —"

"It's me," Mindy explains. "These are my demo tapes from a rough recording session we had down at Silent Beats. We are trying to decide which version would make a better single."

"I'll be darned," my dad says with a tone of admiration. "When my son told me you were a musician,

I thought maybe you like the crazy rap music that's so popular these days. I never figured you'd sing something I could listen to. Maybe I'll take Roxanne to one of your concerts."

"That would be fun. Just let me know and I'll make sure you get VIP seats."

Mindy grows quite still and abruptly yells as she points to the pickup next to us. "Seth, duck! There's a gun!"

From the seat behind me, Josiah scrambles over the seat. He reaches over the front seat and pushes my dad's torso down onto the seat beside Katie. In an instant, she drops back behind the yellow track and darts off the exit.

Josiah trains his gun out the driver side window up toward the freeway until the off-ramp curves away from the freeway. Then he pulls out his cell phone and dials 911. I'm so busy trying to piece together what happened, I only hear bits of the conversation. "Mustard yellow Ford F150 extended cab, repair work left-hand side and rear right panel." Josiah shifts his phone and holsters his gun as he listens to the dispatcher. "Washington plates. Some sort of flag. Only got the first two letters. Bravo – Tango."

Katie pulls the SUV into a parking garage and swings it around so she's facing the exit. She slams the car into park and helps my dad sit up. She gently runs her fingers down his extremities. "Are you all right, Mr. Fischer?"

"I think so," stammers my dad.

She motions for Josiah to hand her his phone.

"This is Katelyn Anthony. I provide private security. We encountered a threat with a weapon. We're hidden on the first floor of the parking garage at Chemekta and

High, in Salem. Suspect's vehicle is a mid-nineties mustard yellow F150 pickup with military plates from Washington. License plate may contain the letters Bravo Tango. The truck has heavy body damage which has been repaired with Bondo. The right taillight is out." She listens for a while. "No ma'am. No shots were fired. We appear to have lost them. We will wait for your officers to arrive. Thank you. No ma'am ... we will not hang up until they do."

Katie rolls her eyes as she hands the phone back to Josiah. "This is so much harder when you're on this end of the call," she signs to Mindy while we wait.

She must not know I am proficient in sign language because she looks surprised when I laugh out loud.

"Why do you say that?" I sign back.

"I used to be a police officer," she signs quickly.

My dad looks at Mindy. "What are they going on about?"

"Katie was just telling Elijah she used to be a police officer before she moved to Oregon."

"Oh… Explains your dynamite driving," he says to Katie.

"Seth, have you ever seen that truck before?" Mindy asks carefully.

My dad leans his head back against the leather seat and lets out a shaky breath. "I wish I could say no. But I am pretty sure that rig belongs to Harrison Conlin."

My eyebrows raise. "From Harrison Brothers?"

My dad nods as tears form in the corners of his eyes.

Katie looks at my dad blankly. "I'm afraid I'm not familiar."

"I worked for the same guy for more than thirty years. His name was Bud Olson. He was as ethical as they come. But, his wife had a series of strokes. He had to put her in one of those care facilities and the co-pay was crazy expensive. So, he had to sell the business. Roxanne and I wanted to buy him out, but we couldn't raise the capital. So, he sold to an investment company."

"Harrison Brothers?" Katie confirms.

"At first, they promised us nothing would change. We would be able to be independent and objective and do our jobs as usual. We would be able to bid the same and keep our high standards and good reputation."

"What happened?" Josiah asks.

"We started getting hired for jobs we would've never bid for in the past. You know, there are certain companies you instinctively know aren't on the up and up and you don't want your name associated with them — even as an inspector. Then when we got on the jobs, people seemed to be expecting us to just sign off on paperwork for jobs we never actually fully inspected. That's not the way I work. I never have."

"Jigger, jig, jig, anyone who knows you, knows that, Dad," I insist.

"The last job was the final straw. They kept pushing around deadlines, and they were asking people to falsify documents and sign off on building materials which weren't safe. I wasn't willing to do it. I was going to call in the Feds."

"Anybody else know about your plans?" Josiah presses.

"Oh, probably everybody. I warned Harrison that it was a safety issue. I wasn't going to play along just to be nice."

We turn and look out the window when we see blue lights flashing.

Josiah and Katie exit the SUV and show the police officers their ID. One officer looks at Katie's identification and says, "Hey, I know you. You were in that officer involved shooting a couple of years back. Way to be on your toes."

"Thank you, but I had a team of people supporting me that day. It wasn't just me. Honestly, everything had to go right for it to turn out the way it did."

The officer looks up in the air as if he's searching his memory. "Oh, that's right you had a young folk star act like your own personal fortuneteller or something. I don't suppose she was here today? You could have probably used a heads up," he jokes.

"Actually, we're really grateful Ms. Whitaker was with us," Katie answers diplomatically. "I'll let you ask her what happened."

The other officer steps forward and sticks his head in the car door. "Before we indulge your love of the paranormal, Officer Brown, perhaps we should ask a few basic questions first. Is anyone hurt?"

Seth shakes his head. "Thank goodness we weren't. My son's girlfriend could sense the danger, and I looked up in time to see a Glock pointed directly at my head before I reacted to her command for me to duck."

"What happened next?" The first officer asks.

Katie picks up the narrative. "I was able to utilize a little evasive driving. I slowed down and dropped behind the pickup briefly before I took the Albany exit onto Front Street and found a hiding space in the parking garage."

"That was incredibly smart thinking. Once you were behind him, there wasn't much he could do to pursue you. Why did you ever leave the force? Clearly you know your stuff."

Katie shrugs and winces. "Not well enough to keep from getting shot. Besides, I lived in Florida and fell in love with the head of security for Aidan O'Brien. Since he happened to live in Oregon, now I do too."

"Since everyone seems to be in one piece, let's go down to the station and I'll get the rest of the witness statements. It might be helpful to issue a BOLO on the truck. I'd like to talk to the owner to see if I can get their side of the story."

"Officer, I understand you can't automatically take Mindy's side of the story, but after you hear her side of the story, jigger, jig, jig, you'll side with her."

The officer stiffens and the muscle in his jaw tightens. "Excuse me? What did you call me?"

My heart sinks to my feet. This is my worst-case scenario. My hand swings up and hits the side of my face. I can feel my cheek grow hot from the force of the blow. "Jigger, jig, jig, nothing sir. I have Tourette's syndrome. These are tics. I can't control them."

The first officer makes a dismissive sound. "Likely story."

Katie straightens herself to her full height. "It's likely a true story. The person whose account you are dismissing is Elijah Fischer and the victim of the crime is Seth Fischer, his father. I'm sure he would be happy to confirm his diagnosis for you." Katie shakes her head in disgust. "Not that it should be remotely required. Even so, if you insisted — any of us or a couple dozen other people would be more than happy to confirm the alleged impairment."

The other officer steps forward and addresses us all, "That won't be necessary. This is all a simple misunderstanding. We'd appreciate it if you could all follow us down to the station so we can get some more information and hopefully find the other party involved. We'd like to get Mr. Fischer some justice in this case and make the streets a little safer."

———————◆———————

My mom and Mindy are sitting at the kitchen table peeling a mountain of potatoes while I unload the dishwasher. For several minutes, there's an awkward silence, broken only by the sounds of Dad, Josiah, and Katie cheering or jeering at one of the teams playing on the TV.

Finally, my mom puts down the vegetable peeler and looks up at Mindy. "I don't know what to say."

Mindy looks down at the bowl of potatoes she's been peeling and quartering. "Oh, I'm sorry did you want me to cut them differently?"

My mom shakes her head. "No, those are fine. I'm not talking about potatoes. I'm talking about what you did for Seth — what you've done for everyone."

Mindy blushes slightly. "I'm glad I was able to help."

"Seth told me you did more than just help. He said you very likely saved his life, and Katie's too," my mom argues stubbornly.

"Katie gets most of the credit for that one." Mindy holds her hand out to illustrate how calm Katie was. "She had nerves of steel under a humongous amount of stress. She could put several NASCAR drivers to shame."

My mom smiles. "Seth called the two of you his guardian angels. He was very proud of you."

I grin as I dry off my hands, lean against the kitchen counter and drink my coffee. "Jigger, jig, jig, I was proud of her too. She was amazing."

"Josiah mentioned they weren't very respectful at the police station."

"Oh … they weren't so bad. Honestly, I've encountered much worse," Mindy hedges.

My mom looks down at the pile of peelings in front of her as she averts her gaze from Mindy. "I'm sorry I was one of those people who didn't believe in what you do. I was wrong."

"It's all right, Roxanne. You're not the only one. Most people have a hard time wrapping their minds around what I do. I understand that I'm wired a little strange."

"Jigger, jig, jig, but you made a believer out of even the most skeptical cop. Tell my mom what happened — " I prompt.

Mindy comes over to the sink and rinses the potatoes. She shrugs as she explains, "I didn't do it to impress him, it was simply the right thing to do. It was like a moral imperative for me."

"Still, it was epic," I interject. "Even though they thought you were trying to throw their questioning off track."

"What did you do?" my mom presses as she watches our interplay with growing curiosity.

"I had to stop the interview because I needed to tell

him he had to take his puppy to the vet."

"Why?" my mom asks with wide eyes.

"It seems the officer's daughter learned to tie without anyone noticing. She got a piece of dental floss out of the garbage and tied it around the puppy's neck. The puppy was about to suffocate in the kennel."

"He didn't believe you?"

Mindy shakes her head. "Not at first — but I guess his commanding officer had investigated the incident with Katie a couple years ago and was more of a believer. His supervisor told him to send one of the beat cops over to do a welfare check."

"What did they find?" My mom clutches her hand over her chest.

"The police officer encountered a very startled mom who had just put her daughter down for a nap. When they opened the kennel, the puppy was almost gone. They were able to cut off the dental floss. When they took the dog to the vet, they found the damage wasn't permanent."

"Oh, thank goodness! I guess you saved more lives than you imagined." My mom lets out a deep breath.

Mindy walks over and stands in front of me. I start to massage her neck. She relaxes into my touch. "I suppose so. I don't really keep score. Usually, I don't hear from people after I share my visions." I place my arms around Mindy's waist and draw her close.

My mom rubs the locket she got from my grandmother. She tends to do that when she's anxious. "Oh dear. How worrisome for you to never know whether people take your advice. They could be stubborn like I was. That would be just awful."

Abruptly, Mindy leaves my arms. She walks over to my mom and wraps her arms around my mom's shoulders. She hugs her and says. "I was never upset with you. You need to forgive yourself. No harm was done. I'm used to people not believing me. I've been like this since I can remember. As a child, no one ever took me seriously. I finally came to the conclusion that if I wasn't the right messenger, God would use someone else."

Mindy sits down beside my mom and grasps her hands in a supportive gesture. My mom looks at her with tears in her eyes. "Are you sure? What about your roommate? She didn't listen to you."

Mindy sighs and pain flickers through her expressive eyes. "I don't know, Roxanne. I don't always have the answers. I wish I did. Sometimes, bad things just happen and even I can't stop them."

CHAPTER TWENTY-ONE

MINDY

MADISON ADJUSTS THE CAMERA and microphone. Somehow, they've figured out how to record this session for a DVD and a live podcast for Madison's television show at the same time. Although touring with Uncle Aidan has really helped me overcome my stage fright, this is surprisingly nerve-racking.

Uncle Aidan sits down beside me and hands me a cup of chai tea. "Take a deep breath. This is supposed to be fun. It's release day. Everyone will love this single. You sound phenomenal."

"I still don't understand why you chose this version. Don't you think fans would have responded better if you were on it?"

"Actually, I don't. I love the simplicity of just you and the acoustic guitars. Besides, you are always worried about people believing you are only riding on my coattails. If I'm not on this album, no one can argue your success has anything to do with me."

A startled laugh escapes. "I've got news for you.

Nothing will ever convince everyone. After all, most people know I call you Uncle Aidan. Most people assume you pounded down doors to make sure I topped the charts. In a way, I'm not sure they're wrong. You certainly didn't stand in my way. If I hadn't had the publicity machine behind Silent Beats helping me, I'm not sure anyone would've known my name."

Tasha comes in and sits on the other side of me. "I used to feel the same way about following in Aidan's footsteps. But now my fan base is almost as big as his. I don't have any doubt yours will be huge too. I was in the recording booth when Joe was laying down a few tracks. You sound amazing."

"I thought I was ready for this. I mean, our duet did really well. It's not like I'm a newbie but I feel like I'm a kid getting ready for my first choir concert."

Jude walks behind me and ruffles my hair. "You are like an *hermosa* to me. I get the same feeling every time Tasha and I go out on stage. Just try to focus it into keeping your energy up. You've got this."

Aidan looks down at his cell phone. "Oh good, they're here."

I look around the studio. Tara, Aidan, Jude, Tasha, Elijah, Madison, Trevor, my parents, and my grandparents are here. Even Seth and Roxanne are sitting over in the corner watching. I can't imagine who else would be coming.

Tasha laughs at the confused expression on my face. "You didn't think I would hold a party like this without our biggest fan, did you?"

Hayden bursts into the room with her tablet in hand.

"Holy moly, Aidan! Do you have your computer team working on this? I don't know if your server will be able to handle the traffic. These numbers are off the charts — "

"Good evening, Hayden and Pennie. It's great to see you guys. How was your flight?"

Hayden looks up from her tablet with a perplexed look on her face. "It was awesome. But you know that because you provided a private plane for us to fly on — which, by the way, is totally epic. Who knew when I was put in charge of Jude and Tasha's fan club, it would come with perks like this?"

Pennie nudges her daughter. "Hayden, most people say thank you."

Hayden stops in her tracks. "Oh … right. Thank you so much. I'm so excited to be here. Tasha wouldn't even give me a sneak peek. I'm going to be as surprised as everyone else. You know I think you are fifty-thousand different kinds of cool, right Mindy? You convinced me my life would still be okay, even though cancer destroyed my arm."

"I'm so glad you could make it tonight. Tasha told me about your scholarship offers," I answer with a grin. "Sounds like life is a little more than simply okay."

"I know! Can you believe it? Now, I have to decide which school to choose. But, we have a bigger problem right now. We don't want your big announcement to crash in the middle. Web traffic is way up," Hayden announces as she looks around the room.

Madison glances at her watch. "Hayden has a good point. Since we're broadcasting this live, it might not be a bad idea to have your computer folks on site in case something goes wrong. You want me to call Jameson?"

"Go ahead, we might as well have extra insurance. I remember when Jamison upgraded our system; He said we were pretty much bulletproof. Something about private networks and limitless capacity."

Madison leaves the room, as she dials a number on her cell phone.

Hayden turns to me. "Are you excited?"

I shrug uncomfortably. "I guess. Mostly, I'm nervous that we've done all this work and the universe will take one gigantic apathetic sigh and just go about its business. For most people, I'm not even a blip in the radar. I'm not sure this was such a brilliant idea. What if I don't raise any money?"

Haley laughs at me. "You sound like Tasha every time she has a new song. It's just jitters."

Aidan adjusts the strap on his favorite guitar. "Mouse, you and I have been having jam sessions since I first started teaching you to play the guitar almost a dozen years ago. Just treat it like one of those." He gestures toward the cameras. "We're simply inviting a few more friends to watch."

Madison enters the studio with a pensive expression. "Well, I have bad news and good news. The bad news is Jameson has the stomach flu and can't be here. But the good news is he's sending Toby in his place. Jameson says Toby is probably a better person to handle this anyway. He'll be right over."

Hayden lets out an inarticulate squeak. "Tobias Payne

is going to be here in this room? Great! There go my plans for being the one who isn't nervous."

I can't hide my giggle. "You know what they say? Misery loves company."

Hayden sticks her tongue out at me. "You only say that because you have a cute boyfriend. You've forgotten how hard this is."

"Oh, trust me — I've forgotten nothing," I assure her.

Elijah leans over and whispers in my ear, "Jigger, jig, jig, this boyfriend wants to take a walk outside. My nerves are getting to me too. Join me?"

"Anywhere you want to go," I answer, with a blush.

Elijah glances over at Aidan. "We've got a while before we go live, jigger, jig, jig. I'd like to take Mindy for a walk to burn off some of our nerves."

Uncle Aidan must have caught my blush because he winks at Elijah. "Uh-huh, I was young and in love once. Heck, who am I kidding? I'm still crazy in love with Tara. Go have fun, but don't mess up Mindy's makeup."

Elijah swallows hard. "Yes Sir, jigger, jig, jig."

I wrinkle my nose at my uncle as we stand up to leave. "Be nice to my boyfriend. He's shy. I don't want you to scare him away."

Uncle Aidan grins. "I'm always nice. I'm just an unrepentant goofball. The sooner he learns that about me, the better. Now, scoot — you guys are burning valuable time."

I clutch Elijah's hands in mine and tuck them into the large pocket of my heavy wool coat as we stroll through the small community park. The weather is crisp and a bit breezy but unseasonably clear for the time of year. Elijah sits on a wooden bench and pulls me down beside him. He takes his jacket off and places it around my shoulders.

"What's all this about?"

"Jigger, jig, jig, I just wanted to tell you how proud I am of you. I know how hard it is to put yourself out there for people to judge."

Elijah leans over and kisses my temple.

"Thank you. Your support means everything. I kinda thought you didn't want me to do this at all."

"Truthfully? Jigger, jig, jig, I didn't — at first. But after the experience with my dad, jigger, jig, jig, I understand the reasons you had to help Tasha stop living in fear. It really hit home, jigger, jig, jig."

"I'm wondering if maybe I set too big of a goal. What if I don't catch Nadine? I don't want Tasha to be disappointed, especially since she's getting married and starting a new life."

"Maybe the fact that you jigger, jig, jig were willing to go out on a limb for her, gave her the courage to move forward. Didn't you tell me she and Jude have been engaged for a long time, jigger, jig, jig?"

"They have. I never really thought about it. I just figured it was because Jude was starting a whole new career and Tasha was taking classes in nursing school. You know, one of those timing issues."

"Jigger, jig, jig, so, even if Nadine doesn't fall for the bait, you helped them get unstuck and you are releasing a super cool Christmas song to help St. Jude's Hospital. So, I think it's a win for everyone."

I groan. "What if no one buys my Christmas song?"

"Jigger, jig, jig, are you kidding me? You know my mom is a state inspector for nursing homes, right? Ever since you announced this project and she found out that you were donating the proceeds to St. Jude's, she's been like a one-woman sales force. She's probably drummed up five hundred sales for you."

I'm in so much shock, I have to remember to close my mouth. "Are you being serious? There were times I could've sworn your mom hated my guts. Out of everyone you've introduced me to, your mother was my biggest critic. I'm sure she thought I was pulling a fast one on you. I'm not sure what she thought I would do to you, but I'm pretty sure she thought it had something to do with fraud and deception."

"You're right. My mom was a skeptic. But you've turned her into a fan. She's profoundly grateful for your help with dad, and the fact that you became her own personal food guru didn't hurt anything either. I took her to the grocery store the other day and she was telling the guy at the bakery counter how to slice his cinnamon rolls. It was a bit awkward, but her heart was in the right place."

An alarm goes off on Elijah's phone.

"We should go back. But I just wanted to tell you that even if you don't sell a single copy of this single — I am so proud of how you stood by your friend. Not everyone is willing to stand up to a bully. You are awesome. I love you."

"You have no idea how much I needed to hear those words. Let's go catch ourselves a bad guy and hopefully raise a bunch of money for the good guys in the process," I say before I reach up and thread my fingers through his hair and give him a thorough kiss.

Elijah pulls away and groans. "Jigger, jig, jig, your uncle is going to kill me. I wasn't supposed to mess up your makeup."

I wink at Elijah and kiss him one more time. "I have a phenomenally talented makeup artist. She has had lots of practice finding the most durable lipstick. Otherwise, Tasha could never wear makeup and Aidan would always be sporting Tara's lipstick. She's learned a lot through the years. I just happen to be the beneficiary of all that experience."

Elijah shoots me a wolfish grin. "Jigger, jig, jig no, technically, I think I would be the primary beneficiary."

"Or, we could call it a tie."

———— • ————

The sound technician counts us down to air with his fingers. I try to take a deep breath and let it out, but my body seems to have forgotten how to do even basic involuntary functions, like breathing. Elijah notices my discomfort and squeezes my hand gently. His presence reminds me that even if everything goes catastrophically wrong with this release, the things which are important in my life are still all okay.

Aidan greets his fans with an ease I doubt I'll ever obtain — no matter how long I'm in the industry. Madison is chatting with Uncle Aidan as if they are just in her backyard having a barbecue. Then again, I suppose they've had plenty of practice honing this routine. Although Aunt Madison and Uncle Aidan are not officially related to me, no one seems to care. Everyone in my parent's circle of friends has always been treated as if they are actually family. So, we have all had many real-life barbecues where we actually have jam sessions.

Madison looks over at me as if she's expecting me to speak and I realize I must have missed a verbal cue. Madison tries again. "I don't know if you all know this, but Mindy Whitaker will always hold a special place in my heart because she officiated my wedding ceremony several years ago when she was a little girl. It warms my heart to see what a lovely young woman she has become. Mindy, can you tell the audience the special meaning behind your release of *Silver Bells*?"

I smile gratefully at the softball question. Holding up my hand to the camera I explain, "My sister and I had an incredibly rough start in life. We had the good fortune of being cared for by incredible doctors and nurses who prevented a bad situation from getting much worse. They were a lot like the nurses who work at St. Jude's Hospital. As you know, Tasha Keeley and Aidan O'Brien have made St. Jude's one of their favorite causes. Through the work they've done there, I've met some patients both past and present. They are remarkably courageous and resilient. I want to do everything I can to make sure St. Jude's can continue their wonderful work."

"Talk about making your mess your message. That's a great way to turn things positive." Madison turns to Tasha, "How do you feel about Mindy picking up the reins of your work?"

Tasha smiles. "I am so glad you asked. I've read some comments on the fan forums which concern me. I guess some people are worried Aidan is somehow using Mindy to replace me and that I'm upset or jealous. Nothing could be further from the truth. If you haven't heard, I've started school to become a nurse. The nursing program is tough. I need to step back from my music career. It was my plan all along. Mindy had nothing to do with that."

"So, if this single does really well, you don't have a problem with that?"

"I'll be cheering it all the way up the charts! Mindy is like my little sister. I couldn't have a better best friend than Mindy Whitaker. If she goes all the way to number one with this song, I'll be throwing her the biggest party ever," Tasha insists.

Aidan gets an evil twinkle in his eye. "I don't know about you guys, although it's fun when they get along — one of these days, I'd like to put them on stage and have them participate in a guitar duel. They are both so good, I'm not sure who would come out on top."

Madison shakes her head in dismay. "You guys and your need to turn everything into a contest."

Aidan grins. "I was kidding — mostly. It would make a heckuva show, wouldn't it? I know the fans are probably dying to hear Mindy's new single, and we've been keeping them in suspense for weeks. What do you say? Should we play the video?"

Hayden pulls the mic closer. "As president of the fan club, all I can say is it's about time! Let's get this show on the road."

The sound guy pushes the button to play the video Joe Summers and I recorded the other day in an old historic church. He silences all of our mics just in time for Toby to do a fist pump.

"I gotta say, I thought you had lost a few marbles. But that was a stroke of brilliance. You reeled her in like a trophy fish," Toby comments with a wide grin.

Madison looks at him blankly. "What do you mean?"

Toby turns his laptop around. He shows Madison a series of comments on the fan forum. It appears to be an argument about Tasha's talent compared to mine. When I look at it closer, I realize it contains so much personal background, it could only be from Nadine. Toby clicks on the comment and opens another window. To me, this looks like total gibberish, but Toby gleefully announces, "The IP address and VPN are the same as the death threat."

"Does that mean we've got her?" Jude asks. I can tell by his pensive expression he's afraid to be too hopeful. They've been close before, but Nadine managed to escape justice.

"I'll send all this stuff to Tristan's cybercrime guys at Identity Bank, but I'd say your mom just got caught red-handed with her hand in the cyber cookie jar."

Uncle Aidan puts his arm around my shoulders and gives me a hug. "Most awesome job, Mindy Mouse. If nothing else happens with this single, you've accomplished your mission. But I have a feeling you have a runaway hit on your hands. Let's check out the fan feedback."

I groan. "Do we have to?"

Tasha chuckles. "Yes, you'll be fine. Your song is amazing!"

As the video concludes, the sound tech makes our mics hot and Madison goes back on the air. "Wow! I know I have goosebumps. What did you all think? Let's take a caller. Who do we have on line one?"

"Oh my gosh! I can't believe I made it on the show! This is Doreen Wickens. I'm a huge fan. I haven't heard anything so beautiful since Crystal Gayle did the song. I love it. I'm going to give it to all my friends as an early Christmas present."

I have to clear my throat. I hoped people would like it but hearing someone saying so out loud makes me emotional. "Thank you, Doreen. Your support means a lot."

"It sure does," Aidan adds. "Every purchase will help St. Jude's Hospital."

Let's take another phone call. "Who am I speaking with?" Madison asks.

"Hey, this is Thad Bolingsworth. I was wondering if Mindy is still single. She's hot. If she is, have her hit me up on Snapchat."

"Umm … thanks for calling Thad. Unfortunately, I'm a little too busy for online flirting these days."

"Okay let's move to the next caller," Madison says awkwardly as she tries to smother a grin. "Who do we have on the line?"

"Hi! This is Liberty Jane. I want Mindy to know I started guitar lessons last month and I'm in my church choir. I'm in the third grade, but when I grow up I want to be just like her."

"We sure appreciate fans like you," Aidan comments as I pause to catch my breath.

"Thanks so much for calling, Liberty Jane. What an awesome name! You know, I started playing the piano when I was in the first grade. So, you are off to a very good start." After a few moments, impulsively, I add. "Hey, Liberty Jane after we're off the air, stay on the line and tell the receptionist your address and I'll send you some fan gear. I want to stay in touch with you and see how your guitar lessons go, okay?"

"Seriously?" she asks me incredulously.

I shrug. "Absolutely. I wouldn't be where I am today if somebody I looked up to didn't totally have faith in a little girl who was full of questions and more hopes and dreams than common sense."

Liberty Jane squeals. "Mama! Did you hear that? Mindy Whitaker wants to talk to me again!"

"You keep up with your music lessons and we'll keep in touch, okay, Liberty Jane? I've got to move on to other callers, but it was great talking to you."

Elijah squeezes my hand and I grin. I never considered myself much of a role model to anyone except my siblings. It's cool to think other musicians might be looking up to me. I take a deep breath and let it out.

"Mindy, I can't tell you how happy I am for you. It seems like your single has struck a chord with the listeners. We've got time for one more caller before you close with a live version. Welcome to our show."

"It makes me sick to listen to all these people fawn all over Mindy. She's nothing but an ungrateful mongrel."

We all gasp in shock as the sound technician cuts the feed to the webcast and the room becomes quiet. He keeps recording and we can still hear her words through our headsets.

Elijah is not wearing a headset. Thankfully, he doesn't hear the vitriol coming from Nadine's mouth. He sends me a questioning look. I silently mouth, "Nadine." His eyes widen.

My stomach churns as I hear Tasha's mom prattle on. It isn't until she says, "I only threatened my daughter, but I can do worse to you, Mindy Jo Whitaker!" that the hair on the back of my neck stands up.

Aidan abruptly signs, "Take your headphones off, Mouse. Need to keep her on the line. Isaac's buddies will take care of her."

My heart pounds and sweat rolls down the middle of my back. I'm torn. I want to know what she's saying, but then again, I don't. Reluctantly, I take off my headset and lay it down on the table. "How?" I sign rather desperately.

"I sent a text message to Tristan and Tyler," Madison signs back.

"Wait … Everyone knows sign?" Elijah signs with a confused expression.

"Been hanging around Uncle Aidan too long, I guess" I answer in sign language as I shrug. "We all just picked it up. We all work with the kids at his day camp."

Uncle Aidan is still talking to Tasha's mom. I'm trying hard not to pay attention because the angry words are making me nauseous. As I glance over at Tasha, I can tell she's having the same reaction. Jude has taken the unusual step of pulling Tasha up into a close embrace and physically covering her ears so she can't hear the heated exchange.

Tears fill my eyes and I start to shake as one of Tasha's memories fills my psyche. In my mind, I see Nadine backhand Tasha's grandmother hard enough that she flies across the kitchen and lands crumpled against the refrigerator. I was so focused on the current drama I wasn't shielding myself against my visions and it takes me completely by surprise.

Elijah sees me turn pale and sway. He catches Madison's eye and whispers in a harsh tone, "Jigger, jig, jig, we'll be right outside."

Elijah slings his backpack over his shoulder before he helps me stand up. He places a firm arm around my waist and quietly escorts me out the door. As soon as we reach the small alcove on the other side of the studio, he throws his jacket down on the ground and pulls me down beside him. We rest against the wall for a moment before he pulls a bottle of water out of his backpack and hands it to me. "Jigger, jig, jig, want to tell me what's going on? This is way more than nerves about your new single."

"Tasha's mom threatened to kill me. I knew she was bad news —but I didn't know how bad."

"Jigger, jig, jig, maybe she's just bluffing. You know, some people get super ticked off and say things they don't mean."

"I don't think that's the case here. I saw a vision through Tasha's eyes. Maybe Tasha doesn't consciously remember it, because the only thing she's ever told me about her mom is Nadine's insatiable desire for Tasha to succeed as a beauty pageant contestant."

"Jigger, jig, jig, what did you see?"

"I saw Nadine physically strike Dottie hard enough to propel her across the room. If she is capable of hurting her own mother, she's capable of harming any of us— it's not simply talk."

"Jigger, jig, jig, thanks to you, she's over played her hand. It's only a matter of time before she's caught.

"It can't be fast enough for me," I declare with a shuddering sigh.

Chapter Twenty-Two

Elijah

Candace Fitzgerald picks at her salad as she looks around the hip vegan restaurant. She sighs. "I guess Oregon is nice enough, but it's not California. Portland shows promise though."

"Jigger, jig, jig, do you understand I don't live in Portland? I merely came up here to have a meeting with you. I live in a much smaller town."

Candace waves my comment away. "Yes, I know. I'll never understand why you want to live in the middle of the woods."

"Jigger, jig, jig, is there something we couldn't talk about over the phone?" I press.

Candace's expression sours. "Although Douglas tells me your manuscript is much improved, he has informed me that you have refused to make the changes the publisher has requested. Is there a reason for this?"

"Yes! I won't turn my main character into a school shooter simply because it's a hot topic and the publisher thinks it might resonate with readers. It's not honest to who the character is based on."

"Need I remind you we paid you an advance for this book and you are writing fiction?"

For once, I'm glad I have a million and a half unrelated errands to run today. I never carry my checkbook, but today I happen to have it with me because I have to go to the bank and order new checks with my new address. With an inner strength I never would have had the courage to show a few years ago, I pull my checkbook out of my backpack and write a check for the amount of the advance. I push it across the table toward Candace.

Her mouth goes slack when she picks it up and sees the amount. "What? Are you serious? Do you know what you're doing?"

"Jigger, jig, jig, yes, I know exactly what I'm doing. I spent most of my childhood and teenage years letting bullies rule my life jigger, jig, jig. I'm done. You might be wearing a business suit and have a fancy title, but you are no different from the people who used to stuff me into my locker."

Candace lets out a horrified gasp. "How can you say that? Our publishing company gave you a huge break!"

"Jigger, jig, jig, you did and I'm grateful. Make no mistake, you got a lot from the deal too. You've made a ton of money off my books."

Candace rolls her eyes at me. "Last I checked, that's how it's supposed to work."

"Jigger, jig, jig, maybe so. But, I think it's supposed to be a two-way street. It's clear you've stopped respecting my integrity as an artist."

"Save me from whiny authors who think your work is sacrosanct," Candace snaps. "You all think writing is the hard part. Wait until you have to market the drivel you produce." She grabs the check from the table and sneers at me. "I wish you the best of luck. Honestly, I don't know how you're going to do it. Your writing is strong, but you can barely put together a sentence in real life."

"Jigger, jig, jig, I am aware. Even so, the people who matter seem to understand me just fine, jigger, jig, jig," I respond, refusing to be defeated.

Candace stomps off in her impossibly high heels. As she struggles with the door, she can't resist one last insult, "You'll see no one else will want to deal with your weirdness either."

"Jigger, jig, jig, I love how you announce it like it's a newsflash. It's more like the story of my life. Yet, somehow, I'm still here, jigger, jig, jig,"

———— ●● ————

I breathe a small sigh of relief when I see Mindy's face pop up on my tablet. "Jigger, jig, jig, can you talk?"

Mindy shrugs. "As long as my hotspot holds out. I don't know why I bother to try to write lyrics on the bus. It never works."

"Where are you headed, jigger, jig, jig?"

"We're headed down toward Roseburg to do several concerts in senior centers and hospitals. We thought a few Christmas songs might be fun. What are you up to?"

"Jigger, jig, jig, I just fired my publishing company. At first, I felt free. Now panic is starting to set in. Jigger, jig, jig, what if I've made the biggest mistake of my life?"

"Good for you!" Mindy cheers excitedly. "What if you didn't? I think this is exactly what you needed to do to take control of your writing career."

"You know me, jigger, jig, jig. I'm terrible at public appearances and I don't know anything about marketing."

"Luckily, you are surrounded by people who are experts at this." Mindy flips her hair over her shoulder and scooches down in the bus seat. I can tell she's resting her iPad on her knees like she does when she's watching movies.

I am so distracted by her grace and beauty, I blurt, "What do you mean?"

She giggles. "Well, in case you haven't noticed, a bunch of us live our lives in the spotlight. Hayden is amazing at social media reach — she's done wonders with our fan clubs. My cousin Gabriel can make websites do magical things. You already know Madison has her own TV show and when you win some fancy-schmancy award, Jordan can dress you to the nines."

"What makes you think your whole family is going to help me if I venture into the world of self-publishing?"

Mindy laughs out loud. She looks up from the screen. "Hey guys, my boyfriend wants to know if you guys want to help out if he publishes a few books?" she yells to the people on the bus.

"Is it another excuse to eat and throw parties?" Declan teases.

I recognize Aidan's laughter. "Dude! Since when do

we ever need an excuse? Seriously Elijah, whatever you need, it's yours. You might've guessed I'm all about supporting Indies."

Mindy looks back down at the screen with a smug grin. "See? I told you so. It's the way we all work. Face it Fischer, when you fell for me — you got the whole gang."

Aidan's face comes into view. "Mindy Mouse, it's a little late to tell him about us now. That's the kind of thing you probably should've warned him about before he fell in love with you."

I snicker. "Jigger, jig, jig, I think I got a good sense of you all on the very first day Mindy and I met. Yet, for some reason, I still stuck around, jigger, jig, jig."

Joe Summers lets out a guffaw of laughter. "Elijah, I was beginning to wonder if you were tough enough to hang out with this crazy group. On second thought, I think you'll fit right in."

Mindy winks at me. "Why do you think I fell so hard and so fast? Elijah fits in my heart like he's always belonged there."

<hr />

"Why do you look so troubled?" my mom asks as she refills my mug of coffee. "Are you having trouble with Mindy?"

"Jigger, jig, jig, things are just about perfect with her. I just have some big decisions to make."

My mom pours cream and sugar in to her tea. "Is that a new creamer set?" I ask.

My mom smiles. "You'll never believe it. Gifts have been showing up at our door practically every day." She eyes me shrewdly. "You didn't send them, did you?"

I hold my hands up in a gesture of innocence. "Don't look at me. Maybe they're from Mariam. What did you get?"

"No! I checked with her too. She said it wasn't her either. The first present was funny. It was a card shuffler with a deck of cards with jokes on the back. The next day, I got fabulous oven mitts. At first, I thought maybe we were getting the neighbor's packages, but then I found little cards inside which had our names in them. Gourmet coffee showed up next and then there were very fancy nuts and cheese."

"Jigger, jig, jig, what a great surprise!"

"But it didn't end there. The next day it was a gift certificate for our favorite bakery. Then it was slippers for your dad."

A slow grin crosses my lips as I solve the mystery. "Jigger, jig, jig, if I counted right, I think you'll probably get two more."

My mom's face lights up. "Hanukkah? Someone is giving us Hanukkah presents? Who on earth would do such a thing?" My mom jumps to her feet and rushes out to the living room.

My dad looks up at us with a startled expression. "Where's the fire?"

My mom goes over and kisses my dad soundly. "Seth Fischer, I had no idea you'd become so wily!"

"I don't object to the kiss, you can do that anytime you like — but I have no idea what you're talking about, Roxanne."

"The gifts, you silly goose!" my mom exclaims as she

playfully bats my dad on the shoulder.

"Why would I give myself presents?" my dad responds with a look of befuddlement.

"You didn't? I thought you did it to throw me off your track. If you didn't buy the Hanukkah presents, who did?"

"Jigger, jig, jig, you guys, think about it. Who knows about your love of card games and your obsession with tea and fine cooking implements?"

My mom is quiet for a moment. "Mindy? Your Mindy did all of this for us? But she isn't Jewish —"

"No, jigger, jig, jig, she's not. I don't know how much of Mindy's past you know, but she had an incredibly rough childhood. She cherishes family and family traditions more than anyone I've ever known. So, when she found out about our roots, she wanted to honor them, jigger, jig, jig."

My mom tears up. "That is probably the sweetest thing anyone has ever done — especially when you consider I wasn't so warm to her in the beginning."

"Mom, I think you can consider it forgotten, I know Mindy has."

My dad clears his throat. "I can't say this enough. You be sure to let that girl of yours know she's mighty special."

I smile at my parents. "I try to do that every single day."

My mom walks over and gives me a hug. "We never got a chance to talk about what was bothering you," she prompts.

"Jigger, jig, jig, you know what? In the grand scheme of things, it's probably not worth worrying about. I'll figure it out."

CHAPTER TWENTY-THREE

MINDY

TASHA HUGS DOTTIE TIGHTLY. "I still can't believe you're here. How in the world did they pull it off?"

"My dear granddaughter, your mother didn't have as much control over me as she thought she did. After the incident a couple years ago, your wonderful boss moved me into a facility your mother couldn't control. She was livid about that, by the way. You know what? I don't care. Your mother's ego was getting way too big for her britches."

"How did you get all the way to Oregon?" Tasha asks with an anxious expression.

"I just got on that lovely plane your boss sent for me. It was a little hard for your mother to get her talons into me from jail," Dottie answers with a gleeful cackle. "She was so sure if she bribed the concierge at her favorite hotel, he would cover for her. She forgot she's been treating the staff at that hotel like dirt for years. They turned her in faster than a winning lottery ticket after she pulled her little stunt on the radio."

"It doesn't make you a little sad?" my mom asks, ever the social worker.

"I mourned the loss of the bright, funny girl I raised a long time ago. I'm not sure what happened to her. I don't know when Nadine became bitter and vengeful. She never used to be that way, and it wasn't how she was raised. I'm just happy she can't hurt anyone else."

"Nana, I'm so glad you're here. You'll love Jude. He is so gentle and kind. I can't wait to finally marry him."

"I know I'm going to love him. He was one of the few who stood up to your mother and put her in her place. He did it because he loves you. He reminds me so much of your papa."

Tears fill Tasha's eyes. "Me too. Jude even understood about the suitcase Papa gave me to conquer the world. These days, Jude makes sure I see the world even if it's only through my studies. Papa would be so proud of him."

Aunt Donda comes into the bedroom. "I hate to be a taskmaster, but I need to work on everyone's makeup. The photographer is going to be here soon."

Maddie puts down the iPad. "Do I get makeup too?"

Donda puts her finger to her lips like she's keeping a secret. "Maybe a little lip gloss — but we'll keep that just between us."

Maddie grins. "Cool! A secret, just like the big kids."

Tara grimaces as she runs a brush through Maddie's hair. "I'm not even sure I want to know what that means."

My mom snickers. "Not that I'm making any predictions or anything, but it could mean you're going to be in for some challenging teenage years."

"You have met her father—" Tara says with a raised eyebrow. "I knew when I married Aidan, our children were going to be spirited."

My mom looks at me and winks. "I don't know… spirited children can be a very good thing."

Tasha walks over and puts her arm around my shoulders. "Obviously I don't know what it's like to parent one, but I can tell you they make awesome friends. Thank you for being my best friend."

Jude's sister, Fernanda, stands beside me, adjusts her bridesmaids dress. "What does that make me, besides your tamale dealer?" she jokes.

Tasha glances up at the clock on the wall. "*Mi familia.* In a few minutes, you're going to be the sister I always wanted — and never thought I'd have. I am so honored to be part of your family — and not just for the awesome food you make."

Fernanda shrugs. "Well, at least that's something."

"To me, it's everything," Tasha asserts.

───── ◆ ─────

It's amazing to think how much has changed since the first time I was in a wedding where Aidan and Tara walked up the aisle. The configuration is slightly different this time. Tara is helping their daughter Maddie, who has cerebral palsy, walk up the aisle. Because of her balance difficulties, in order to throw out flower petals, she has to stop and adjust the grip on her crutches. She's made so much progress in the time since Aidan and Tara have adopted her, it's hard not to cheer out loud for every step she takes.

Joe Summers is walking Jude's sister up the aisle and I follow behind with Elijah. He looks so handsome in his rustic version of a tux he takes my breath away. We all turn around and watch as Aidan and Dottie carefully escort Tasha up toward Jude.

When Tasha arrives, Jude carefully draws her veil back from her face. He is such a quiet guy I'm surprised to hear him whisper, "*Sirena, te amaré para siempre no importa lo que.*"

Although my Spanish is rusty, I know it must be good because Jude's mother tears up and sighs.

Madison and Trevor's old barn is the perfect romantic setting for a spur-of-the-moment wedding. They recently built new facilities and use this one only for the equine therapy program Trevor has established for veterans in the community. It's charming and weathered. There are Christmas lights and crystal beads hung everywhere. With the soft light from the lanterns, it looks enchanting. Jordan did a great job designing denim dresses with a touch of lace, which look both formal and right at home in this rustic environment. Tasha's lace wedding dress fits her like a glove.

Family friend and former Oregon Supreme Court Justice William Gardner surveys the small crowd seated before him. He winks at Tasha. "I don't know what it is about you guys; it's almost as if you're playing an elaborate game of musical chairs. Last time I saw this one, she was singing at one of your weddings and now she is an enchanting bride."

Howard steps in front of the judge and snaps a few pictures. "Isn't she magnificent? My brother would be so proud of her."

William raises an eyebrow and gives him an stern glare that would've made anyone in his courtroom wither. "In my experience as an officiant, usually, the photographers try to be a little less obtrusive."

Howard has the good grace to blush. "Sorry, Your Honor. Occupational hazard. Besides, Natasha is my niece."

"I'll let it slide this time — but just be careful you don't enjoy yourself too much at this wedding and overshadow the couple," William warns.

Howard hustles to sit down in one of the wooden chairs. "Duly noted."

Justice Gardner takes a sip of water from a bottle sitting on the stool beside him. "As I was saying, I've known this couple for a long time and I've seen them grow together and fall deeply in love. Even though they live their lives in full view of the public, in reality, they are both quite shy and reserved people. If you are here, consider yourself privileged. It means you play a special role in their life. They've elected to keep things simple to help celebrate the way their love began — with a small act of friendship which grew into love. Jude and Tasha have a few words to say to each other."

Elijah moves closer when he sees me tear up. He reaches into his pocket and hands me a tissue. Then he holds out his hand for me to grasp. As soon as our hands touch, I feel a sense of peace.

Jude clutches Tasha's hands as they face each other. "I'll try to stick to English, but sometimes when I'm emotional a little Spanish slides in."

Tasha rolls her shoulder in an elegant shrug. "It's all right. I'm bilingual," she teases.

Jude chuckles. "As luck would have it, so am I. When I met you, I was just a guy with a dream. Honestly, at first my dream didn't have much to do with you. Mostly because I figured you wouldn't have much to do with me."

"Little did you know I had a huge crush on you from afar," Tasha says with a smile.

"No one ever said I was the brightest. Anyway, you believed in me even when I was too scared to believe in myself. You loved me through my fear and made me a better man. I love you Tasha Keeley and I can't wait to chase dreams with you for the rest of our lives."

Tasha swallows hard and dabs at her eyes with a tissue before she says, "You may be a man of few words, but when you say them, they matter." She pauses for a moment to collect herself before she adds, "When you saved me from falling — literally — I was lost. I was stuck between my past and my present. That left me completely paralyzed when it came to deciding my future. You gave me the courage to stand up for what I believe — even in the face of incredible pressure. You never backed down and took the easy way even when things were hard. You helped me face down my monster. Your belief in us made it possible for me to reconcile my past with my present and plan for the future. You set me free to be me. Judas Vicente Hernandez, *te amo*."

Tasha reaches up and hugs Jude tightly as tears flow down her face.

Justice Gardner hands Tasha a cotton handkerchief. "Are you ready to say your vows?"

Jude nods. "I've been ready for quite some time."

"I understand. You may begin when you wish."

Jude clears his throat and then in a clear speaking voice says, "Natasha, I promise to be faithful, supportive, and loyal and to give you my companionship and love throughout all the changes of our life. I vow to bring you happiness, and I will treasure you as my companion. I will celebrate the joys of life with you. I promise to support your dreams and walk beside you, offering courage and strength through all endeavors. From this day forward, I will be proud to be your husband and your best friend."

Tasha fans herself and wipes away tears. She looks back at the crowd. "I swear, I'm usually better at controlling my emotions. Darn it, I knew I should've gone first. I don't know if I'm going to make it all the way through. I thought I had everything memorized, now I'm not so sure."

"*Sirena*, our love has never been about perfect, it has been about getting through our mistakes with grace. I think everyone who knows us would expect us to flub up our vows at least once or twice."

"Once again, I can count on you to tell me the total truth," Tasha says as she tearfully laughs.

"I kinda thought that was what all this is about," Jude says as he gestures around the room.

"Right," Tasha says with a smile. "I guess I better get on with it. Jude, I promise to be faithful, supportive, and loyal and to give you my companionship and love throughout all the changes of our life. I vow to bring you happiness, and I will treasure you as my companion. I will celebrate the joys of life with you. I promise to support your dreams, and walk beside you, offering courage and strength through all endeavors. From this day forward, I will be proud to be your wife and your best friend."

Hayden comes up to the front of the room. She stands in front of the microphone and looks out at the crowd. "Hi, I'm Hayden. You might not know who I am. These guys are some of the most important people in my universe — besides my family, of course. I met Tasha and Jude during one of the lowest times of my life. The doctors had just cut off my arm because of cancer. Still, they never looked at me as if I was any different. In fact, Tasha made me the head of her fan club. She gave me a reason to get out of my funk and attack life again — even though I didn't even know how to tie my shoes. They gave me the courage to go back to school and face my friends even though I was different. Because of them, I'm headed to college with a scholarship … well lots of scholarships, truthfully. I can't even express how much they mean to me. So today, I'm going to tell you a little about their rings."

Hayden laughs at the surprised look on Tasha's face. "What? Do you think you're the only person capable of pulling off an epic surprise?"

Tasha just shakes her head in disbelief as she mutters to herself, "Well, I guess not."

Hayden grins before she continues, "The ring set Jude is going to give Tasha once belonged to her grandmother. Her grandfather bought it in Paris."

Tasha swings around and gives Dottie a surprised gasp. "Are you sure you want me to have these? They're from Papa."

"I'm sure honey. Your grandpa got me three wedding sets throughout our marriage. This is the first set he ever gave me. My fingers were so slim in those days — just like yours. There is no way I could ever wear those rings with my arthritic fingers. Wear them in good health. I know that you will carry our love story forward to the next generations."

Tasha picks up the train of her skirt and runs down the aisle to give her grandma a hug. "Thank you so much. I love you, Nana." Tasha runs back to her spot and looks up at Hayden.

"The ring that will be presented to Jude is compliments of Howard, the bride's uncle. This ring was worn by Tasha's grandfather on her father's side of the family. Her Uncle Howard is honored to pass the ring down to his niece because he believes it's what his brother would want."

This time, both Jude and Tasha turn around and give a very startled Howard a hug as he's quietly taking pictures from the sidelines. "You guys are bound and determined to turn me into a pile of mush today. I just want to thank you for all those years you silently stood watch over me when I had no idea who you were. I appreciate all you did to protect me. I'm glad you're part of my life," Tasha says as she wipes her eyes.

Jude steps forward and shakes Howard's hand. "I appreciate the gift. I will wear it with honor."

"I'm sure you will. I am so glad you will be watching over my Natasha."

William softly clears his throat.

Holding hands, Jude and Tasha rush back to the front of the room.

William chuckles as he hands the rings to the couple. "I assume you want to get on with this so you can get to the fun part —"

They both nod as Tasha blushes.

"Tasha, repeat after me," William says somberly as Jude holds out a somewhat shaky hand.

"I give you this ring as a symbol of my love, my faith in our strength together, and my promise to learn and grow with you."

Tasha's eyes tear up as she slides the ring on Jude's finger. "Oh, that's so perfect! I couldn't have chosen better words myself," she whispers.

"I give you this ring as a symbol of my love, my faith in our strength together, and my covenant to learn and grow with you."

William looks at Jude and starts to repeat his instructions. Jude holds up his hand. "I've got this."

William laughs out loud. "Okay, this is your show. I'm just here for the cake."

Jude turns to Tasha and holds her hands for a moment before he takes a deep breath. He slides the ring on her finger as he says, "*Te doy este anillo como símbolo de mi amor, mi fe en nuestra fuerza juntos y mi promesa de aprender y crecer contigo.*"

Tasha looks at William as she pleads, "That was so beautiful. Can I kiss him now?"

"By the power vested in me as a member of the judiciary in the state of Oregon, I now happily pronounce you husband and wife. Yes, Tasha, you may kiss your husband."

"I thought that was gonna take forever," complains Maddie as she sits on her mom's lap.

After Jude finishes thoroughly kissing his new wife, he looks up and winks at Maddie. "You weren't the only one, little one. For years, I thought the same thing."

———◗•◖———

Elijah is resting his chin on my head as he holds me tight. We are doing what I would call a waltz-ish as Joe Summers sings a cover of the Kenny Chesney classic, *You Had Me from Hello*. I've decided Elijah's arms are just about my favorite place on the planet to be, even if he isn't a stellar dancer.

Suddenly, Joe takes a break. He steps off the stage and hooks his phone up to the sound system and starts a playlist. He high-fives Uncle Aidan as he steps off the makeshift stage.

"Jigger, jig, jig, this. This is what I want," he whispers against my temple.

"This what?" I ask, distracted by the sight of my parents dancing to an old Randy Travis song filtering through the air. "A phone playlist played through speakers?"

Elijah pulls me closer for a gentle, but thorough kiss. "Jigger, jig, jig, no, I mean this." He gestures around the room. "When we get married, jigger, jig, jig, I want it to be just like this."

I gulp and swallow hard. "Umm … are you asking me to marry you?" I stammer.

"Jigger, jig, jig, jigger, jig, jig, not right now — but someday soon," he blurts. "I mean … right now there is too much going on in our lives to even consider something so huge. But, someday I plan to ask you the right way, jigger, jig, jig. I just want you to know, I have this perfect vision of us together and it looks a lot like what we're experiencing in this very moment."

I throw my arms around his neck and hug him tightly.

"I couldn't agree more. I love you, Elijah Fischer and when the time is right, I'm sure I'll say yes."

"Is that what your special senses tell you, jigger, jig, jig?" he teases.

"I need no precognition skills to tell me that. All I need to do is listen to my heart," I answer as I lay my head on his chest.

Tasha rushes over and starts pulling on my arm. "If you're done flirting with your handsome boyfriend, I need you on stage."

"Me? Why?" I ask as I follow her up toward the stage.

"Jude and I have decided we want you to sing *Silver Bells* for our ceremonial first dance."

I shoot her a puzzled glance. "Are you sure? It doesn't seem like a very romantic song."

Jude puts his hand on my forearm. "I don't think you understand. To us, it's the most romantic song in the world because it helped set us free. Tasha can answer the phone without wondering if she'll face a barrage of venomous words. My wife is now free to pursue whatever career she wants to without judgment and hate. We can have children without worrying how Nadine will poison them against us. I don't think it's possible to understate the gifts you have given us. That's why we want you to sing your single for us."

Tasha looks at me with tears in her eyes. "Jude doesn't usually say very much, but those words 'my wife' mean the world to me. You made it possible. There aren't enough words in the universe to say thank you."

Swallowing hard, I pick up my guitar and flag down Joe Summers from the audience. We take our place on the stage. As Joe and I take a moment to tune our guitars he says, "I knew it was a big gamble to throw it all in the air and trust that fate would figure it all out, but that's exactly what seems to have happened."

I shrug. "My whole life seems to be about tempting fate and beating the odds. So far, I seem to be on a winning streak."

CHAPTER TWENTY-FOUR

ELIJAH

MINDY NERVOUSLY CHEWS ON her fingernail as she examines the stuff we've put on the table. "Do you think this is enough? It's not very fancy. My grandma and mom make this look so easy. I never realized how stressful it would be to have company in our home."

I know her reference is inadvertent, but her use of 'our home' makes me feel good anyway. Even though Mindy still lives with her parents, she spends most of her time at my place. She decided to take a year off of school to promote her music. When she's not touring with Aidan, she helps her grandmother out at the floral shop. "Jigger, jig, jig, I'm sure it will be fine. Everything looks beautiful," I say, as I envelop her in a hug. "Jigger, jig, jig, I especially love the irises. Did you know they are my mom's favorite?"

Mindy gives me an enigmatic look. "I may have had a little inside information," she confesses.

I shake my head. "I can't believe I always forget about your extra special skills, jigger, jig, jig. Of course, you knew — you can see everything."

"I can't see everything," Mindy corrects with a laugh. "Just some things. In this case, that's not the type of inside information I'm referring to. A couple months ago, Seth asked me to pick some up for your mom as a birthday surprise."

I blush. "Sometimes, simple works." I lean forward and give her a leisurely kiss. Suddenly, my back door flies open.

"Uh oh, we caught the young'uns smoochin' again," my mom teases.

"I don't know about you, but I haven't forgotten what it's like to be young," Seth remarks as Josiah lifts his chair over the threshold to my townhouse. "It smells amazing in here. What did you cook for us today?"

"Nothing terribly gourmet, I'm afraid. I made my grandma's famous stew recipe and some sourdough rolls. My mom had some starter, and I decided to give rolls a shot. We are a little behind schedule because they took longer to rise than I thought they would," Mindy explains nervously.

My mom walks over to Mindy and puts her arm around her shoulders. "First time entertaining company?"

Mindy nods. I can tell she's fighting back tears.

"Breathe. It's okay. I've been cooking for a very long time and I still struggle with getting all of my food out at the same time. Homemade bread is worth waiting for. It'll be fine."

As Mindy relaxes, I suddenly remember the Hanukkah gifts she left out in the car.

She looks up at me with surprise and covers her mouth. "If you'll excuse me, I'll be right back," she says as she rushes out the back door.

As I'm thinking of a way to explain what just happened to my startled parents, an odd thought enters my brain. Unexpectedly, I hear Mindy's voice in my head as clearly as if she's standing right next to me. "Thanks for reminding me."

Disconcerted, I look around the room to find the source of her voice. I even check my cell phone to see if she's sending me a live message over Facebook or something. Yet, the phone is completely silent. My breathing goes tight for a moment as I realize I've just had a small taste of what it's like to be Mindy.

Mindy rushes through the back door carrying two gift bags. She hands one to my dad and the other to my mom. "Interesting — my son was right. It was you. Why were you being so mysterious?" my dad asks.

"Honestly, I didn't mean to be sneaky. Initially, I planned to be around. The single was a surprise hit and Uncle Aidan added a bunch of extra gigs to our schedule … and then there was Tasha's last-minute wedding. I'm sorry I didn't get back to you for the final two presents — but I wanted to give them to you in person. I hope you don't mind that they're late."

"Nonsense. We are just surprised we got presents from you at all. Which one should we open first?" my mom asks.

"Honestly, it doesn't matter," Mindy says.

"If that's the case, I'll go first," Dad says as he digs into his bag. He pulls out two CDs. "They look exactly the same," he declares in a puzzled voice.

"Almost. See the little holographic sticker on the back of the one? Uncle Aidan always gives the artists the first one off the assembly line. This is the very first copy of my version of *Silver Bells*. I included an extra CD in case you actually want to listen to it too."

My dad swallows hard before he asks, "I love it. But why would you give me such a precious, irreplaceable gift?"

"There are a couple of reasons. You've come to mean a lot to me. You *are* worth it. The other reason may seem silly, but you were the first person to give me honest feedback about the song when you didn't even know it was me. I don't get that kind of candor very often. I appreciated your feedback."

"I can't believe a few nice words would lead to something like this —" my dad says as Mindy reaches down and gives him a hug. "Will you sign them?"

She grins. "For you, sure."

I reach behind me to the breakfast bar, grab a Sharpie, and hand it to Mindy. She quickly signs the CDs and hands them back to my dad.

"I should get a shadowbox or something for this," he says to me as he holds one up in the air. "You better open your present now, Roxanne. I can't handle much more of this. Elijah, this gal of yours has turned me into a bucket of tears."

"Jigger, jig, jig, don't worry about it, Dad. She gets me sometimes too."

My mom digs through the gift bag and carefully pulls out her present. Mindy has wrapped it in several layers of tissue paper. My mom carefully takes off each one and folds it. When she finally gets to the present, she draws in a sharp breath. For a long time, she silently studies it, slowly looking at each page. Finally, she looks up at Mindy with tears in her eyes. "Did you make this? It's beautiful!"

Mindy nods as she twists her hair between her fingers. "My Aunt Donda is an artist. When I was a kid, my parents were always searching for things to keep my busy brain and body occupied. So, one summer I spent time with Aunt Donda learning to make stained glass and write things in calligraphy."

My mom holds up the book and shows my dad a page. "Isn't this magnificent?" She turns to Mindy. "Are these your recipes?"

"Yes, they are all my family's recipes. Some of them are from my grandma and my mom. I included a few from my dad and grandpa — mostly ones involving fish. There are even a couple of recipes for quick bread and yeast rolls, I developed from scratch. Aunt Heather even allowed me to give you her recipe for hummingbird cake. Trust me when I tell you it is phenomenal."

"I'm sure it is. I will cherish every recipe in here. I've never had anyone do anything so nice in my whole life," my mom says as she wipes away tears. "I'm sorry. I was so wrong about you. When we first met, I thought you were fake — but I've come to know there is nothing fake about you. You are the most real person I've ever met. It is clear that you love my son with your whole heart."

Mindy nods tearfully. "I do. I have for a while now."

"These gifts show me that you've come to love us too. I'm not sure we deserve it, but I am completely grateful."

"You deserve my love, don't be silly." Just then, the oven timer goes off. "Oh! My rolls are ready. Elijah, can you put the stew on the table please?" Mindy asks before she runs into the kitchen.

I look up and try to find Josiah to tell him dinner is ready. In all the drama of the presents, I didn't notice him leave the room. That man is as quiet as a jungle cat.

As I'm about to say something, Josiah comes through the door with a grim expression on his face. At the same time Mindy comes back into the dining room with oven mitts still on her hands. She is pale and shaky.

Before I can ask any questions, my dad looks at Josiah and demands, "What's going on?"

"Dinner will have to be postponed. I just got a heads up from Isaac. The Sheriff's office needs to speak to you."

My heart sinks to my toes. "Jigger, jig, jig, how could my dad be in trouble?" I blurt. But, even as I ask the question, I remember how accusatory the law enforcement officials were with Mindy when she had nothing to do with her roommate's death.

Josiah shakes his head. "I don't think that's the case here. I don't have a lot of details, but I didn't get the impression that's why Seth is needed."

I turn to Mindy as my anxiety flares. "Can you tell us anything? Obviously, you saw something."

Mindy chews on her lip. "Shoot! This is an impossible choice. You know this doesn't fit the rules. I've lived by the rules my whole life."

"Jigger, jig, jig, does it matter that it feels like it's a matter of life and death and it's not good for my dad to be under this much stress?" I press.

Mindy sighs. "Of course, it matters! I love you. I love *all* of you." Mindy stands silently for a couple seconds as she fingers the frayed edges of my oven mitts. "Okay, I'll tell you this: I just told you it's not a matter of life and death so it doesn't fall within my rules."

My mom searches my face for answers. "That has to be good, right?"

Mindy stands as still as a statue. "Listen carefully. Whatever you do, trust what Tyler Colton says."

"I need to get Mr. Fischer to the Sheriff's office. This might take a while. You'll probably want to put the food away for later."

"As much as I hate to miss a good meal, I need to take care of this first," my dad says as he struggles to put his jacket on.

———◆◆———

Mindy agrees to wait in the waiting room with my mom as I escort my dad back to the interrogation room. She is rubbing her temple as if she has a colossal headache. I can't say I blame her. She told me that she never wants to see the inside of the police station again.

Someone who does not know the whole story would never guess merely stepping through the doors of her uncle's workplace now makes Mindy nauseous. Yet she's here, calmly talking to my mother about recipes as she tries to distract her from the stress of the moment. Yes, there is something extremely special about Mindy Whitaker that the rest of the world can't possibly see.

When he sees the size of my dad's scooter, Tyler changes the location of the meeting to a conference room. "Hello Mr. Fischer, I'm Sheriff Colton. I understand you've been working with the folks from Marion County?"

My dad nods. "Not to be rude or anything, but why are we here?"

"From what I gather, you identified a suspect in a gun incident a while back. There was a BOLO issued. When that vehicle was located, the owner became nervous and fidgety. As the officer approached, the driver managed to shoot a hole in his floorboard, grazing his own thigh. This occurred in our county. That's why you're here."

"Are you telling me Harrison Conlin almost shot his own junk off?" my dad asks with a surprising amount of mirth.

Tyler lets out a surprised burst of laughter. "That pretty much sums it up, Yep."

"Jigger, jig, jig as my friend Sadie is fond of saying, 'Karma bites!'

"As far as I'm concerned, he didn't get close enough to his family jewels after all the misery he put my family through. It'd be nice if he would've given himself a reason to be a soprano for a while."

"You want to tell me about what happened the day of the accident? I can read the file; but I'd rather hear your take," Tyler prompts.

"Honestly, I don't remember much. They beat the snot out of me and most of my memories got scrambled that day too. Mindy says the guy who tried to shoot at me is the same one who clobbered me."

"That right there is a mixed blessing. In my experience, Mindy is never wrong. Unfortunately, proving that in court might be a different thing. It would probably be best to try to get a confession from Mr. Conlin."

"Jigger, jig, jig, I've got no objections to the guy singing like a canary. He had a gun pointed at my dad's head. How do we make that happen?"

"It seems Mr. Conlin gets a little discombobulated when it comes to talking about you, Mr. Fischer. If you positively identify him, I think a carefully controlled encounter might just push him over the edge toward a confession."

"Is that safe?" presses my dad. "What if he's all the way around the bend, if you know what I mean? The guy aimed a Glock at my head, you know."

"Hence, the carefully controlled portion. Mr. Conlin will be handcuffed at all times with an armed officer on each side. We will keep you safe," Tyler assures us.

"Jigger, jig, jig, what do you think, Dad?"

"Listening to Mindy has saved my life before, I've got no reason to doubt her now. Let's do this. Besides, I want to look that jerk in the face and ask him why he thought he had the right to destroy my life."

"You know, that actually sounds like a solid strategy, but are you sure you're up to it? This guy seems to have a lot of issues," Tyler cautions.

"Tell me about it. I've gone toe-to-toe with him before. If words are his only weapon, I win," my dad confidently proclaims.

Several minutes later, officers arrange for my Dad to sit in a room with a large window. Tyler and I are watching from another room. Part of me wants to be in there to protect my dad from the pain. On the other hand, ever since the accident my dad's resolve to do the right thing is stronger than ever. I know he is driven to see this thing through to the end, regardless of the cost.

A lineup of men file into the room across from my dad. The officer gives my father instructions. He tells him the suspect might not even be in the lineup, but before he finishes my dad interrupts him. Without hesitation, my dad identifies the guy as suspect number four. The officer brings a card with Mr. Conlin's picture on it for my father to sign.

My muscles tense as I realize what's coming next. We spent a long time talking about the pros and cons of this step. However, my father insists he wants to do it. I pray that Mindy is right and her uncle can protect my dad.

As we arranged, Tyler is escorting us down the hall when my dad makes his scooter malfunction. At the same time, the other officers are escorting Mr. Conlin down the hall. As soon as Harrison sees my dad, he stops in his tracks. The veins in his neck bulge and his eyeballs look like they're about to pop out of his head as he seethes, "You! Why the freak are you so hard to kill? It was only supposed to take a couple of whacks. I can't believe you didn't die from your injuries the first time. Then, the stupid goons I hired to finish you off couldn't tell the difference between you and a random stranger standing right next to your son. I finally decided to take you out myself. But, you've got some sort of bodyguard team around you like you're some freakin' CEO or something."

"Harrison, I know you and I didn't see eye-to-eye all the time, but you promised to take care of Bud's company when you bought it. What happened? Why go after me?"

"Are you stupid?" Conlin roars as he lunges toward us. Before I can even blink, Tyler Colton places his large frame between my dad and the enemy. He subdues him and hauls him over to a bench in the hallway. With one hand Tyler removes his handcuffs from his waist and loops them through Conlin's existing cuffs and the rail of the bench.

Harrison Conlin picks up right where he left off before his face was planted on the ground. "I can't believe with all your advanced degrees in engineering and all that bull crap, you still don't get it," he taunts. "Harrison Brothers owns companies at every step of the process — either in our own name, or under shell companies. We could have ruled the whole field of construction and run it any way we wanted. We were making money hand over fist. But you had to get all self-righteous and put lives over our profit. You were all that stood in our way. You had to go." By the time he finishes his rant, he's shaking with white-hot rage.

My dad looks at him with total disbelief. "Money means that much to you? You were willing to kill me because I wouldn't sign paperwork? What about my family? Heck, what about *your* family?"

"You and your stupid ethics. My family understands I do what needs to be done to get to the top," he scoffs.

Tyler walks over to Harrison Conlin. "Mr. Conlin, I hope for your sake your family understands the cost of your decisions. I am placing you under arrest for the attempted murders of Seth Fischer and Chester Franklin."

"Who in the heck is Chester Franklin?" Harrison spits.

"The guy you arranged to have shot," Tyler explains.

"That was a mistake! Those goons were supposed to shoot Fischer," he protests.

"Their lousy eyesight doesn't make their bullets any less deadly."

The gravity of the situation must have just hit home. Harrison Conlin leans up against the wall and hangs his head. "I probably need a lawyer," he mutters.

My dad breathes out a frustrated sigh. "Count yourself lucky, that's all you need." He points to his scooter. "I'll probably need this for the rest of my life. The doctors say my pain may never go away because of the nerve damage. I hope when you try to sleep at night, you remember that and ask yourself if it was worth what two families lost just to chase a few dollars."

My dad looks up at Tyler. "I guess it's time to move on. I hope you have enough to lock him up for a long time — but I'm done giving him another thought. I've got more important things to accomplish in my life."

Tyler puts his hand on my dad's shoulder. "I understand more than you can possibly know. Sometimes, you just have to let it go."

Epilogue

Mindy

MY LITTLE BROTHER IS literally pulling me down our driveway. "Why are you late? You promised you'd be here. This is important! It's like the most important day of my whole life."

I ruffle his hair as I try to disengage my arm. "I'm sorry, Charlie. Registration was crazy. They were trying to figure out all my AP credits from high school and the online courses I took while I was touring this last year. They were having a hard time figuring out which classes I needed to take. I guess I'm not a true freshman."

"Shoulda sent a text," he counters.

I smile. "You're right. I should have. I'm just not used to you having a cell phone. Is everybody here?"

Charlie nods eagerly. "Uh-huh, even Maddie. She got a new wheelchair because she's too tall for her old one. Gabriel is teaching her to play basketball. I didn't know people in wheelchairs play basketball — because Mom doesn't. But Gabriel knows someone from his college who plays basketball on a team like the Trail Blazers.

They're called the Wheelblazers. Maddie didn't believe him, so he showed her a YouTube video. Now, she wants to grow up and be on the team."

"That's all kinds of cool."

"Not as cool as me," Charlie insists.

I smirk. "A little humility might be helpful," I suggest.

"What's to be humble about? I'm getting a book published today!"

"Okay, you might have a point. You've earned bragging rights today," I concede.

"Well, come on!" Charlie says as he holds the door open. "Elijah says he won't do it unless you're here to watch."

I walk into Elijah's living room where he has two computer monitors set up. Gabriel did a masterful job of colorizing Charlie's drawings and turning them into digital art. Of course, I'm a little biased, but that cover is going to sell like gangbusters.

Elijah stands up to kiss me. As he does, he whispers in my ear. "Missed you, jigger, jig, jig. Did it go well?"

"I made it through," I answer candidly. "Large groups are always hard on me. I can't always filter everything out and there were a lot of anxious people there today."

Elijah sits back down and puts Charlie on his lap. "There were a lot of anxious people around here today too. Are you ready to see if our gamble was worth it?"

"Absolutely," I answer as I sit down in the office chair next to Elijah's. Maddie wheels over. "Can I sit on your lap too? I can't see."

I scoop her up and place her on my lap.

I start to read the story to her as Elijah slowly flips through the pages. Maddie puts her finger to my lips. "*Shh!* I do it myself."

My grandpa Denny laughs out loud. He points to my mom. "Kiera, Maddie sounds just like you did when you were little."

Charlie and Elijah anxiously watch Maddie as she reads each page to herself and smiles at each picture.

When she gets to the end, she grins and points to Charlie. "CJ looks like you, but walks like me. That's cool."

Maddie looks around. When she spies Tara she asks, "Mom, I thought you said we were coming to look at a book. This isn't a book. It's is a computer."

"I think that's what we're here for today," Tara explains. "I think Elijah and Charlie are going to publish their book. We'll get real books in the mail in a couple weeks."

Maddie looks over at Charlie. "For reals?"

Charlie nods.

Maddie grins. "Can you come read it to my class? I'll tell them you drew it."

Charlie looks at my mom for guidance. "Can I?"

My mom looks like she's about to burst with pride. "I don't see why not. After all, you're officially an illustrator now."

Elijah interrupts, "Jigger, jig, jig, not quite yet. To make it official, Charlie has to push submit."

As Charlie shifts on Elijah's lap something catches

my eye on the back cover. I look up at Elijah in surprise. "Did you really call your self-publishing company Jiggernut Publishing?"

Elijah shoots me a self-deprecating smile. "Jigger, jig, jig, I did. I figure if I ever make one of the lists again it'll be a thumb in Candace's eye. She thinks I won't be successful because of my Tourette's syndrome. Jigger, jig, jig I'm determined to show her otherwise. If I'm wildly successful, she'll have to read the name of my publishing company in all the press releases and be reminded what she missed out on, jigger, jig, jig."

"Sounds good to me." I smile at my brother. "Are you ready to help Elijah start his plan to dominate the publishing world?"

Charlie gives me a high five. "Let's do it!" He clicks on the button which says submit. "Wow! This is cool. We just made everyone's dreams come true."

"I think you're right, Charlie. This is the start of a brand-new dream," Elijah responds. "Thank you so much for helping me pull it off."

Maddie pulls on my sleeve. "Can I get down now? I want to go play with Charlie."

I smile at her enthusiasm as I place her back in her wheelchair. She reminds me so much of myself when I was little. I used to follow Gabriel around with the same amount of devotion.

After the kids leave the room, my mom wheels over to Elijah. "I just want to thank you. Charlie has been feeling a bit lost and out of place recently, but you gave him a whole new outlook. Even if this book doesn't sell a single copy, you've changed his life. Thank you for making a difference."

"Jigger, jig, jig, I appreciate the compliment," Elijah responds. "But I'm only paying it forward. There was a time in my life when I didn't think very much of myself. Someone believed in me and my skills. She gave me the courage to stand up for myself. Jigger, jig, jig, that's all I was doing for Charlie."

My mom pulls Elijah's face close to hers and kisses him on the cheek. "I can see why my daughter loves you so much. Thank you for making her dreams come true too."

"Jigger, jig, jig, I've never been sure if it was God's will or an accident of fate or if Mindy was the culmination of all the dreams I've ever had, but from the moment I met her, I knew we'd be together."

Just then a vision which has always eluded me clicks into place like a slide in a slide projector. I look at him with complete awe. "You're telling the truth! You knew years ago! Even when I didn't know, you've always known. Why didn't you tell me?"

Elijah looks uncomfortable. "To be honest, everyone always thought I was weird anyway. I wasn't sure if what I saw was wishful thinking or just a fantasy. Until I met you and Tara, I'd never met anyone with any kind of special abilities. I thought I was simply imagining things. You know, like an extra-vivid version of my storytelling?"

My dad walks over and puts his arm around me. "Mindy Mouse, I wouldn't be too rough on your guy. How often do you carry around secrets because it's not the right time to reveal them?"

I put my head down and study the floor. "All the time," I admit.

Elijah stands up and holds his hand out for mine.

When I offer my hand, he pulls me up to a standing position. He escorts me into the kitchen where we have a little privacy. "I'm sorry I didn't tell you. I guess I was afraid if I said it out loud and let it out into the universe, it would be like tempting fate and you would disappear from my life."

I thread my arms around his neck and stand on my tiptoes to kiss him. "You know what this means, right?"

Elijah shakes his head.

"It means I was never wrong about us being a couple. I simply couldn't see the vision. I see it now, and it's beautiful."

Elijah pulls away. "If our life is anything like what I see in my head, we've got it made."

THE END (for now)

Note from the Author

Dear Reader,

I hope you enjoyed Tempting Fate, If you love Mindy and her family and friends, the adventures continue in my new sweet contemporary romance novel, The Letter.

As a paramedic, Rocco Pierce is no stranger to making life-and-death decisions and delivering devastating news.

But he has never faced a situation quite like this.

What exactly do you do with a letter informing you that your wife is dying of breast cancer when you've never been married?

Is it a bureaucratic failure or divine intervention?

Crime reporter Mallory Yoshida is used to getting odd fan mail, so why should she pay attention to this guy who wants to talk to her about a mysterious letter?

After all, it's not like it's a matter of life and death.

Or is it?

Tempting Fate

You'll love this sweet interracial romance with big heart.

Thank you for your support.
Happy reading

~Mary

Because love matters, differences don't.

ACKNOWLEDGEMENTS

The entire time I was writing *Tempting Fate,* I had to pinch myself. It was surreal to be writing a second generation love story. Yet of all my characters, Mindy's voice has always been the loudest. It's almost as if she couldn't wait to grow up and have a love story of her own.

I had to choose carefully for Mindy. She needed someone who would understand what it was like to be different and misunderstood. When I wrote *If You Knew Me,* initially my idea was that Sadie and Elijah might eventually fall in love. However, often characters don't behave the way you expect them to. That was the case with Elijah and Sadie. They have a beautiful, supportive relationship, but it was never a traditional love story because they ended up being best friends. At the time, I wasn't quite sure what to make of that. Then Mindy had a cameo appearance in *If You Knew Me* and suddenly it all made sense.

I hope you loved reading *Tempting Fate* as much as I enjoyed writing it.

I have several people I need to thank. Without them, writing a book would be immeasurably more difficult.

Kathern Watts — you started out as a beta reader but you have become so much more. Thank you for your last-minute research, your cheerleading skills and your willingness to proofread an entirely raw document filled with voice recognition errors.

Kathy Faltinson — thank you so much for following me on social media and liking every post. It helps me believe that someone pays attention to what I do. Thank you for taking the time to read my books even though I know your job is crazy.

LJ Redding — Thanks for keeping me organized and visible to the public. My life has become so much calmer since you started assisting me.

Brianna Tubbs — Thanks for your help. Editing my words can be a thankless task. You're a trooper.

Becca Draper-Ristanovic — Your thoughtful critiques keep me on my toes and to make me always want to improve.

Justin Crawford — Yes, I know my commas need work. Thank you for meticulously proofreading my book.

Dr. Brandon Crawford — thank you so much for not diagnosing me with an odd psychiatric condition when I ask you to diagnose and treat fictitious characters for me. I am so proud of you and the work you are doing.

Leonard Crawford — thank you for still listening to me when I ramble about characters as if they are real people. I love you and I could not do this without your support.

To all my beta readers — thank you so much for your feedback. You make my writing stronger.

Lastly, to the fans who support books featuring atypical characters, I can't thank you enough. With your help, we will change stereotypes and make the world of fiction a better place.

A SMALL REQUEST

Studies show readers trust the word of other readers. Your recommendations mean a lot. If you enjoyed this book, I would be honored if you would recommend it to other readers. Even if my writing style isn't your cup of tea, your feedback is valuable to and I may take it into account as I write other books.

A review does not have to be long and complex. You can simply say what you liked about the book, what it meant to you or what you'd like to see more of.

If you would like to leave a review, you can do so on Amazon by following this link: Leave a review for Tempting Fate.

If you would like to leave a review on Goodreads, you may do so here: Leave a review on Goodreads.

ABOUT THE AUTHOR

I have been lucky enough to live my own version of a romance novel. I married the guy who kissed me at summer camp. He told me on the night we met that he was going to marry me and be the father of my children.

Eventually, I stopped giggling when he said it, and we've been married for over thirty years. We have two children. The oldest is a Doctor of Osteopathy. He is across the United States completing his residency, but when he's done, he is going to come back to Oregon and practice Family Medicine. Our youngest son is now tackling high school, where he is an honor student. He is interested in becoming an EMT.

I write full time now. I have published more than thirty books and have several more underway. I volunteer my time to a variety of causes. I have worked as a Civil Rights Attorney and diversity advocate. I spent several years working for various social service agencies before becoming an attorney.

In my spare time, I love to cook, decorate cakes and, of course, I obsessively, compulsively read.

I would be honored if you would take a few moments out of your busy day to check out my website, MaryCrawfordAuthor.com. While you're there, you can sign up for my newsletter and get a free book. I will be announcing my upcoming books and giving sneak peeks as well as sponsoring giveaways and giving you information about other interesting events.

If you have questions or comments, please E-mail me at Mary@MaryCrawfordAuthor.com or find me on the following social networks:

Facebook: www.facebook.com/authormarycrawford

Website: MaryCrawfordAuthor.com

Twitter: www.twitter.com/MaryCrawfordAut

Made in the USA
Columbia, SC
16 June 2023

17981968R00181